The Devil's Son

JENNIFER LOREN

Books by Jennifer Loren

The Devil's Eyes Series

THE DEVIL'S EYES

THE DEVIL'S REVENGE

THE DEVIL'S MASQUERADE: THE POISON

THE DEVIL'S MASQUERADE: THE REMEDY

The Finding Ava Series

FINDING AVA

RECKLESS

THE HAND THAT HOLDS MINE

http://www.jenniferloren.com/

First published by Jennifer Loren, 2012
This edition published by Jennifer Loren, 2013

ISBN: 0985702982
ISBN-13: 978-0985702984

Representation and Management, More & More Professional Literary Services
http://www.moreandmorepls.com/

Acknowledgements

Content Editing: More & More Professional Literary Services http://www.moreandmorepls.com/

Copyediting: Erinn Giblin, Yours Truly, The Editor

Proofreading: Jacqueline Tria

Cover Model: Lionel Clerc

Cover Design: Hang Le, By Hang Le
http://byhangle.com/

Interior Design: Polgarus Studio
http://www.polgarusstudio.com/

Prologue

Nick

They tell me that father was, at one time, much the same with me as he was with my other siblings: apathetic and unmoved by our cries. That is, until one summer day when everything changed between him and me. My mother worked for him; she always worked for *him*, the only reason I believe he stuck around. My mother, however, was so infatuated, *no bewitched*, by him that she could see no one else, including me. She barely acknowledged my birth, and once I was able to sit up, she was content to leave me alone with no concern.

They said it was boiling hot that day. Everyone in the neighborhood sat outside trying to find some kind of shade, some kind of relief from the sun. Thankfully, my mother was kind enough to leave me playing under a tree while she hung laundry. Humming her hypnotic tune, she never noticed the man who had taken a sudden interest in me or his rapid approach to take me from my playpen. But my father did, and something inside him raged to the forefront like never before. With everything he had, he chased the man down and took me back into his own arms. There were no words spoken, no hands lifted even, as the man fell to his knees and cried out in pain.

They say they thought it was the embarrassment of his sickness that caused the man to surrender so easily; it seemed reasonable to assume such. It seemed reasonable until they saw … him … *them*, the power in his eyes, the controlled rage that boiled and concentrated in the man's heart. That man collapsed at my father's feet and was left there to go cold in the blazing sun. My mother once said my father had the power of a thousand men within a blink of his eye. The "rage of the devil," they say, that's what killed that man and that's what kept people from ever crossing my father, the devil himself, and me … *the devil's son.*

Chapter 1

Nick

I have considered my options for days. Even considered making Brady disappear, but once I saw my sister's blissful expression in her new wedding dress, I was convinced to think otherwise. I have never seen her so happy. My disgust for Brady is clearly outweighed by the love I have for my sister. For her, despite him, I have to figure out how to keep that fool alive so she can remain happy. Brady's constant pursuit of The Barron has caused me major headaches. I have done everything to cut him off and detour him away from the right path. I wasn't exactly sure who The Barron was until Estrella confirmed it, but I have always had a good idea. The Barron, otherwise known as Dennis Savage, is not one you cross or even attempt to think about crossing. I don't like putting myself in his path, but I am hoping that I can thwart Brady's determination to destruction with an honest plea to an old family *acquaintance.*

I have known of Dennis Savage since I was a kid. I remember hiding behind my father's coat tails as the man looked me over. No one dared to cross him, and the man never, ever, seemed worried. He feared no one, and you knew it from the moment you met him. I only saw him angry once, and my father was the object of his rage. Ever since, I have managed to stay out of his crosshairs and keep a civil respect between the two of us.

I am not surprised that he agreed to meet with me, but I am surprised that I agreed to meet him at his home. Am I brave or stupid? Of that, I am not sure. No matter, I drive myself and go alone. I don't want to risk my own people going up against him, and no matter my uncertainty about this man, I know one thing for sure - he wouldn't hurt me.

The gate opens up to my car as soon as I pull up, and the front doors are already standing open with greeters as I get out. One stands out from the others, frigid and silent. He simply nods and waves his hand towards the doors. Crossing in front of me, he guides me into the house, and with his head held low, he walks a perfectly straight line down the marbled path. The cold muteness that sits in the air weighs heavy, but the stiff emptiness of my greeter sends chills down my spine. The only thing worse is the ominous, gothic décor of the home. It is rich and beloved by its owner but lacks the warmth I would consider for my own home. My sons would run screaming from this house, like a Halloween nightmare. The silent man motions for me to wait in an office while others come in, offering me food and drink as if I am going to stay for longer than I wish. Everything about this room is uncomfortable, but nothing more so than the highlighted artwork that sits behind the commanding desk chair. The demon, encapsulated in the artwork, stares at me with desiring eyes, heating my flesh to its devouring temperature.

Savage walks in, or rather floats in, with his confidence carrying him like he is on a cloud. He clutches a cane as if he desires to look feeble, but the ruby-eyed dragon at the head causes him to look anything but. Its fiery eyes beam in my direction as Savage stands it straight up at his side, readying it for attack. "Nicholas," he hisses. "So happy to see you again." I stand and greet him with a handshake that causes our eyes to meet and a smile to deepen into his unmarred face. "I see you admiring my favorite piece. It is Asmodeus." I glance at the demon once again, recalling the name of the lust-filled devil, *The King of Demons.* "I don't know why I treasure it so. Maybe it is because it just seems so fitting in this room."

Nodding respectfully, I wait for him to sit before speaking. "Mr. Savage, thank you for meeting with me," I say, doing my best to disguise my impatience to leave.

"Please, call me Dennis. All this time and you still don't feel comfortable calling me by my name? We are, after all, old family friends," he says, analyzing my expression to see how much I recall of our family history.

"Dennis, then. I am going to get right to the point of my visit, Dennis, I wanted to warn you that the police are aware of who you are. They now know you are The Baron." He doesn't even budge or does his smile diminish any. "They are coming after you, and one in particular is determined."

"I appreciate you letting me know. I assure you, though, it will not be a problem. This person, whoever he is, will not be a problem for me," he says, calmly sitting back in his chair.

"I have no doubt about that, but I would like to ask that you forego destroying this person, and instead, give him a smaller bone to chew on, a victory to appease him long enough for me to talk him out of coming after you."

Savage sits up and gazes over at me as if he is trying to read my mind. "Why? Why, Nicholas, are you so intent on sparing this man?"

"Let's just say, I owe him one."

"Just one?" he asks, but I simply raise my eyes to his and wait as his smile emerges once again. "Well, this is interesting, something new for me to ponder today." He sits back. "I do love new things. Life has become too routine lately. Sometimes, I wish things weren't always so easy; there is no excitement anymore. I tell you what, I will not touch a hair on the man's head *if* you come and work for me, Nicholas." He sings my name with want, and suddenly, the sounds of my father's voice ring loudly in my head.

"You know I can't do that," I say as he laughs softly to himself.

"I do not like hearing that. What is holding you back? Your father is gone now. If you join me, you would want for nothing."

"I already have everything I want. I don't need anything more."

"Yes, I have watched you grow into a fine man. A family man, even. Your wife is quite beautiful. Kayla, right?" I nod simply. "And *two* sons is it now?" Glancing up at him, my muscles tense, my heart pounds, and I breathe, carefully. "The oldest resembles you quite a bit. I saw him once with his mother." There is nothing I can say right now. I know well enough to stay quiet and speak nothing of my son. "Yes, Nicky I believe, he is quite something, much like his father indeed." My silence amuses him, but he moves on. "If I recall correctly, you were never going to have children?"

"I was young when I said that. I grew up and changed my mind."

Savage laughs fully. "You changed your mind? I doubt that. No, Nicholas, you didn't change your mind at all. She …" he says, looking me over to verify his accusation. "… yes, *she* changed your mind. Interesting woman, I must say. She walked right past me one day, leaving nothing but her invigorating scent for me to inhale," he says, trailing off as he closes his eyes and hums his appreciation for my wife's fragrance while I do my best to remain calm. "Now, Nicky," our eyes meet, and I instantly meet him face to face with clenched fists. "Are you ready to take me on, Nicholas? Ahhh, you are so much like your father, trying to hide your precious secrets from me. I already know the boy is special, but is he as special as his father? That is the only thing I don't know for sure." Eyeing me carefully, he continues.

"Tell me. How did Saldean die? How did Dante ...," Savage stands back with a sudden understanding while I finally admit the truth to myself. *Saldean, I can still recall my father saying his name, screaming his name before, he died.* "Nicky... does he ...?"

Before he can finish that question, I step away towards the door. "Thank you for meeting with me, Dennis. I appreciate your time to hear me out, but I think our business is done."

"What's the rush?" Savage sits back in his chair, salivating over his new knowledge.

"My family is not something I am willing to discuss with you. And just so you know, like my father, my son is one boundary I won't allow you to cross." I wait for him to nod before turning my vulnerable back to him.

"Oh Nicholas, about your request, the cop, a Brady Simone, correct?" Looking back, I catch sight of his knowing expression and nod. "I will not harm him, and you can rest assured that he will be kept busy with plenty of rewards soon. If he has done you such an important favor, then it is certain that I owe him, too." Savage leans back in his chair again, staring out the window with a searing smile. "And do please say hello to your family for me. I do hope to meet them all one day." I don't bother responding, despite my objection to him ever coming near my family. My only goal right now is to wash away my past, get home to my family, and protect them with every muscle, every ability, and every power I have.

Chapter 2

Nick

Walking along my side, Nicky holds tightly to my hand as he tries his best to duplicate my swagger. It's difficult not to laugh at my miniature self, but I also have to admit, I couldn't feel more proud of him. My son is special and, unfortunately, not only to me. The recent events have me watching over him more than usual. I want to take some time to talk to him and make sure he understands who he is and, most importantly, who will not understand. The downtown creamery is quiet this time of day, and my son's eyes light up at the sight of all the possibilities in front of him. "Now, let's not tell Mommy we had ice cream for lunch, okay?" Nicky nods, folding his little hands in front of him, eagerly waiting for our server.

"Hello gentlemen. How are we today?" The waitress says, smiling at my son and turning to me with freshly moistened lips.

"We are good," I say, watching my son roll his eyes as the waitress eyes me up and down. "We want two specials with two mint chocolate chip ice cream bowls, but we are going to have our ice cream with our meal instead of after."

"Oh, being naughty already today," she says with a wide smile.

Before I can respond, Nicky huffs his way back into our conversation. "We can't tell Mommy because she won't like it."

"Well, cutie, I will certainly keep you and your daddy's secret," she says before turning back to me. "I am very good at keeping secrets, especially from Mommies."

"That's good 'cause Mommy carries a gun, and she is not afraid to use it," Nicky says, causing the waitress to glance his way before looking back at me to verify. I nod and indicate with my hands that is a sizable gun.

"Well, I will get your food right out to you," she exhales and rushes off.

"She's annoying. And not as pretty as Mommy," Nicky huffs.

"I agree. She doesn't even come close to Mommy," I say.

"Daddy, look! A dog!" Nicky jumps up and points out the window. A large mutt passes by and wanders into the alley, snooping for food. "He looks hungry. We should bring him some food."

"Maybe when we're done. Nicky, turn around and sit in your seat before you fall." He does as I ask, but his eyes continue to linger to the stray dog. "Nicky, look at me. I need to talk to you about something. Do you remember what we talked about the other day? About our secret?"

He nods. "Don't do it anymore unless you say it is okay. And don't tell Mommy cause she'll worry."

"Yes, and I want you to be careful around people you don't know. They don't always want to be nice to you, but you let Daddy take care of that, okay?"

"Okay, Daddy. But can I …?" I shake my head, and his shoulders instantly sink, only perking back up when his ice cream is placed in front of him. He pushes his sandwich far aside and takes full ownership of his favorite flavor.

Before I can say anything else, Ryan calls. "Eat your ice cream, Nicky, and at least a bite of that sandwich so we can tell your mother you did. Okay Ryan, what do you need?"

"Nick, I swear this woman is driving me crazy!" he grumbles.

"If you would just listen to me for once, we could have been done hours ago." Kayla snaps in the background.

"You see what I am putting up with? I thought you said for me to handle it. Why is she here?" Ryan gripes.

The arguing between these two lately is going to send me to an early grave. "Put her on the phone."

"Your husband wants to tell you to shut up and listen to me," Ryan smarts off.

"Hi, Baby. Are you having a good day? How is Nicky? You remembered to pick him from school, didn't you?" Kayla says sweetly, but I can tell she is cursing Ryan behind her hand.

"Yes, I did. He is eating lunch with me right now. Kayla, why are you with Ryan? I told him to take care of it," I ask her with frustration in my voice.

"Nick, I thought he could use my help. I am so much more effective with these things than he and …"

"Oh bullshit! You're just trying to get even with me for teaching Nicky how to greet women," Ryan yells.

"It wasn't proper; it was disgusting! You're disgusting, and if you would just shut up and realize I know more …"

"Kayla!" I snap, hiding my frustration from my son.

"Yes, Nick?" she asks with shock.

Rolling my eyes, I have to force a breath to calm myself as I try to figure out a solution that will get these two to stop bickering. "Can you please let it go? I know he has been pushing your buttons a lot lately, but can you find another way to annoy him that is not at the expense of our business? Please, Princess. I promise I will make it worth your efforts." Pondering my offer, she is silent for some time, but I know my wife and what she likes. Hiding my mouth, I whisper, with great detail, every place on her body I plan to pay special attention to tonight.

"I suppose, Nick, but you better make it worth my effort… every day." Her smile echoes through my phone.

"Oh, Princess. You know I will. Thank you. I love you."

"I love you too. Your brother, however, is a nuisance, and if I hear one more disgusting thing come out of my son's mouth, I am going to hurt him severely," she says as Ryan huffs in the background.

"Understood. I will talk to him when I get home, and then I will take care of you." Kayla happily gives me my way for now, and I can have peace for a little while longer. Hanging up my phone, I look up to an empty seat and immediately begin searching for my son. "Nicky!" My muscles tense as I stand up, frantically searching for him. After what seems like eternity, I spot him across the street in the alley with the dog. Sighing, I throw some cash on the table and rush off to get him. "Nicky!" I yell to him, but my efforts are drowned out by a group of punks approaching my son. My world begins to move slowly around me as I attempt to hurry traffic along to get to him. I try to remind myself to remain calm, but everything within me starts to heat up.

"Stop! You're hurting him!" Nicky yells.

"Who are you to tell us to do anything?" one punk yells.

"I'm Nicky Jayzon!" I round the corner as the teenager walks up to my six-year-old son and grabs him, forcing him to watch as his pathetic friends beat the dog. Before I can stop him, the punk releases my son and crashes to the ground, writhing in pain.

His friends turn in shock. "What did you do? You want a beating too, kid?" Nicky fists his hands and stiffens, standing his ground despite being outnumbered. My son, definitely my son, oh how he reminds me of my own stubborn past …

The day my father first held me in his arms, he stared at me for hours with my mother continually asking if he was okay. He shushed her and sat down with me in his lap, carefully watching me as I looked up and met his eyes - dead on and with no fear. He didn't trust my mother to watch me after that day, so he took me wherever he went: the store, the post office, and the home of whatever woman he had met along the way. He didn't understand children, and he certainly didn't understand how to take care of one. He would give me a book or a game with no understanding of what might be appropriate for my age. When he realized I couldn't read yet, he sat me down and read one book to me until he thought I had memorized it well enough to "read" it on my own.

The older I got, the more I learned. What I couldn't learn from books, I learned from him and his female friends. My father was never one to shy away from women, or they from him. His exceptional taste in style was only outmatched by his extraordinarily good looks, and he knew it. I always watched him, curious as to why people treated him the way they did. Everyone he encountered was ensnared in his spell, much like my older brother, Connor's, mother. Connor was the bane of my existence, and he hated me even more than I did him.

My first meeting with Connor was when I was six years old. My father had taken me out with him on his usual patrol for new women. He dressed me as he would dress, impeccably. The man never had a hair out of place and always dressed like he owned everything, yet we still lived in the worst part of town. Strolling through the city with no place to go, my father talked to me like I was his equal, like I could understand every adult issue he had. I think talking to me made him feel better, especially since I rarely spoke.

Connor and his mother were on their way to meet his stepfather. Connor was seven years older than me and quite aware that we shared the same father. His mother, like all my father's women, was infatuated with him, and as much as she wanted to pretend to hate him that day, she couldn't. She, with Connor at her side, approached us with an angry face.

"Hello Sylvia," my father sang in his seductive tone.

"Oh Dante, I've missed you." Sylvia embraced him, instantly falling into his arms.

"I am sure you have, but you're married now." Gripping my father tighter, Sylvia whispered her desires to him, begging for his attention. My father looked around and noticed the creamery at the end of the block. "Nicholas, would you like to get some ice cream?" I nodded, and my father escorted us all to the creamery where he set me up in a booth and ordered a bowl of mint chocolate chip, my favorite. I didn't notice my father and Sylvia leave, but I did notice Connor crashing into the seat across from me.

"So are you going to share that ice cream, jerk off?" Connor asked. I silently looked up at him as he twisted his expression into something more menacing. "So, give it to me." I shook my head and continued eating. A growl pushed through Connor's tight lips, and with an understanding of his intentions, I quickly moved the bowl from his reach. "You better give me that ice cream or I will make you regret it." I smiled and stuffed another spoonful in my mouth, enjoying our game. "You think that's funny?" Connor said, reaching over the table to grab me, but just before his hand reached my face, I eyed him dead on, causing a painful, trembling energy within his hand. Wide eyed, his fury came at me with both fists until my father pulled him off me.

"Sylvia, take your son and leave my sight," my father said, grabbing Connor by the arm and handing him over to her.

"But Dante!" she begged.

He pushed the desperate woman away from him, and shouted, "Now!" After they left, my father sat me down and looked me over, cleaning the blood from my lip. "You have to be careful of your anger, Nicholas. It will cause problems for you as you get older, especially against those who have similar blood."

"I can take him," I said firmly, causing my father to smile.

"I am sure you can, but let's give it a few more years before you try again. I have a lot more to teach you first." Scooting my ice cream back in front of me, he sat back and with pride he watched me dig back in.

I ate calmly until my father sat forward and began to listen to the room. He stood up suddenly and waited as a man came in and faced him with his chest out. He was Sylvia's husband and Connor's adoptive father, Bruce Daniels. Surrounded by his men, Daniels threatened my father, causing everyone in the creamery to leave. My fathered eased his way in between mine and Daniels's glare. "Is there a problem?" he asked smoothly. My father's calm demeanor kept me from becoming alarmed, so I finished my ice cream.

"Yes, there is, and either you or that boy is going to make up for it," Daniels said.

"I don't think so. I think you are going to admit you are wrong and apologize to me and my son," my father said as Daniels laughed and then gasped. There are no more words spoken from anyone. All I noticed between bites was a simple twitch of my father's hand before he slid it comfortably into his pocket. "Come, Nicholas. It is time for us to return home." Taking my father's hand, I scooted out of my seat and looked back at Mr. Daniels's trembling, sweating form and waved goodbye.

It was about disrespect for Daniels, but after that day, it was about Connor. After that day, Connor became Daniels's prized child. He made sure he never wanted for anything and gave him whatever he desired, including a position in his crooked business.

Chapter 3

Nick

"Nicholas," my father whispered to me in my sleep. "I want you to get under your bed and stay there until I tell you to come out," he said, picking me up and helping me crawl deep underneath my bed. "We are going to play a game, son, so be as quiet as you can and don't come out until only I tell you it is okay." My father disappeared into the darkness while I wondered what kind of game we were playing. Either way, I was determined to win, but when I heard a strange man's voice, my curiosity diminished my winning determination.

"I assumed I would never see you again, Dante, or I had hoped, for your sake, that you had run and hid like the coward you are."

"Oh no, Saldean. You know as well as I do that *he* would find me somehow."

"Then why did you leave us?"

"I want better, and you should want the same. We could work together …" my father said with a groan before I heard something crash into the wall. The blistering and thrashing of noises was non-stop thereafter. I began to crave to hear my father's voice again, something to guarantee that he hadn't left me there, hiding under the protection of my bed. When the backdoor broke open, I rushed to my window to see my father fighting with another man. There were no fists between the two, just some kind of fiery brute energy between them. Their eyes were locked, their chests stiff, but their legs rumbled from the ground and up into their hands that were wrapped around each other's throats. A sudden fear washed over me, provoking me to run. My desire was not to run away. No, I wanted to run to my father. He needed me. I felt it, and I feared losing the only person I could count on. My heart raced faster than my tiny body can carry me. I didn't know what I thought I could do, but the images began to blur the closer I got to the two men.

"Nicholas!" my father screamed the moment he saw me. Picking me up off the ground, he rushed me back inside and into my bed. My heartbeat seemed to shake the entire house, and my body felt on fire while my eyes resembled rapidly cooling embers. My father's hazy face slowly became clear as he brushed his hands over me and through my hair. "Everything is okay now, son. Close your eyes and go to sleep. I will stay right here with you." It takes some time for my body to calm completely, but with the help of my father's soothing voice, I was able to drift off to sleep again. "Everything is going to be okay because of you, Nicholas. I know it."

The next morning, a limo arrived in our driveway. My father quickly ran after me as I was playing in the yard and pushed me to the opposite side of him as a tall, angry man approached us. I stood to my father's side, looking up at the man before staring into the eyes of the ruby-eyed dragon sitting atop his cane. The dragon's skin draped along the neck and down below the man's hand. The glimmer in its eyes provoked me to reach out and touch it, feeling its golden scales and bright red eyes. I gasped, looking up at the man again as he eyed me with an unyielding glare.

My father instantly pushed me further behind him. "There is no reason for you to be here, Dennis, and I don't appreciate you showing up at my home unannounced," my father said sternly.

"I didn't know I had to be announced, Dante. When did we become so formal? Besides, I believe you might have information I need. I am looking for my son. I was told he came to see you last night."

"You would know. You sent him," my father said through his teeth.

The man sighed with a deep smile. "I was hoping you two could work out your differences."

"Yes, we worked them out, and he agreed to my terms." My father smiled.

Taking in a deep breath, the man simmered before speaking again. "Impressive Dante, *very*. I would not have thought you to have the ability to counter Saldean. So, how do we work out this issue from here?" the man said, looking down at me with piercing eyes. "Your son? I wasn't aware you had children, not that I am surprised. I am, however, surprised I wasn't told."

"He's not mine. He's my wife's. I am looking after him while she is at work." The man laughed harshly, and instantly, my father was in his face. "You have no reason to be here. We parted ways a long time ago."

"You parted the organization only, Dante, and don't forget that. Your responsibilities still hold true to the family, especially now that, thanks to you, my son is gone. And that boy …"

"This boy has nothing to do with the organization. He is unimportant."

"You owe me, Dante."

"I owe you nothing," my father said, facing the man with a fear I have never felt from him before. Peeking up at the man, I crouched behind my father and hid. The moment was silent, but the surrounding air cooled and heavied, bringing a hardened chill to my lips. My heart sped up as a stinging sensation pierced my skin. I wanted to run, but my hands wouldn't let go of my father. I clung to his leg as my head began to swarm. Suddenly, my urge to run was interrupted by a dog barking. I instantly searched around me for the source, and spotted him running towards another. Their playfulness caused me to laugh, and I let go of my father and ran after them. "Nicholas!" my father yelled, picking me up and rushing me inside. Over my father's shoulder, I looked back at the man who stood wide-eyed and stiff as he focused in on me. Setting me down in front of him, he said, "Nicholas I want you to listen to me and never forget what I am about to say to you. That man, Dennis Savage, do not ever go near him. He is not to be trusted. He only wants bad things for you. Promise me, son, that you will never go near that man?" I nodded, silently of course.

Chapter 4

Nick

My father experienced many women, and many of them with me watching. For the most part, I cannot recall their faces, and certainly not their names. That is, except for one. This woman, as I remember, was so beautiful that, even as child she captured my attention. She had my father's in the same instant.

With me in tow, he walked up to her while she was ordering coffee in a local diner. He looked her over, head to toe, until she turned his way. "Hello," he said with his usual deep, velvety voice. Her eyes smiled, and her knees went weak, forcing my father's hand to take hold of her bare arm. "Hmmm, you are so soft. I could caress you all night and never get tired. Maybe you will let me sometime," he said, letting her go and leaving her with a simple goodbye. "Absolutely beautiful." She nearly knocked me down trying to get to him before he walked out the door. Rianne, we visited her often. She was nice to me, but I was indifferent to her until I met Ryan.

I remember hearing him cry as a baby, even seeing him a few times as a child, but it wasn't until I was ten that I understood who he was. He was nearly six then: shy, skinny, and hard to ignore. Believe me, I tried. My father told me to watch him while he entertained the boy's mother, but he wouldn't sit down. He continued to pace with his raggedy bear in his arms, whimpering for his mother. I finally asked him if he liked cartoons, and he nodded. His attention immediately shifted back to his mother, and he asked for her, over and over.

"What's your name?" I asked him.

"Ryan," he said, hugging his bear with its one eye hanging down the side of its face, seemingly longing for Rianne as much as Ryan was considering its sad state. "When will they come out?" he asked, grabbing my shirt sleeve to make sure I didn't ignore his question. I tried to tell him they would be done soon, but he went back to waiting for his mother at the edge of her door. I huffed at him and told him to stop being such a baby and to get over it. My indifference to his issue was not appreciated. Ryan dropped the bear from his face and turned to me with churning fury in his eyes. That was first time I ever saw his anger, but it was certainly not the first time I had seen a display of unmistakable fury.

"Who is your dad?" I asked and watched him point to his mother's bedroom. I shouldn't be surprised, but the thought of having a younger brother is not something I had ever considered. He didn't understand, but I did. From that moment on, I took it upon myself to teach him what I knew and made sure no one would ever hurt him. This meant keeping him a secret from our older brother.

Ryan and I had plenty of time to get to know each other. My father and I visited them often, allowing Ryan and I to grow together and become true brothers. Some of our favorite memories are when we were left alone. We always left the cramped apartment to entertain ourselves, but most of the time, I walked him to the store on the corner where the owner was easy to manipulate. She gave us so much candy and cookies that we had a hard time eating it all.

One time, when we returned to the apartment, Ryan came back home with his pockets full of sweets and looking absolutely ridiculous. His mother caught us as he frantically tried to stuff all he had in his mouth. It would have worked except he got sick seconds later and spewed the colorful evidence all over the floor, in front of everyone. Of course, my first response was, "I don't know where he got that." Neither Dad nor Rianne was happy about the situation. I assumed his mother would yell at me, but instead, she approached me and put her hand to my forehead.

"I think he had too much, too. Let me make him a bed," she said.

"No, he is coming home with me," my father said, taking my hand and pulling me away from her.

"Don't be silly. He won't make it that far, not without throwing up. Unless you want to take care of a sick child, Dante, I suggest you leave him here. I already have one sick little boy keeping me up tonight, and one more won't make much of a difference." She didn't wait for him to speak before she took my hand, found me some clothes, and told me to change. My father refused to leave me, but he allowed the woman to clean me up and put me into bed, tucking me in tight after she gave me some medicine and put a cold cloth to my head.

"If you get sick, yell for me, but you should feel better in the morning," Rianne said, fingering my hair to the side and smiling at me. "You look so much like your father, another heartbreaker in the making for sure." With another kiss to my head, she checked on Ryan and left us to sleep.

I told myself I didn't like her. I complained about having to go to her house every time my father forced me to, but in reality, I can't wait to be around her. She would make me dinner, and I would find new reasons for me to, *have to,* stay overnight. I don't know if she ever met my mother, but I think she had some idea about her, and she definitely knew my father. Eventually, my father allowed me to stay by myself with her.

One night, I pretended to be asleep when they finished, and after my father left, she whispered into my ear, "Okay honey, you can go to bed now." With a kiss to my head, she bid me a goodnight, "Sleep well sweetheart." I didn't know what love was until then, and I loved Rianne.

As much I like spending time at Rianne's house, it made my time at home that much worse. I hugged my mother one time, and she held her arms open and looked down at me as if I were some kind of alien creature. I never bothered to try again. My mother went through life with no emotion, and she never cried, never got angry, never seemed to care about anything. She worked with numbers and could figure out any equation there was. I could ask her what 24,640 times 52,438 was, and she would tell me as simply as if I had asked her what time it was. My mother worked in a big building with a lot of people, doing some secret work that no one could talk about, and she never did.

My mother, Gillian, met my father, Dante, on her way home from work one night. She made the mistake of stopping and buying some soup at a nearby café. Dante was talking to one of the waitresses at the time while she tried to tabulate his check. She became confused and flustered until she said the numbers out loud, prompting Gillian to say the total of his bill for her. My mother cost my father money that day. He said he was impressed and that was why he pursued her. I don't believe that. I think it was revenge. She cost him money, and he was going to make her spend her life paying for it. He spent almost everything she made, and usually before she could even make it. I never met my grandparents; I assumed my father was never actually born but rather appeared out of the depths of the earth. My mother's parents were happy to hand her over to my father and rid themselves of her, disappearing soon after my mother and father married.

The only family of hers who stayed behind was her brother, Tanner, a drunk who wouldn't have survived at all if I hadn't snuck him food and fresh clothes.

The first time I met Tanner, he showed up on our doorstep, plastered and looking for a place to crash for the night. My father, despite my mother wanting to allow Tanner in, screamed at him to leave. Tanner begged for anything: food, water, clothes, a place to rest his head. Anything. My father was not sympathetic to my inebriated uncle; he simply closed the door in his face. What my father didn't realize was that Tanner didn't leave, and instead, he set up a place inside the neighbors' dilapidated shed. I watched him come and go from there through my bedroom window, and after my father fell asleep, I gathered food, water, blankets, and some extra clothes for him. I filled a large trash bag with the items and lugged it across the yard. When I arrived, I knocked on the rickety door like it was any other home.

Tanner scrambled inside, knocking over whatever home life he had set up. He nervously peeked out the door before noticing me. "Hello … uhhh … oh, Nicholas. Right?" I nodded, shoved the trash bag inside the shed, and ran back home before anyone could discover I was gone.

My childhood was not one of normality, and my parents were not ones to be at PTA meetings or cub scouts, but somehow, I survived. My father even managed to keep me in school up through most of high school, and he only slept with a couple of my teachers in the process. However, that wasn't entirely his fault. Both teachers had met him prior and requested his presence to discuss my education. My teachers thought I was special, or so they said, and needed more attention in order to develop to my full potential. They eagerly volunteered their time, for free, to help me. As it turned out, they weren't all that free after all. I couldn't wait to get older and go to school by myself. High school was even better because I could talk the teachers out of ever talking to my father and convinced them to deal strictly with me. My father had taught me well.

Chapter 5

Nick

At eighteen, I was restless and hungry for something more than what school could ever offer me. The decision to leave school was easy; it had nothing more to offer me. My life was destined for something special, and it wasn't some fancy degree.

I began stealing cars for Harvey Rice before I even had my license. By the time I was sixteen, I was the best he had. I was not an official member of his crew and neither were my friends. We all were working for him in hopes of getting being offered a position with him after proving our loyalty and skills. Rice was not the most trusting man, and his distrust was heightened when faced with three punk teenagers. I had met Luke Norton, my overzealous friend, while we were both trying to steal the same car three years ago. We nearly got arrested arguing about who had the rights to the steal, a bond that we still laugh about.

My other friend and the third member of our trio was Elijah Stevens, my best friend since… forever. Our fathers knew each other and seemed to have some kind of special relationship, enough so that Mr. Stevens took it upon himself to look after me whenever my father wasn't around. A respectable man, Mr. Stevens owned his own electronics shop. He was also the one that helped teach Elijah and me how to handle every tool imaginable, it's one of the reasons we can get in and out of cars with no problem at all. We never let him know that; instead we joked that it helped us get into girls' bedrooms without their fathers knowing, also something we have no problem doing, but we don't need any tools for that. Mr. Stevens also happened to be a great cook and always had homemade meals available for us to eat. He loved to cook, and always made more than enough for us to eat ten times over. I think he also knew that two growing boys would always come home if a table, full of food, awaited them, and we did. We even included Luke once we added him to our small crew.

Luke and I are great friends because of our differences, and Elijah and I are friends because we are so much alike. We have similar interests and similar tastes in women, too, something that made for great competitions at times. Elijah considers himself charming and irresistible, and true or not, I consider myself even more so.

My two friends and I spent most of our time working for Harvey, but when we were done, it was all about getting laid. The club we frequented was always busy and always full of women. Luke knew one of the body guards, and he always let us in through the back for an even exchange of what he needed. After we got in, our time there wasn't about dancing or drinking, but it was all about relieving our stress of the day. One particular evening, the three of us immediately scatter upon entering the club. Standing quietly in my jeans, t-shirt, and much abused leather jacket, I look innocent enough, but I am nothing more than a devil in disguise. I scan the area until I found the right one, and then, I wait, calmly confident in what will happen when she looks my way. It is a simple strategy, one that I learned from my father. The moment we make eye contact, that's my cue. She is surrounded by friends, but I stay focused on her and walk towards her with a hungry gaze. I want her. I want to feel her. I want to fuck her like she has never been fucked before. Staring deep into her eyes, I hold my hand out to her and simply say, "Hi, I'm Nick." It works every time, and this time is no different. She takes my hand and I draw her into my arms. With a soft exhale, I graze my lips across her cheek. The world disappears around us as she weakly peers into my eyes. She's mine. "All I want is to be alone with you." She hums her address while her friends gasp behind us. "Take me there, and I am all yours." Not even a second passes and we are out the door and on our way. She offers me a drink after we get there, but I shake my head and, again, hold out my hand to her. "I don't need anything, but you." One soft kiss to her lips and her dress unzips. A soft caress of her ass into my erection drives her right into my arms, allowing me to carry her to her room and strip her completely naked. She crawls into bed with her bare ass stuck out in front of me. I take advantage and bury my readied dick inside of her. With a sudden gasp, she fists the sheets in front of her and backs her ass further into my hips. My whole body calms as I rub her ass, massage her breasts, and graze her most tender areas with a light touch of my fingers. Her cries of lust are loud, so I whisper some calming words into her ear. She comes all over me, and I do the same for her, exhausting her and making it difficult to wake her enough to do it again. After the second time, I give her a break and make myself something to eat while she sleeps.

Sitting in her kitchen with a sandwich in hand, I hear her door open and see another girl coming in with someone right behind her. "Do you live alone?" Elijah says, coming through the girls' door.

"No, I have a roommate, but she is probably sound asleep by now." Leaning back in my chair, I look around the corner at him and wink, causing him to shake his head.

"Oh, I would say she is certainly sound asleep by now." He smiles, making sure she doesn't look my way, but up at him.

"So… do you want to come back to my bedroom and talk?" she asks, biting her bottom lip.

"Your bedroom? That sounds dirty," Elijah says, cozying up to her as she leads him to her room. "Okay, but be gentle with me. I have never done anything like this before." The girl giggles with excitement while Elijah winks back at me, nodding.

"Never done this before – dumbass," I mumble to myself.

"Nick, are you coming back to bed?" Amanda stands in her doorway, naked and ready to go again. The night gives me an opportunity to sleep somewhere other than home, something I savor every chance I get.

By morning, I rush home to clean up and change before I meet up with Elijah and Luke to get back to work. There is a corner store we meet at most days, and today is no different, except my brother shows up soon after I do and before Elijah and Luke. Connor is determined to make me miserable. His hate for me nearly matches mine for him. Catching sight of his car, I step back into the shadows, trying to hide, but he knows I am here, and there is little I can do against his crew by myself. Connor's father has access to more weapons than the military and more drugs than the entire city could high on. Connected? Yeah, he's connected and dirty. Dirty as hell. So, his stepson, my half brother, is connected by association. Ever since he moved up the ranks, Connor has formed his own crew for no other reason than to help him harass me.

They surround me with delight as they walk up on me. I prepare myself, but before I can decide on who to attack first, a bag is thrown over my head, and the beating begins. I know the beating is over when my brother's laughter causes his breathing to be labored. They leave me, twisting in pain and depending on my friends to help me home.

"You know, Nick, if you would just agree to Harvey's terms, you would be in his crew, and your brother would not come after you anymore," Luke says.

"No, he would still come after me. Harvey doesn't scare him, no matter how much power he has." My father greets us at the door, shaking his head as his woman of the day dresses herself. "Don't you dare say a word to me," I scowl before crawling into bed and hiding from the world.

"Don't worry, Nicky. We will take care of things for today. I will call you later," Elijah says, leaving me to remove my destroyed clothes by myself.

He doesn't speak as he stands at the edge of my door, but I can feel his eyes on me. "Just say it! If you have something to say to me, then just say it!" I yell, glancing over my shoulder at him.

"I have told you already. You're stronger than him, but you refuse to understand. One day, you will get it, and I just hope it's before he kills you."

"There were five of them, and they threw a bag over my head. What would you have me do?" I ask, knowing I am right and that he has no clue what he is talking about.

Approaching me, he looks me over and then pokes me in my chest, "Here. Here is where you need to feel it. Concentrate your anger here, and you will understand. You are *trying* too hard, and you don't *want* it enough."

"Oh, I don't want it enough because I like getting my ass kicked?"

"Nicholas, you have everything you need within you, son. Just believe in yourself," my father says before walking out of my room with a sigh.

"Gee thanks, Yoda. What I could really use is a bandage and a cold pack… you know, something for my wounds. Useless …" My father was never one to be nurturing, but compared to my mother, whose eyes dart away instantly from mine as she passes my door, he is Florence Nightingale..

My father walks back into my room, handing, me some bandages, an ice pack, and a key. "One day, when you're ready to face who you are, you let me know, and I will take you to where this key fits."

"Dante?" my mother says, peeking her head back in but still avoiding my eyes.

"He is old enough, Gillian, unless you want him to continue coming home looking like this?" my father snaps at her. She doesn't respond to him; instead, she quietly goes back into her world. "It is your choice, Nicholas, but don't take too long. I would hate for you to be killed before you could ever make a decision."

"Ha ha, asshole!" I yell as he leaves my room with a smile. *Damn Harvey is going to kick my ass for not working today. Maybe I can boost some extra cars for the next few nights and make it up.*

Chapter 6

Franky

I have been working at my father's shop since I was twelve. I cannot imagine my life away from this place or away from my father, but college looms, and I cannot wait. A girl can only take so much routine before the repetitive motions lose their appeal.

Taking my place at the front of the store, I help the few customers left for the night while my father prepares the daily deposits. Giving me a concerned wave, he hesitates about leaving me, but I frustratingly wave him on. We are closing in less than an hour, and the police patrol this area quite regularly at this time of night, so there is no reason he should be worried. After the last customer leaves, I decide to prop up my text book, wrap my lucky scarf around my neck, and study for my exam the next day until it is time to lock up. Everything is quiet and working its way to another uneventful night, but then, with ten minutes left until closing time … *he* walks in. I am not sure if I am going to be able to concentrate for the rest of the evening, and I am going to have to hope for the best on my exam because there is no way I am getting anything in my head, but him. He's tall, dark, and deathly handsome, so much so that it hurts to stare at him…Nicholas Jayzon. I don't see him much anymore since he quit school, but every once in a while, he stops by the store, usually with his friends in tow and always making my father uneasy. "Hoodlums," my father would say under his breath, watching their every move until they would leave. They have never stolen anything and always buy something, but still, my father believes they are casing the place. The moment he glances up at me, I instantly look back down at my book.

The longer Nick wanders around the store, the more uneasy I get. *Maybe he is going to rob us*? Clearing my throat, I sit up straight and try to speak, but the moment he looks up at me, I lose the ability to. "Yes? Do you want to say something to me?" he asks in a frustrated tone.

"I was … ummm, just wondering if …" *what was I wondering? Oh yes.* "If you need help finding anything?" I say, feeling relieved that I managed to say something coherent, not something I have been able to do around him in the past. Last year, some boys at school purposely shoved me, causing me and my books to go flying across the floor. The only hand that was held out to help me up was Nick's. He asked me if I was okay, I nodded, and then said, "Ankle you." *Ankle you?* A combination of my "ankle is twisted" and "thank you". Apparently, he doesn't speak my language of gibberish, so he, and his puzzled expression, left me to glow in my embarrassment.

From that point on, I have been fascinated by him, curious to say something more than, "*Ankle You.*" I have seen other girls speak to him, but they never do a lot of talking. Conversations with him are short lived. He prefers other one-on-one activities with girls, something else I have always been curious about. I have never met anyone to share that kind of activity with. I am not exactly the kind of girl guys dream about, and I am certainly not Nick's type; however, I have, more than once, daydreamed about his arm around me or his luscious lips on mine. Unfortunately, I don't know enough to even daydream much further than first base. I am a sad spectacle, but when I go to college, yes, there is where I am going to have my time. I hear that everyone loses their virginity at college. *Everyone!* I just have to wait my turn.

"Excuse me? Do you have any of these bags in black or a darker color of some kind?" Nick asks, holding up one of our new tool bags.

"I can check in the back?" I say, stumbling off my stool and into the storage room. Tossing items from one side to the next, I quickly rummage through our inventory until I find one black tool bag. As soon as I turn around, Nick runs up on me and presses me against the wall. Hovering over me, he looks down with a serious look, piercing my eyes with his own. "My father has already taken the deposits. We don't have much money left here. If you want the bag, just take it and …"

"What? No, I am not trying to rob you. I need you to be quiet," he says. He holds his finger to my lips and adjusts to get closer to me as he listens closely. I should be scared, nervous even, or at least curious as to why I have to be quiet, but instead, all I can think about is his body pressed tightly against mine. His arm wraps around my waist as his hands hold me firmly still. "Just be very quiet," he says, waiting for me to nod. Nick looks around the corner, his hot breath steaming up my neck, causing my entire body to go weak. I can barely breathe, taking in the scent of him as the feeling of being guarded by him consumes me. My mind begins to wander to a place I have only read about, and watched once at my cousin Mark's house. That was creepy. I wish I hadn't finished watching it, *sort of.* I wonder if Nick is wearing anything like that guy had on underneath? Or has anything like that? He must have something nice, considering … how … oh, he smells so good. I feel a dopey smile form, and my mind goes deeper into trouble. My euphoric daydream is abruptly interrupted by a loud crash within the store. As soon as I open my mouth, Nick presses his finger back to my lips. "They are looking for me. Are you a good liar? You can't tell them I am here." *Lying? Me?* "Yeah… I thought that might be the case, so just stay quiet instead. Please. They will leave once the cops go through." I trust him for no reason other than I enjoy this moment of having him pressed against me.

With his attention occupied with what is going on within the store, I rest my hands against his chest and slowly drag them over his body, leading him to glance down at me. "You're kind of close."

"Just … be … quiet," he whispers harshly. Once we hear the chimes from the front door, Nick releases me and cautiously investigates the store. "They are gone. You can come out now."

Stepping back into the store, I instantly panic at the site. "Oh no!" The store is completely wrecked. *How did I not hear this being done?* One look at Nick, and I realize why. "This is a … my father is going to kill me."

"Don't worry. We will get it back together," Nick says picking up a display.

"Who was that? Why did they do this?" I demand to know.

"My brother, actually. He is determined to kick my ass especially after …" He glances my way and stops short of telling me everything.

"After you what? I can't imagine what it might be that would cause your own brother to be this angry with you."

"You don't know my brother. He doesn't need much of an excuse to hate me, but in this case, I took something of his and put it in an awkward place." Nick smiles, seeming to fight back a laugh.

"Well, I don't care for your brother at all if this is any indication of what he is like," I say, and Nick instantly smiles and kisses my cheek. *Although, I really love you.* My dopey smile reappears without my consent.

Nick does stay and help me clean up, even taking off his shirt to help reset some light fixtures. A tattoo across his ribs is something I have never seen before, a fiery design that doesn't seem to be completed. "What made you get that tattoo?" I ask, tracing its outline in the air.

"Another incident with my brother left this bruise along my ribs. My friend Luke said it looked like I was on fire, and I liked the idea so …" he says before stepping down off the ladder and looking down at me. "It's not finished yet. I plan on it stretching from my shoulder all the way down …" He laughs when I gasp at his hand dropping below his waist. "Don't worry, I don't plan on tattooing my dick. It's fine just the way it is. Don't you think?" he asks.

"What? I wouldn't know!"

Leaning in close to me, Nick nearly touches my lips with his. "Do you want to?" he asks, sending my knees diving for the floor. Shaking his head, Nick takes hold of my arm and guides me to another area of the store. "We are nearly finished. Let's concentrate on getting done so we can both get on with our lives." I, suddenly, don't want to ever finish. "Just one last thing, come here …" Taking my waist, he lifts me up so I can adjust some items on the wall. His sudden touch startles me, and I forget that I am wearing a skirt. Thankfully, I think clearly enough to do what I need to do. When he sits me down, I quickly realize that my underwear is showing and push my skirt back down. "Nice panties," he smirks.

"You are not much of a gentleman, are you?" I snap at him, my words shocking him and myself.

"I am trying to help you. I could have left you here or left you alone with my brother's henchmen, and I guarantee you, Kitten, they are certainly no gentlemen," he says, winking and turning away from me.

I forcefully grab his arm. "I think you actually still owe me."

"How do you figure? I just helped you clean this disaster up."

"You helped clean a mess up that you caused! They were looking for you. I could have screamed and turned you over to them. I doubt they would have cared much about me once they had you. Hell… there is probably a reward …"

"Reward? What am I, America's Most Wanted? I stole his car, Kitten. I didn't kill his wife," Nick says with a huff.

"Still, you still owe me."

Shaking his head with a sigh, "Fine I owe you. What do you want?"

His question lingers around me with thoughts and ideas multiplying so fast they begin to blur, but for some reason, a thought pushes its way to the front and out of my mouth before I can stop it. "I want … I want to know about sex." *I can't believe I just said that.*

"What? You want to have sex with me?"

"No! I only want to know about it."

"How else do you learn about it? Wait, are you a virgin?"

"That doesn't matter. All I want is to ask you questions and for you to answer honestly."

"About sex?" He laughs as I nod. "Wow. Sure. Okay, Kitten, whatever you want. Ask away."

"No, not here, not now. I have to get home before my father freaks out. Tomorrow, at my house. My father stays at his girlfriend's after work on Fridays, so you can come over and we can work on my study then."

"Your study? That's a new one," he says, winking in my face.

"I am not trying to have sex with you!" I scream, pushing him away from me.

"Okay, it's for your … *study*, I suppose. Call me when you want me to come over." Nick takes my phone and types in his number. "I have business to take care of tomorrow night. Once I finish, I can come over." I agree, biting my bottom lip to keep from screaming for joy.

Chapter 7

Franky

It's Friday night, and as soon as my father leaves, I pick up my phone and nervously dial Nick's number, breathing several times before I finally hit the call button. *Hi Nick … Hey what's up … ummm. So it's me … Get your fine ass over here now …*

"What's so funny?" Nick asks.

"Ummm, nothing … I … I … ummm … Hey." *Oh no. What is wrong with you?*

"Hey. Listen, I really thought you were kidding about this coming over shit, so I made other plans. I am sure you can find someone else to help you out with your study," he says, snickering.

"But I wasn't kidding, and what do you mean you made other plans? You owe me," I insist.

"Yeah, okay, I will try to make it up to you some other time, but right now, I have to go. I will talk to you later," Nick says and hangs up the phone.

That fucking asshole! Oh, I hate him! I can't believe he did this to me. Well, never again. I am never talking to him again. I steam for sometime before I start to feel guilty for hoping that he calls me back. No, *I am not going to sit around here and hope that he changes his mind and shows up after all.* Making a quick call, I agree to meet my one available friend, Brandi, for pizza, and drown my disappointment in pepperoni and cheese.

"Sorry about Nick, but he isn't really your type anyway. He is kind of scary even," Brandi says, sipping on her soda. I know she is trying to help, but her straightforward response doesn't really help me feel any better. Brandi is level-headed and smart, but more naïve than me which is saying a lot. She was home schooled up until about two years ago, and has been scared shitless to talk to boys since I met her. Brandi is not exactly the authority on men that I am looking for tonight, but she was my best answer at the last minute. Brandi continues on with some other mindless chit chat while I nod in agreement whenever it feels right to do so. All I can think about is him changing his mind and showing up to my empty house. What if he had some family thing and that is why …

"So, Nicky, did you manage to get laid before we forced to leave?" Elijah says, following Nick into the pizza shop.

"I crawled into her bedroom later. She always leaves it open for me anyway," Nick says, laughing along with his friends.

"Lucky bastard," Luke says with a shake of his head.

"I can't believe he is here. That asshole is actually here!" I stare at Nick in disbelief until he looks over at me and nods with a smile. "Hey."

"Hey," he says, walking out the door again.

Before I can think about it, I get up and run after him. "Nick!"

He turns around, wide-eyed and greets me with a frustrated, "What?"

"Do you have nothing to say to me?" I snap.

"I said Hi." He shrugs.

Stomping my foot, I cringe with anger. "Go to hell, asshole!"

"Okay," he laughs, continuing on with his friends. With Brandi in tow, I follow after him. After a couple of blocks, Nick turns around in annoyance and approaches me, "What are you doing?"

"I am going to follow you until you apologize for breaking our agreement," I reply.

"*Franky*, go home! I will talk to you tomorrow. I am sorry I couldn't make it, but I have business to take care of right now."

"No, I want to go this way, too." Nick shakes head, but continues walking, only faster to try and lose me I assume. Now even angrier and even more determined, I concentrate on keeping up and following his every move, despite Brandi's constant complaining for me to stop. Nick takes some sharp turns before leading down to an area I am not familiar with. I look down the dark street before finally noticing Brandi has stopped trailing behind. *No point in going back alone. Might as well stick with someone I know.*

I continue following them to a bar where Nick checks behind himself one more time and growls with impatience before shaking his finger in my face. "Go home, Franky. This is no place for you. You're only going to get yourself hurt." Nick pushes me back in the opposite direction while he goes forward with his friends into the bar.

I am not a little girl. I can handle a bar if he can. Following him in, I take in the heavy smoke and the unruly crowd with less excitement than I had before I entered. I am pushed away from the door before I know it and standing near some prostitute bargaining with a man for her time. My interruption is not welcomed by either of them. This bar is nothing like I thought it would be. Searching through the smoldering air, I try to follow Nick, but the crowd quickly surrounds me, and he moves too deep in the back for me to keep track. Nick and his friends have completely disappeared, and now, I am alone. *What was I thinking? Why didn't I just go home?* Working my way through the crowd, I slide across the wall, searching for some kind of exit until I find a fire door. Anxious, I quickly make my way out and into an alleyway, a dark alleyway.

"Who are you?" someone says, grabbing my arm.

"No one, I was only trying to go home," I say, trying to pull away from the repulsive man.

"It's too early to go home, girly. Do you need a pick me up? I can certainly help you out with that." He hands me something and rubs his hand down my side, harshly pulling me into him. "Go ahead. Take it. I promise you will feel a hell of a lot better."

"I don't want it. I am supposed to meet someone. I need to go!" I cry out, hoping to draw attention from someone, somewhere.

"But I don't want you to go. I want you to stay here and be my friend for the night." He smiles wide, and tears well up in my eyes. "I bet I can find a few friends for you tonight. What do you say? Want a make a little cash?" His toxic breath releases into my mouth as I ready myself to scream. "I can't speak for the others, but I'll be gentle."

"NO! Get away from me!" I scream.

Suddenly, my arm is jerked away from him, "Go find someone else, Pearls. This one is not for you. She's mine," Nick says, pushing me behind his back and meeting the man face to face.

"I saw her first, Nick." The man takes out a knife, shining his bright smile once again. Nick reaches back and pulls out his own. Breathless and wide-eyed, I grip Nick's shirt wanting to do something, anything to keep him from fighting this man.

In an instant, Nick slams the guy backwards and holds his knife to the man's throat. "I said go. If you can't do that peacefully, then I will make sure you lose your …"

"No, I'm good. Sorry, Nick. Please, I only thought she would like a pick me up," Pearls drops his rusted knife and holds up his hands. "You know I have friends right around the corner Nick …"

Elijah and Luke come out another door, drawing their guns on the man and silencing him. "Oh yeah, I got friends too. Get the fuck out of here before I lose my temper any more than I already have." Once the man leaves, Nick turns his anger back towards me. "I thought I said go home." I have no words, and all I can do is cry.

"Oh fuck, she's crying. I hate when girls cry," Luke says.

"Shut up, dumbass," Elijah says, shoving Luke. "Nick take her home. We will run the money back to Harvey and pay you later."

Nick nods and wraps his arm around my waist, forcing me down the street. "What is wrong with you? I speak to you once, and now you are following me around? Don't you have better things to do?" I have nothing to say to him. I can only cry harder. "Please stop crying. I can't be mad if you're crying."

"I don't want you to be mad at me. I am mad at you," I whimper while he laughs. "Don't laugh at me! You promised me, and then you brushed me off like I didn't matter. I have every right to be mad at you," I yell, halting my pace. "I am so sick of people like you looking down on me and treating me like I don't matter or that I don't have feelings. So what? I am not the sexy hot chick you like. Who cares if you are not willing to go out of your way to crawl through my bedroom window. I am beautiful, too. You know, you are just too stupid and full of yourself to realize it. You'll see. One day, you will get tired of the airheaded fools you are falling all over yourself for and want someone who you can actually have a conversation with, and guess what?"

"What?" He smiles sarcastically.

"You will be too late – that's what!"

"Oh no, I'm late. I'm late. For a very important date …" he sings as I smack him until he stops.

"You are such an asshole!" I yell, continuing to smack him as he resumes laughing.

"Okay, okay! I'm sorry, but some business came up at the last minute, and to be honest, I didn't think you really wanted me to come over. You have never even talked to me before. You and your father look at me like I am a loser. I assumed it was a joke, and I wasn't about to participate in it."

"It wasn't a joke. I really wanted your help. I wanted your help with … oh never mind. I will find someone else to help me. Go back to your friends. I can make it the rest of the way by myself."

"No, I am walking you home, and making sure you get there safely. I would feel terrible if something happened to you now," Nick says, fighting a smile.

"Feel terrible then because I don't want to be around you anymore." I push him away from me and stomp towards home. I curse him under my breath most of the way, and he snickers behind me with every grumble and protest I make. With my house in sight, I check behind me one more time and see Nick continuing to follow me, watching our surroundings closely. "Go away and stop following me!" I yell one more time, but he still continues to follow, and then waits for me to go inside. Running into my room, I catch sight of him from my bedroom window as he continues to stand outside my house. I have to wave him away in a threatening manner before he finally nods with a cynical goodbye.

After I settle in for the night, he calls, and I purposely ignore him, but I don't ignore his voicemail: *Goodnight Franky - I enjoyed walking with you, I mean behind you. I hope I get to stare at your ass again sometime soon. I promise, I won't be late for that.*

He is such a jackass. I hate him. I smile deep into my pillows through the entire night.

Chapter 8

Nick

To get back at Connor, the other night I stole his precious classic car that he spent nearly a year customizing for himself. While he was wining and dining his new wife at the country club, I slipped into the valet parking lot and drove it right out with no one ever noticing a thing. It was easy and quite gratifying. The only thing I could not decide was whether I should wreck his car and return it that way or make it disappear altogether. I drove it around for some time, trying to decide until I came up with the perfect solution. I parked it at the city impound lot, unaccounted for and untagged. I have an old friend who let me hide it in the back and among the many until I was ready to make a move with it. Today, I got wind that Connor is deeply involved with business, so I feel safe enough to move his car from its hiding place and sell it for a nice profit. Knowing that Connor will never see his priceless car again is all I need to feel good about my steal, but the money makes it even better.

Ruge circles the car several times while he looks it over on top and underneath, verifying the quality. My brother's prized possession is going to help give me an extra boost to my own dreams. "You did real good, Nick, but how much you want? Keep in mind, I am your best connection for more leads." Rolling my eyes, I look down and hold up my hand to his instant sigh. He knows I am also the best he has, and the number I am holding up is more than fair for this car. He tries to take a strong stance, but I step forward, adding an additional hand to my number. "Fuck, Jayzon! Fine. Here. Don't spend it all in one place," Ruge says with his usual dryness. "Where are your buddies anyway? You shouldn't be out by yourself tonight. Connor will bury your ass if he finds you after this."

"Don't worry about me Ruge, I can handle myself." Shaking his head, he laughs and sends me on my way so he can shut down the shop before the cops patrol the area. A quick call to both Luke and Elijah, and I am assured they are on their way to meet me. I am confident, but not stupid. Knowing my streets like I do, I decide to cut through an alley to meet up with my boys. Huge mistake. The eerie silence begins to sends chills up my spine until I have to stop dead in my tracks. I feel him near, and then I see it. A quiet puff of air soars out from the corner near me. It's him, and there is no where I can run and no place I can hide.

From out of the darkness, Connor steps out with some of his crew. It figures I would run into him tonight. Harvey has made it clear that we have to complete all tasks that we are given for the next few weeks if we want any chance of earning a better positions on his crew. Now, my brother is going to make sure I screw up on night one. There are five, not including Connor. I quickly weigh my options, but I don't get much time before my head is covered and my beating begins. Thankfully, Luke and Elijah send Connor and his crew running but not without a promise to return for me.

"Nicky?" Elijah runs up on me while Luke confirms my brother is gone. "What the hell happened?"

"Same as always, but I guess he decided to make a special late night effort for me tonight. I stole his car and just sold it to Ruge." I smile as Elijah laughs.

"You're an idiot. Have you not gotten enough beatings from him? What, are you asking for them now?" Elijah immediately takes hold of me, and with Luke's help, they shove my shoulder back into place, sending me cursing to the ground. I take a few minutes to walk off the pain and move my arm a little before tying it up with a ripped up t-shirt from Elijah's car. Despite the pain, I move forward with my night, completing our tasks before heading home with Elijah to hide out from my father for one more night.

I thought my night was over until Elijah and I walk in on his father fighting off robbers, street thugs trying to score some high-priced tools from his shop. We both immediately jump into the fight and enjoy inflicting our own punishment before sending them limping away with an understanding that they are never to come back.

"Elijah!" his father yells, falling to the ground and clinching his chest. Elijah runs, screaming for his father. The fear in his eyes is evident. I have to snap Elijah's focus on his father and help get him to the car. I race through the streets to the nearest hospital while Elijah cries to his father to hold on. Elijah's pain sinks deeply into my own heart; I have never seen my friend so broken, and I never want to see it ever again. Elijah and his father disappear into the whiteness of the hospital while I stay behind and wonder where to go and what to do now. Elijah reappears a few hours later, arguing with a hospital suit about the costs. His stressful, teary-eyed tone makes it clear he is about to break.

"Sir, I understand your issues, but we are simply not able to take care of your father here. I promise you, the city hospital will be more than helpful to you. We will even be happy to transport him safely."

"Transport him? His is not a crate of garbage - he's my father!"

Taking hold of Elijah shoulders, I move him away from the situation and assure him I will handle the hospital suit while he sees to his father. "So how much do you need to keep him here?" While the suit rolls his eyes at me, I pull out my car money and hold it up. "I will count it off. Just tell me when to stop."

"Yes sir," he says, stepping closer to me with more respect. That's the feeling I want to feel again. *Respect, instant respect. There is nothing like it.*

After I make sure Elijah's father is set for the night at the hospital that his son chose, I return to the Stevens' shop and clean up before crashing on their sofa for the night.

"Hey." Elijah smacks me on the head. "Knucklehead, I got you some breakfast." Sitting up groggy, I welcome the coffee he hands me and the bag of food. "You gave up your brother's car money, didn't you?"

"No, I threatened to call the media on them or shoot up the place until I got my way. Either way, it would have gotten unwanted attention for them."

"I am paying you back, every dime, Nicky."

"I don't know what you are talking about. I got plenty of money. This is good food. You obviously didn't get this from the hospital, thank you for you that." He nods, smacking the back of my head playfully. "How is your father doing?"

"He's going to be okay." Elijah holds out his hand to me. "Brothers for life, right Nicky?"

I take his hand in agreement, "Brothers for life, Eli."

I am able to hide out at Eli's for a couple of days before needing to return home for more clothes. Hoping my father is off on one of his women runs, I wait for my mother to go to work and sneak into the house to shower and crawl into my own bed. Unfortunately, my father returns quicker than usual. I can already feel his eyes on me. "What do you want?" I ask, avoiding turning around and showing him my new bruises. His low growl curls into a knowing, heavy sigh. "Please go do whatever and leave me alone."

My father approaches me, takes hold of my face, and looks over my chest at the still healing bruises. "It was him again, wasn't it? He won't stop. He enjoys it too much. It's in his blood, and his parents only encourage the behavior, which will only make him more deadly as time goes on. I can take care of him for you and make sure he never bothers you again."

I jerk away from his hand with a strong glare. "Leave it alone. In fact, leave me alone!"

"He's jealous of you," my father insists.

"Oh yeah, that's it. All my riches and glory drive him crazy." I laugh harshly and fall back into bed. "Please, Dad, just leave me alone."

"You are better than this, Nicholas. You should be in school. You are too smart for your friends and smarter than Connor for sure. I still can't believe they let you test out of all your classes. How could they possibly allow that without my consent?" My father leans over my reclining body to look into my eyes for the truth.

I simply wink at him, giving him all he needs to know; however, his instant huff only encourages me. "You should know Dad. You taught me everything I need to know to get what I want," He slides his hands over his face, sighing. He knows exactly what I mean; it's the same method he uses to appease himself. It was easy. It wasn't what I had planned, but it worked out just the same.

That day I walked into school, I could not imagine being there one more day. My counselor would say otherwise, but then again, she had also sucked my dick during one of our previous Nick-needs-an-attitude-change meetings. The more we talked, the hotter she got. She is barely out of college herself and has a definite, hot-librarian look about her. The moment she let her clip slip out of her hair and her dress ease up her thighs, I knew something was going to happen. I wasn't sure I could get away with it, but I reached over and unbuttoned her blouse, pulling her breasts out and fondling them against my lips. I sat back, watching her with my cock hard and ready to go, and then, she came to me. Dropping to her knees, she unzipped my pants and took it out, taking it deep into her mouth. I was sure someone was going to walk in on us, but the longer we took, the more excited I became, so I had to fuck her. Jerking her up off her knees, I bent her over her desk, pulled up her dress, and pushed her panties down her legs, spreading her easily before pushing my dick inside her. It was such a rush, watching the door and listening to her pant.

I asked her, "What will happen if someone catches us? Catches you bent over your desk with my dick inside you?" All she could do was moan and push her ass into my cock even more. She found the perfect position, with one leg up on the desk, so I go sink deeper inside her. We memorized it for the future. Pulling back her hair, I whispered against her ear, "What would they think of you coming all over me, all over your desk?" The more I talked, the more excited she got. Gripping her hips, I watched her ass tighten as I began to come. She collapsed with a whimper. When we finished, she stumbled her way to her chair, forgetting her panties and allowing me to take off with them. I wondered how long it would take her to realize she didn't have them, but she never seemed to recognize they were gone.

I passed her several times that day in the hall, even grazing her ass with my hand, and still, she never seemed to be bothered. In fact, I was ordered to her office again before the end of the day, so I could sign my paperwork and be given a full physical examination to confirm I was able to complete my studies on my own. I didn't bother to study, and why spend weeks studying for exams I knew I could pass? Why bother shooting for a grade that didn't matter? My sexual interaction with my counselor became comical to my friends, but it helped me get out of school. However, I was advised to continue to still meet with my counselor due to me being *troubled and stressed.* The only good part about school was my counselor.

"Nicholas, I think you should stay home tonight," my dad announces, shaking me out of my erotic daydream.

"You mean here with you, Mom, and your girlfriends? No thanks. Don't worry, Dad. I have something new to do tonight, and it is nowhere near Connor and his men. In fact, I am sure it is a place he would never think to look for me." After my father leaves my room, I make a call and do my best to make amends. Hopefully, I can earn a new place for myself to sleep in peace.

Chapter 9

Franky

Forgiveness. It is something I believe in, but it is not something I would have thought Nicholas Jayzon would ever be asking from me. His plea was nice to hear, and it is easy to forgive him. I mean it's … *Nicholas Jayzon*, the boy who makes my entire body quiver whenever he looks at me. How can I possibly say no to him coming over and spending a night alone with me? No other girls to compete with, no father to look over us disapprovingly, no smart mouth friends to drive me insane, only him and me. Nick Jayzon and me. Alone in my room. My whole body begin to tremble, and I fall back into my bed, spreading out and curling back over myself again, simply thinking of *my study* and nothing but my study. Since our conversation, I have spent days preparing questions, and I should certainly, at the very least, ask him some. Only, I didn't realize how many questions I had until I started writing them all down. There are so many things I don't know, and so many things I am not sure I can ask him, so I saved those questions for last.

I cleaned the house, especially my room, and then I spent three hours trying to find the right thing to wear. Luckily, I don't have that many clothes to choose from. Whatever I wear has to make me look as good as possible, but still look casual, like I don't care. *Because I don't care. He's a disgusting loser, and I don't care what he thinks about me. Huh … almost believed it that time.*

Once my father leaves, I sit at my desk with an open book in front of me. I haven't read a word in two hours, but I still continue to turn pages as if I am. Just as I begin to believe he isn't going to show, he calls me to check to see if everything is still good. I can't wipe the smile off my face. As soon as I hear the knock at the door, butterflies engulf my stomach. Adjusting my hair, my glasses, and my sweater, I finally feel good enough to answer the door, but I try my best to do so casually. Nick stands on my front porch, leaning against the door frame. "Hi," I say, nearly fainting when he looks up at me.

"Hey, how are you?" he asks, walking in around me and giving my house a thorough inspection.

"My father left a couple of hours ago. He won't be back until morning," I reassure him.

"Okay, so now what?" Nick asks, looking me over and suddenly adjusting himself.

"How about something to drink?" I offer nervously. While I get him something to drink, he searches our pantry for food. "Are you hungry?" He nods. "We have left over pot roast?" His excitement is clear, so I warm him up a plate and sit with him as he eats.

"Did you make this?" I nod, fidgeting with my hands. "It's good. You're a good cook."

"Your mom doesn't make you pot roast?" I tease.

"My mother rarely makes anything for me." He cleans his plate quickly before looking back at me for what to do next. "Thank you, that was good. So, what do you need me to do? Answer some questions or something?" he asks, seeming almost as nervous as I am. I jump up and run for my list in my room, and he follows. When he shuts the door behind us, I nearly pass out. This is what I wanted, but now that he is here, I am more nervous than I thought I would be. "So … ask away," he says, crashing onto my bed and stretching out with his hands behind his head.

I take a seat at the edge of the bed, bracing myself for a second before I can work up the energy to begin, "Umm, thank you for doing this." He nods with a roll of his eyes. "Okay, fine. Question number one, how do you know when a girl is interested in you?"

Rising up, he looks at me with his arms out. "That's your question? You don't know that one already? You are a girl." I huff, and he sits back. "Fine. There aren't many girls not interested, but it is pretty clear when they go out of their way to talk to me or touch me, look me over." He laughs at my expression. "You know checking *it* out."

"Oh, so what kind of girls are you interested in?"

"Franky! Ask the sex questions already, and stop stalling. I don't care to be spending all night doing this." Nick tries to get me to look at him while I turn the page of my notebook, searching for the questions he is expecting.

Suddenly, Nick grabs the notebook from my hand and starts reading, "Hey! That isn't for you," I yell at him, wrestling to try and get my notebook back, but it is no use.

"Okay… here we go. Do you like blowjobs? That would be a definite *yes*," He laughs "How do you like them? Umm, long and wet and by a naked girl." He smiles wide, glancing up at my frustrated expression. "What? I am answering your questions"

"But that isn't what I want to know." I pout, sitting back and turning away from him.

He watches me carefully as I cowardly look down at my hands. "Oh. You want to know how to give one?" I stay silent, but my silence only confirms his question. Tossing my notebook to the side, Nick scoots next to me on edge of my bed. "Why are you asking me these questions? And no bullshit answers. Tell me the real reason. We have never even talked before the other day, and suddenly, you want me to teach you how to have sex?"

"I don't want you to teach me!" I say wide-eyed.

"Bullshit! Why me, Franky? If you don't tell me, then I am going to leave, and you can figure this out on your own." Crossing my arms, I huff and ignore his question. "Fine, good luck then." He gets up and walks to my door.

"Because you are really good at it!" I blurt out, causing him to turn back to me. "Or … that's what I have heard. I was curious, and I thought it best to ask someone who definitely knows how. And you are …"

"Uh huh, I got it." Nick leans down in front of me, but I refuse to look at him. "I will tell you whatever you want to know, but don't bullshit me. Just ask. Deal? Now, do you want to have sex?" My jaw drops, and he laughs out loud. "Calm down. I didn't mean right now or with me, what I meant is, is there someone you are hoping to impress with all this knowledge you are wanting to gain?" I don't know what to say, but the excuse he gives me is a good one, so I take it. Nodding, I hope he doesn't ask for a name. "I won't ask you who, but I am curious." I shake my head. "Okay, then." Nick suddenly stands up and looks down at me. "Okay, so, do you have any bananas?" I am confused at first, but then I understand clearly. "Unless you want me to offer my …," he says waving his hand near another option that causes me to stare directly at it.

"No, I will go get some," I quickly reply, jumping to go get them as he laughs at me. I hand him a banana, and he shakes his head. "No? But you said …"

"You think I am going to do it? No, the best way to learn is by doing, Kitten. Now, sit down right here." He takes my glasses off and positions me a certain way as I hold the banana in my hands. "Open your mouth and breathe out." The sensation is strange, but he controls my hands and coaches me into the motions. "Whew, stop. You are making me hard. I think you've got it Kitten, now what?" He sits down and watches me, but I don't know what to ask. "You really are clueless about all this, aren't you?"

"Don't make fun of me, please," I say, curling over myself and sinking my head into my knees.

"Hey, don't do that." Nick pulls me back to him and forces me to look at him. "I am not making fun of you. I am fascinated by you actually. I have never seen a girl so innocent before. Hell, my first time was with a whore." My eyes go wide. "A birthday present from my father," he explains. "Can I ask you something? I promise I won't judge you at all, but I think, for any of this to work, I need to know how much you don't know. So, how far have you gone with a guy?" I sink deep into my seat, and he sighs, "That much, huh? You haven't even kissed a guy?" I shake my head. "Wow, no wonder you are so curious. Well, we have a lot to cover. I hope this guy you are trying to impress is worth it."

"You don't have to help me. It is probably pointless anyway." I lie on my back and stare up at my ceiling, wishing I had never started any of this.

"Franky, you know the only way to learn is …" I look at him as he comes towards me. Hovering over me, Nick eyes me from head to toe, moving his lips in a motion that begins to hypnotize me. His hand massages my body and positions my face as he leans down and touches my lips with his. His warmth and softness maneuver in a way that entices me to follow. His sudden inhale causes a reaction in my body I have never felt before, and I find myself wrapping my arms around him, cradling his head and running my fingers through his hair. His tongue touches the tip of mine, which causes me to jump. Nick sits back with a smile. "It's okay. You're doing good, Franky. Real good, actually."

He leans down on me again and takes in my lips, one after the other. My head begins to spin, and I barely notice his body moving, repositioning, moving my legs, and slipping down in between them. It is not until I feel the pressure that I lose my breath. Nick takes hold of my face and moves it to the side before beginning to kiss down my neck and unbuttoning my shirt. This is what I wanted, but now that it is happening, I am beginning to panic. His hips move against mine, and my eyes flutter. I want to tell him to stop, but then it feels …

Nick suddenly sits up and rolls us over, leaving me sitting up on him and saying, "Your turn." When he realizes I am confused, he gently takes my hands and places them on his shirt. I begin to unbutton each button while he moves his hips up into me. His eyes watch every flutter of mine and every breath I gasp. Removing his shirt, he helps me out and takes off his t-shirt, allowing me to feel his bare chest. His skin is smooth, his muscles so defined. I have no problem feeling his body, enjoying the sensation of his warm skin against my lips, the moans rippling through his muscles, his erection rubbing and pressing between my legs. Kissing down to his bellybutton, I hesitate and gulp. Nick sits up again, grasping my hips while pushing my shirt off behind me. He takes hold of my tank, stops, and waits. Looking into his eyes, I raise my arms up over my head, and he pulls my tank off. His lips caress mine with a smile, and I relax until I feel him undo my bra.

Taking hold of the straps on my shoulders, he pushes them down partway before I sit back, away from him. "Umm, Nick I don't know …"

"Shhh, come here. You look beautiful, amazingly beautiful," he says, kissing me and rubbing my body back into his arms. It feels good, but

I still can't let go of my bra. Stopping, he looks at me while I look around the brightly lit room. "Don't move." He lifts me effortlessly off him before getting up to turn the light out. He pulls down the covers of my bed and then takes hold of his belt. Releasing it, he immediately begins unzipping his pants, pushing them down his legs and off onto the floor. His erection is nearly coming out of his boxers, and I begin to feel a little proud of myself for being able to get him so excited. Sliding into bed, he lifts me back on top of him again. Undoing my pants, he leaves them open and slides his hand down the back of them, gripping my butt and kissing me deeply. "Are you going to let go of this?" he asks tugging at my bra. "I turned the lights out for you."

"They are really not that much to look at so …"

"Franky, let me decide that, please." I shake my head. "You have to get naked at some point. You think this guy you like is going to want you to leave it on? I will close my eyes, okay?" He closes his eyes, causing me to laugh at his goofy smile. I drop my bra, lean over, and kiss him. "Mmm, taking the initiative. I like that," he says, slowly moving his hands up and down my stomach before taking hold of my breasts and kissing my neck down to my chest. He fondles my breasts with skill as he kisses my nipples, "Breathe, Franky," he says as he wets the tips with his tongue. Nick hums against my skin.

Picking me up, he gets on his knees and turns us both around. Smiling wide with his eyes open, he blatantly looks down at my breasts. "Oops." Lying me down on the bed, he jerks my pants down and off, into the floor before I have a chance to say a word. Sliding up my body and in between kisses, I watch his penis become more and more visible. His heated skin melts into mine, sending incredible rushes of pleasure through my body. He is so strong and feels so good. I don't want any of this to end. Nick's hand goes to my panties, pushing them down before gripping my butt once again. He slips his hand further between my legs and releases a gasp from my mouth and into his. Nick kisses me deep while fumbling with something along the bed. "Shit!" he snaps. "Fucking Luke!" He sits up going through the pockets of his coat and pants.

"What's wrong?" I ask holding a blanket in front of me.

"My dumbass friend took my last condom. Like that idiot is going to be able to get laid tonight." Nick looks at me apologetically. "You don't happen to have any condoms do you?" I shake my head slowly, and he grimaces. "Fuck."

"What does that mean?" I ask, still covering myself.

"It means, Kitten, that it isn't going to happen tonight. Sorry. Got us both all worked up for nothing." Nick leans in to me and kisses me quickly. "Sorry, maybe some other time." Climbing in next to me, he slides under the covers and looks at me funny. "What? You said I could stay the night if I came over, right?" I didn't realize that was what he meant by staying, but I did agree. Nick, still in his boxers, sort of, makes himself comfortable in my bed.

I search the floor, find his t-shirt, and slide it on, taking in his scent as it slides over my face. It smells like him, and now I smell like him. I lie down softly on my pillow, watching and waiting for him to peacefully fall asleep. Feeling safe to do so, I slide my hand over his chest. Surprisingly, he pushes his fingers in between mine and holds my hand against his skin. My smile is so wide it hurts.

Chapter 10

Nick

I sit up in bed when I hear a strange man coughing. *Oh shit, Franky's Dad!* Since I smell bacon, I assume he decided to come home early to cook his daughter breakfast. Her father is surely not going to like finding me here. Letting go of her hand, I get out of bed and search for my clothes so I can get out of her house before I start more chaos than I care to this early in the morning.

"Nick?" Franky says, looking up at me half asleep.

I crouch next to her bed and whisper, "Your dad's home, so I am going to take off. Thank you for letting me crash here. I will talk to you later, okay?" She nods and lies back in her bed, wrapping herself in blankets and smiling a big goofy smile. For some reason, she causes me to smile, compelling me to kiss her as if she is my new girlfriend. Before I can get away, she grabs hold of my face and kisses me back with more want than I intended to spark from her. "Oooh, Franky, don't start that. Your dad is home, and no condoms remember?" I pull away from her, laughing behind my hand when she sighs in disappointment. "Does your window work?"

"Yes," she says. I quickly slide her window up, and move halfway out before giving her a quick wink. "Bye, Nick. Have a good day today." I don't think I have ever seen a girl look so innocently at me. I almost believe she likes me more than for a sexual education.

I take a quick shower at home before meeting up with Luke, and to my surprise, Harvey is with him. Harvey asks Luke about me all the time, curious as to why I am so hesitant to join his organization. It never occurred to the man that someone might boldly say no to him. In most cases, it would have probably got me killed, but I continue to make him money. So, even though I am a free agent and not a dedicated minion, money is all that really matter to Harvey.

I wasn't ready for this conversation right now. I was hoping to make him wait a few more weeks while I work up a game plan to get my brother Connor. Once the plan is in place, I intend to sell to Harvey as a money making scheme. Considering I am surrounded by guns, it doesn't look as if I have a choice but to discuss my future right now. I give Luke a stern glare before being told to get into Harvey's car. The large, cigar smoking man taps my leg with his cane and grunts with approval. "Nicholas, Luke tells me you are unsure about the position I offered you. I can't imagine why. Have I not treated you well, given you opportunities that others would not have? Helped you make more money than anyone your age?" *He can't possibly think I am that stupid.* Opportunities my ass. He doesn't pay me shit for the jobs I do for him, and I am the one taking all the chances. I am the one that will go to jail, not him. I sit back, trying to decide how to respond, carefully analyzing his posture while I consider all the things I want. "Nicholas, I have wonderful opportunities for you. You could stand to make more money than you have ever made."

"By doing what exactly?" Leaning forward, I get bold. "The way I see it, I am the one taking all the chances. I'm the one doing the dirty work.

You want me, Mr. Rice, then prove it. I don't want to work the rest of my life doing these trivial jobs for you. I want to learn from you. I want to work with *you,* become a true valuable asset to your organization, and not one you can easily replace." Harvey sucks on the end of his cigar while he looks me over with a sour expression, his usual pensive routine. I know I have his interest peaked, so I sit back with confidence. "Listen, Harvey, I got ideas that will make you a lot more money with little to no risk." His eyebrows raise at the thought, and I begin to talk about the basics of my plans before leaving him with the understanding I need more than the elementary opportunity. I want a piece of the pie.

Showing his appreciation for my time, Harvey hands me a few hundreds before I leave them, so I head straight to Ryan's. His mother didn't look so good the last time I saw her, and I am worried they may be struggling due to her recently discovered illness. Ryan answers the door with a muffled greeting, vastly different from his normal comedic style, but I do still receive the brotherly hug that we never share in front of anyone else. "How's it going, Nick?" Ryan sits down in front of a bowl of cereal bigger than my head. The boy can eat twice as much as me, but it doesn't seem to go anywhere on my bean pole little brother.

"Hungry?" I laugh at him when his mom walks in. She speaks to me, but I can barely hear her, and her hug is frail. She looks even paler than she did a few days ago. I take a quick glance towards Ryan as she tries to speak to me. He shakes his head, and that's when I know things are worse than I thought. "Well, you are looking beautiful as always, Rianne." Kissing my cheek, Rianne holds my face for a few seconds as she looks at me with a wide smile. She is another one of my father's victims, bewitched and forever in love with him. I know she sees him when she looks at me, and I assume that is why she still lets me crash here. It could also be due to the fact that she is the nicest woman I have ever met. Rianne Milio is the mother I wish I had, and I wish she wasn't dying so my baby brother could have his mother for as long as he needs. Last week, I made her a promise that Ryan knows nothing about. I will protect my brother at all costs. Rianne leaves us to return to bed, and I take the opportunity to question Ryan. "What did the doctor say?"

"They think its Leukemia. She needs to see a specialist to be sure. She needs to see people who know what they are doing and are not worried about seeing the other fifty patients they have in an hour. I have called everywhere for assistance, but all I can do is get on a waiting list." Ryan shrugs, holding back the frustration that is clearly building up inside of him. "We barely have enough money to pay the regular house bills, and now her medical bills and the nurse they said she needs … I don't know what to do, Nick. Do you think you could get me a job with Harvey? Maybe with a few jobs a week so I can make enough to pay the bills and not have to be away from her so much."

"No, you are not going to work for Harvey. You shouldn't be working at all. You should be in school," I say, ignoring his huffing.

"Nick! You quit school," he snaps back at me.

"I tested out actually, so I still technically got my diploma. You still have a lot of time left." He opens his mouth … "No, Ryan! You worry about school and be here for your mother. Let me worry about everything else."

"If Dad would …"

"Well he isn't, and you know that, so forget about him." Ryan huffs, readying himself to come back at me with a better argument. "Come on, let's go get your mother her medicine and some food, too, since you seem to have eaten everything that I just bought for you guys three days ago."

Smiling wide, Ryan shrugs, "What can I see Nick? I am a growing boy."

"Growing where?" I ask, laughing at him as he proudly shows off his body.

Ryan changes his expression, and instantly begins unzipping his pants, pulling out his dick to show to me. "Check it out! Milk does a body good, Bro." I roll my eyes as he laughs. "What? You asked where I am growing."

I push him out the door. "I did, but you still have a ways to catch up to me, *baby* brother," I say, standing taller than him and gripping my dick with pride. We joke around all the way to the store, but we don't miss noticing the girls coming and going around us. Ryan may be my baby brother, but he does have something about him that seems to attract the girls. I watch him carefully as he slyly eyes a young girl near his age until she waves at him. He simply nods towards her, causing her to giggle. I shake my head at him, and he just smiles.

"What can I say? The girls are always on me. I am pretty sure I'm too hot for this world to handle," he says as I laugh. "Shut up," he says, smacking my chest when another girl passes. "Hi, what's your name?"

"Natalie," She nervously laughs as he takes her hand.

"Natalie, I'm Ryan," he hums, leading her away from me. He comes back with a large smile and her number. "See, now you know."

"Shut up, dumbass. You didn't show me a damn thing," I say as he smiles all over himself. I hold up my hand to him, forcing him to wait while I show him how it is done. I spot a woman down at the other end of the aisle. I slide in next to her, looking over the same items. When she notices my presence, I look down over her and wait. She smiles instantly. I don't say a word; I simply mouth, "Hi." And the woman promptly gushes. I hand her my phone where she types in her name and her number. I kiss her cheek before whispering my name in her ear. I have to fight my smile, when she has to grasp her cart to hold herself up. Walking back to my brother, I smirk. "And I didn't have to do all that unnecessary talking to get what I wanted."

Ryan shakes his head and moves on ahead of me, grabbing food and ignoring my ego until he finds another way to compete with me. We continue to battle playfully until we get back to his house.

After helping him put all our purchases away, we crash into the floor to watch movies, eat junk food, and talk about our biggest dreams, just like we use to do when we were kids. It helps us both forget about the world around us and dream about the worlds we wish we lived in. I wake up in the middle of the night, covered up and taken care of much the same as we were when we were much younger. *Damn, I love that woman.*

The next morning, I leave Ryan with money for the week and head off to take care of my next family duty. My baby brother is my top concern, and I am my older sister's. I got a message from Lena that she is in town for a few weeks. She has been away at college, the only one of us to be able to do anything like that. She is incredibly smart and ambitious. It helped that her mother was a hard-ass and never allowed Lena to get out of control. Lena is much like her mother when it comes to her concern for me.

Lena's hard headed mother hunted my father down one day and stormed into our house, ready to give him all kinds of hell. Of course, that didn't work out like she had planned. Much like the rest of my father's conquests, she fell into his arms and lost her determination to demand anything from him, but granted his wishes instead. I was too young to remember much about that day, but from what Lena tells me, she heard me cry in my crib while she waited for her mother. She waited for someone to see to me, but when no one did, she crept into my room and looked down on me. The moment our eyes met, she instantly fell in love, or so she says. She has mothered me to death ever since.

Lena is waiting for me outside of her mother's clothing shop when I round the corner. She already has her motherly stance formed as I walk up to her. "What is wrong now? Don't most people go away to college? Why are you always here?" I tease as she hugs me.

Suddenly, she smacks the back of my head. "Someone told me that you quit school and that you are going to work for that Rice guy? That better not be true, Nick."

"What difference does it make, Le, I was bored at school. It is not as if I am going to college anyway."

"Did you talk to your counselor like I told you to do? She should be able to help you figure out how you can." Smiling, I shake my head. "You didn't meet with her?"

"Oh, I met with her."

"What did she say?" I smile and moan my own name to her instant annoyance. "Son of a bitch! You are absolutely hopeless. I don't even know how that could happen."

"Well, she put her leg up like this, and then I …"

"Shut up Nicky! I don't want to know either. Just, please, do not work for that Rice guy." I nod, and nod again, until she feels that she has exhausted that argument. "What about Connor? Is he still giving you a hard time?" She shouldn't have to ask, but since she did, I give her an honest answer by shrugging my shoulders and looking off into the distance. "You know, I saw him the other day. His wife came in here, buying up everything and being a total bitch, and then … he brought one of his girlfriends in the very next day. I *really* hate him. Do you know that asshole actually smacked me on the ass and tried to hit on me?" she snaps before realizing what she is setting off within me.

Suddenly, I feel everything begin to churn inside me, and I lose focus of what she is saying until she shakes me back to her attention. "Nick, let it go. It was nothing. I don't want you to get into trouble." Lena grabs my face and forces me to look at her. "Do you hear me, Nicholas? Please try to stay good for a little longer, and I promise, I will get you out of here."

"Oh, I am getting out of here, Le, don't you worry about that. You worry about you, and I will take care of me. You are too busy studying to be that big fancy doctor, which I am going to need when we get old and senile," I say, earning a kiss to my cheek for trying to be positive. Lena is hanging on by a thread, trying to stay in college. Even with scholarships, she is struggling to make enough money to survive. We both know she can't afford to help both of us, and I am not going to let her worry about me when she needs to get herself out of this mess we live in.

Before her break is over, she hands me a bag with some new clothes in it. "And make sure you call me more often. I worry, you know?"

"I know, Le, and I worry about you, so get back to work before your mother fires you again," I wave to her mother before pushing her on her way.

With most of the day behind me, I head home to try out my new clothes. I am nearly there when Connor appears out of nowhere. I try to dodge him and his group, but they stalk me up and down the streets, circling me into a corner. When Connor finally corners me, he merely throws a package at me. "Don't worry, little brother. I only have a present for you, candy actually. You will like this stuff a lot, I promise. If you want more, just let your big brother know, and I will be happy to get it for you. Hell, Nicholas, if you really like it, I bet you could sell it for me, too. All this fighting between us is no good for either of us. Let's make amends and work together. What do you say?" he asks with a smile I will never trust. "You still don't trust me? It's understandable, I suppose. Try the gift and let me know what you think. We can talk about working together another time."

I hand his gift back to him. "No thanks."

His smile instantly turns into a frown. "I am giving you the best shit I have, and you are throwing it back in my face?"

"I don't need your drugs, Connor, just like I don't need you. Now, leave before I find a better place to put your cheap ass drugs," I say, dropping my bag of clothes and fisting my hands, reminding myself how much I hate him. It doesn't take much else to get me going, and Connor knows it. He wants to befriend me for some reason so he backs off. "What's wrong, Connor? Afraid I might embarrass you in front of your employees? You know damn well you can't beat me on your own," I laugh, walking away but knowing exactly what I stirred up within him.

Connor's roar comes at me fast, but one on one, he can't beat me. I get to take out all of the frustrations I have out on him. His guards jump in to save their boss, but before they can take care of him, someone else jumps in. He throws each of them on their asses and out of my way. I am grateful until he grabs me and forces me to run.

A few blocks down, I stop and face off with him. "What the fuck are you doing?" As soon as the last word leaves my mouth, I hear the sirens.

"Yeah genius, you might want to pay attention to what is going on around you and not be so dead set on kicking someone's ass for no reason."

"I had a damn good reason, and who the hell are you to tell me anything?" I look him over to see if I remember him from anywhere in the neighborhood.

"Listen, wise ass, I don't want another neighborhood kid getting picked up by the police because he beat up on some *Richy* from uptown.

We don't need cops down here harassing us anymore than they already are. So, do me a favor and think a little more about what you are doing *before* you do it," he says with a sharp smile as he walks away from me. "Oh, and if you want to learn how to fight for real, you should come to the Whittaker Street Center. I could teach you how to fight more controlled and with more power. Your emotions are all over the place, and that will only get you killed. What you need is to learn control, control over your fear and, most of all, control over your anger. Interested? Nick, is it?"

"Yes, Nick Jayzon. How do you know my name?"

He laughs at me. "I make it a point to know everything interesting about my city, and you're one thing I made a point to know. There is something about you, Nick Jayzon. I don't know if it is good or bad yet, but I am curious." He looks down at his watch. "Wow, I have to go. I have some other interesting things I have to look into before the end of the day." He smiles energetically. "If you decide to take me up on my offer, Jayzon, just go to the center and ask for Bo, Bo Sirra."

Shaking my head, I turn away for a second before looking back his way, but he's already gone. My curiosity gets the best of me, so I run down the street and up again, searching for Bo, but it is no use. The man has simply disappeared.

Chapter 11

Nick

"What do you mean you gave it back to him?" Luke bitches to me. "I hear Connor has some good shit, we could …"

"Don't listen to this fool, Nicky. He doesn't have any brain cells left to know better," Elijah says.

"You two are the most uptight pricks I have ever met. I don't know why I continue to deal with you," Luke complains, kicking the edge of the table.

"Me either," I laugh. "Sit down. Where are you wanting to go anyway?" I ask him.

"There is a party tonight," he says, watching us both roll our eyes. Luke has a tendency to find parties that are filled with women, none of which are women Elijah or I would ever be interested in. The last time we went to a party with Luke, some freaks tried to drug us and get us into bed. Luckily, I avoided my drink long enough to notice Elijah starting to sway and feeling up the disgusting mess sitting next to him. He said he was in love, and she said she was going to fuck him until his dick fell off. He smiled up at me, cheering happily, that is until she announced she was going to have his baby and marry him. Then, he grabbed my arm and asked me to shoot him. I quickly shoved him out the door, yelling at Luke the whole way home.

Luke suddenly stomps his feet, jarring us both back to his attention. "Come on! I get your backs every night, and the one time I ask for you to return the favor, you both let me down. It's been months since that awful party. You guys owe me another chance," he whines until we finally agree, but as soon as Luke meets up with his girl, Elijah and I slip right back out of the lame party.

"You want to see a movie? Lots of girls out tonight seeing that new girly movie. Dark theatre, girls …" Elijah smiles, and I agree to follow him. A friend of Elijah's lets us in from a side door, and we can make our way to the expected packed theatre: however, there are barely a handful of people. "What the …?" I give Elijah an exasperated look and take a seat. "Where is everybody?" he gripes. I shake my head, laughing at his obvious frustration. "This sucks!" The modest crowd turns around and gives us a dirty look, including someone I know. I nudge Elijah and move us to better seats. Crashing into the seat next to Franky, I force Elijah to crash in next to her friend. He checks her out for a second before putting his arm on the back of her seat and facing her. "So do you want to make out?" he asks the poor girl, causing me to laugh.

"Excuse me?" she asks him in shock. "I am trying to watch a movie."

Elijah looks at the screen in confusion. "Why? I am much better looking than that guy."

"He was horribly disfigured in a car accident," she huffs.

"Well, that explains his hideous appearance. So do you want a make out now?" My laughter only encourages him, but I just can't help it. Luckily, Franky starts to laugh too, loosening up her friend a bit. Elijah takes her hand and begins to invoke his charm. "Come sit over here by me. I have this terrible fear, and I have to sit near the corner. Please don't make me feel abandoned and alone because of my disability. I only want to be loved like everyone else."

"What kind of disability is that?" she asks, seeming concerned about him but glancing back my way to verify her safety.

"It's called BBD. You know, blue balls disorder. Come help me overcome it." He somehow gets her to follow him and then smiles back at me in triumph.

Franky looks over at me as I shrug, "Sorry about that. He has had a rough night."

"Oh really? He hasn't been able to find anyone to screw all night?" she smarts off, shocking me.

"I can go get him and leave if you want me to?"

"No!" she exclaims, jumping to the edge of her seat. When I look over at her, she instantly blushes and curls back into her chair. "So what about you?"

"No, I haven't got laid either, but I am still hoping." I smile at her, and she, surprisingly, smiles too. "Have you? Is your man here somewhere?" I ask, looking around the empty theatre.

"No. And no!" she stresses. "Brandi and I have wanted to see this documentary for awhile."

"Documentary?" I ask, suddenly paying attention to the screen. "I thought this was supposed to be some girly movie?"

"No, but there is some romantic comedy next door, and it is pretty girly."

"But this one is Love … something?"

"Love Thyself. It's about finding inner peace with who you are." I start laughing, immediately realizing why we couldn't find any girls in here. "That's funny?" she asks, confused.

"Yeah, it is, but I can't explain why," I glance over at Elijah who is too involved to be interrupted now. I sit back in my chair, noticing her sweet smile and smile back. "So do you want to make out?" I ask, making her laugh. "Your Dad came home pretty early this morning. He decided to make you breakfast?" She nods. "That was nice of him, scared the shit out of me, but nice for you. I tried to leave without waking you, but I guess I wasn't as quiet as I thought …"

"No, I was glad I got to say goodbye to you. Although, you barely made it out in time. I didn't have time to get the window down before my father came in. He griped at me for leaving the window open."

"Yeah, you should be careful, you never know what kind of scumbags may come through there." I nudge her, watching her try not to look at me. "Is that my shirt you're wearing?"

"Yes, I threw it on at the last minute. I will wash it tonight so you can come by and get it whenever." I nod, again watching her blush and look away from me. "Umm, and thank you for helping me with my questions, too."

"No problem. It's not like I didn't enjoy it. Even the banana part was kind of nice. Although, I wish it hadn't of been a banana but my …" Franky looks back at me, biting her bottom lip to keep from smiling. "I thought, for sure, you would slap me before I could finish that comment." Shrugging, she shakes her head. I move my thumb across her bottom lip and release it. "You shouldn't do that. Your lips are too nice to be hidden." She licks her lips, and I am shocked to see her preparing for me to kiss her. "Do you want me to kiss you? What would your true love say?" She backs off and squeezes back into the corner of her seat. "Hey, what's wrong?" I nudge her playfully, but she retreats to watching the movie. "Are you horny?" I ask with a laugh, but she only tenses more. "It's okay. It's normal. You would be the only one in this theatre if you weren't." She doesn't respond as she focuses harder on the screen. I sigh and sit back in my own seat.

Franky suddenly jumps to the edge of her seat. "You know, you didn't finish teaching me or answering my questions."

Confused, I look her over. "You want to finish? Do you want to have sex with me? I would think you would want your first time to be with this great man you are so in love with."

"No, I want to make sure I know what I am doing. I don't want to be embarrassed," she says, looking at me strangely.

"Kitten, I think you got it down now. The next step is all on him. If he can't do that, then you have bigger issues."

"But there is more to it than that."

"Yeah, but you have the gist of it down. Touch him, kiss him … put your tits in his face, and he will be happy as hell. Trust me."

"I don't know about my tits." She instantly shrinks back into her seat again, this time with her arms folded tight against her chest.

"You worry too much. They're fine. If you're so concerned, then wrap those gorgeous long legs around him and let him grip that tight ass of yours. Tits or no tits, he won't care about anything else but you at that point." Curling over herself, she looks so sad. "Hey, you'll be fine. If he really cares about you, all your concerns won't matter." She nods with a forced smile. She is nervous for no reason, but I guess, for girls, the first time is a pretty big deal. Taking hold of her face, I lean in, and touch her lips with mine. I give her an encouraging touch of my tongue to remind her that she knows what she is doing. She relaxes so much in my arms that I get a little carried away and pull her into my lap. I find myself squeezing her ass and rubbing her legs, moaning and kissing her hard.

"Excuse me! I am trying to watch this," a lady snaps at us from across the aisle. "If you are going to do that, go somewhere else." She plops back down into her seat with a deep frown.

I place Franky back in her seat and laugh. "Sorry, I get a little carried away sometimes."

"It's okay. Nick I really …"

"Oh Eli," Brandi moans suddenly. Franky and I both snap our heads in their direction.

"Your friend… is she experienced at all?" I ask. Franky looks shocked to see her friend wrapped around Elijah. "I gather that is a no. I can get him out of here if you want?"

"No. Why?" Franky grabs hold of my shirt, trying to keep me in my chair.

"Kitten, if I don't get him out of here now, your friend is going to get fucked. And this is no place for a girl's first time." I get up quickly and grab Elijah.

"What?" he snaps.

"We need to go, Eli."

"Right now?"

"Yes. Rice just called and said he needs to see us," I say, motioning for him to get up and come with me.

"Are you fucking kidding me? Son of a bitch!" He moans some more, still not letting go of the girl who barely has her clothes on at this point.

"Eli, come on. Now!" He reluctantly gets up and gives me a dirty look as he fixes his hardened dick back into his pants. Smiling, I give Franky a wink before guiding my frustrated friend out the door. "Calm down. I have a better idea for you." I push him into the other theatre where he looks around and smiles at the wall to wall girls.

"Oh, this is much better, Nicky," Elijah says. He is off into the dark before I can count to three.

I take my own look around and find a great option for myself. Taking her hand, I take her attention off the damn movie. "You want to come to the balcony with me?" She nods and happily follows. I pull her into the dark corner and sit her down next to me. "Hi," I hum, blatantly looking her over with a lick of my lips. I gently whisper in her ear all the things I like about her, and she melts. Feeling her body, I press her against me and let her feel mine. She easily lets me kiss her and pull her into my lap. She begins rubbing her ass against my cock, and her eyes flutter. I am under her clothes and taking hold of what I want within seconds. I take a look around us before I undo my pants and pull my erection out. She lifts her dress up, and I help her adjust her panties so that she can sit down on me. Breathing heavily, she sits up and sits right back down on my cock. Fucking me hard, her ass moves quickly against me. Rubbing her bouncing ass and her tight thighs, I encourage her every movement. "Oh you're doing good, baby," I moan. With her tits in my hands, I open my mouth as she leans back and takes in my tongue. When she begins gripping the chair arms, I start to feel her come, signaling that I need to hurry. Taking hold of her hips, I move her up and down on my dick, managing to come before she collapses completely. I quickly dress and ditch my condom in someone's cup as we exit the balcony. *I hope they were finished with that.* As we wait outside the theatre for her friends, my girl curls up next to me, taking hold of my arm and continuously kissing the side of my face.

"How did you know I was here?" Amanda asks.

"I remember you saying something about a movie, and I searched every theatre to find you," I say, wondering if she will actually believe that bullshit.

"Oh Nick, I knew we had something special." With a wide smile, she lays her head against my shoulder and I roll my eyes. Once the movie is over, she sits up with her hair still a mess. "Do you want to come out with us?"

"No, you go have fun with your friends. I will call you later," I say, kissing her goodbye and taking off to find Elijah. I find him in the back corridor of the theatre, finishing up his goodbye. "Your night get better?" I ask when he walks up to me, clearly content with his night.

"Oh yeah. Where did you go? Back to that Franky girl?"

"No, I found Amanda to entertain me."

"It looked like you were getting entertained by Franky from what I saw." I shake my head. "Okay. What was that then?"

"A confidence booster," I say simply.

He laughs and begins rubbing my head with a serious expression. "Oh, Nicky. You are a fine looking young man. Don't worry, I am sure your cock will grow one day."

I push him off me. "Shut the fuck up. It wasn't a confidence booster for me, you idiot."

"So, did you pull me off that other girl so you could get laid too?" Elijah asks.

"No because she was a virgin and didn't need to be corrupted by you." His jaw drops.

"That girl was a virgin? Holy shit. She didn't act like a virgin. Hell, I had my hand … well, in some really nice places. She has some huge tits, Nicky. I won't tell you where her hand was, but it was on something huge too," he says, waiting for me to glance at his arrogant smile. Shaking my head, I glance his way and roll my eyes. "Hmm a virgin. Well, that's one thing Kim wasn't. That girl was ready to fuck in seconds. I have to say, I am getting drastically better at my game. If I get any better, all I am going to have to do is snap my fingers, and women will be all over me." *The dumb things he says sometimes.*

When we walk out into the parking lot, we come face to face with Franky and Brandi. Elijah instantly cozies right up to Brandi's side. "So, baby, I didn't get to say goodbye. Do you think maybe we could get together sometime soon, very soon?" She giggles, trading numbers with him, and before I know it, his tongue is down her throat again.

"Eli, damn, come on!" I say, pulling him away.

"Sorry Franky. You should take your friend and go find some guys that are more suitable for you two," I say, continuing to push him forward.

"Nicky, why do you keep pulling at me when my dick is all hard? Are you trying to kill me? I got needs! Damn! I haven't fucked since …"

"Since we were indoors… two minutes ago," I yell at him.

He looks my way with a confused expression. "Oh yeah. Huh. I am having a damn good night." I laugh at him until he finally smiles. Once I have him moving forward again, I look back to make sure the girls didn't hear his nonsense, but instead, I catch Franky's eyes on me. Her expression affects me, and suddenly, I have an urge to leave with her instead, and I am not sure why. I stop briefly, but shake the feeling off. *I am not her type. I am too much of a thug for her.*

Chapter 12

Franky

Brandi looks completely dazed. Talking to her at this point is pointless. Instead of talking, I simply try to make sure she looks presentable for her parents and then rush her into her room before they have a chance to ask her any questions. She smiles all the way into bed, mentioning Elijah more than once. Asshole will never speak to her again; I hope she realizes that. As soon as I have her in bed and curl up in the other, Brandi jumps up and runs to her window. Elijah climbs through, pawing at her instantly.

"Brandi, are you crazy? Your parents are going to kill you," I steam.

"Please, Franky. We only want to talk," she says as if I am supposed to believe that bullshit.

"Where is Nick?" I ask Elijah, hoping he is waiting somewhere outside.

"He went home. You want me to call him for you? I don't think he is doing anything special. I could probably get him to come over too," Elijah says, barely looking my way as he undresses.

"No, why would I want that? I was simply wondering if you left him standing outside by himself," I say before burying my head in my pillows when they start kissing again. I sit up to yell at them, but Elijah is already naked and climbing into bed with her. With my eyes wide, I breathe out slowly. *Wow, he is … not bad looking at all. Damn, I hate her.*

"Be gentle with me, baby. I have never done this before," Elijah hums into my friend's ear. *Oh my God!* Brandi giggles in agreement. *Really, she can't be that stupid?* There are some quick movements in her bed, and the next thing I know, Brandi's clothes are flung to the floor. "Damn, baby, why are you hiding this body?" he moans, kissing her and causing her to moan with approval as he travels down her. I try not to look, but Brandi's tense fingers grip her sheets so tight that I am afraid she is going to explode. The sounds are making me insane, but it only gets worse. I thought they were finished, but then, he takes out a condom. *Ah! I just want to rip my head off. Oh why didn't I just go home?*

The shop is dead today. I have drawn about twenty different trees in my notebook and twice as many Nick Jayzons, each scratched out until they are unrecognizable.

"Hi," I jump from my seat and instantly catch his hypnotizing eyes. "Sorry, I didn't mean to scare you," Nick says with a smile. "I forgot to get my bag the other night, and I need it for a job today."

"Oh, I could have mailed it to you or something," I mumble, realizing halfway through that we don't do that here.

"Well, that wouldn't have worked. I wouldn't have got to see you," he says with a smile that weakens me all over. Blushing, I shy away from his seductive eyes and try to regain my composure. "I have to admit, I was also curious about you and your man. I wanted to find out how you are doing with him." For some reason, my voice stops working, along with my brain, so all I can do is shrug at him. "Eventually, you are going to have to talk to him, Franky. I mean, what if you start talking to him and kissing him and find out he is no good at all, and he isn't what you thought?" Nick leans in closer to me. "You don't want to spend all your time thinking about a guy that isn't worth your time, do you? There are too many other guys waiting for their chance with you." His eyes peer deeply into mine, and I begin to feel something strange between us, but before I can ask, we are interrupted.

"Franky? Is everything okay?" my father asks, peeking around the corner at us.

"Yes, everything is fine. He left without his purchase the other day," I say as Nick and my father exchange glares.

"I don't think your father cares for me too much," Nick says, pulling out some money and holding it up for my father to clearly see before handing it to me. "Thanks for holding it for me." I shrug with a nod, my usual confused response. "There is a party tonight. You should invite your man and take the opportunity to get to know him better. Lots of great hiding places. And, if you decide you don't like him, I will be there … to get rid of him for you." He smiles with a wink. "Here is the address if you decide you're interested." A warm touch of his hand, and I steal the piece of paper from his palm, quickly stashing it in my pocket before my father sees it.

There is no way I am going to miss this party, and there is certainly no way I am going to show up in my usual attire. I need something that *he* will be attracted to, but I also need my backup, Brandi, just in case I chicken out. It was simple to convince her. One mention of Elijah's name, and she isn't about to miss the party either.

Brandi invites me to her place to help prepare my hair and makeup. I bought a short skirt and heels after work, and paired with a borrowed low-cut sweater from Brandi's closet, I'm satisfied. I even dug out contacts from the back of my drawer that are now burning my eyes like crazy. I am perfect, if only I could walk in these heels and stop tearing up from the contacts.

Brandi borrows her father's car, so thankfully, we don't have to walk, but we arrive much faster than I am prepared for. These people are not the usual ones I would be around, not that I usually attend parties or hang out with anyone other than Brandi… and my father. *What I am doing here?*

Arm in arm, Brandi and I maneuver through the crowd, both of us feeling farther and farther away from security as we move deeper into the crowd. Suddenly, Elijah pops out of nowhere with girls already hanging all over him. I look over at Brandi as her jaw hits the floor. Before she tries to run back to the door, I selfishly grab her and hold her next to me. *I did put up with their disgusting display the other night. She owes me.*

Surprisingly, Elijah drops the others girls and picks Brandi up. "Hi." He smiles wildly, bringing out Brandi's nervous giggle.

He starts to carry her away, but I grab his arm to stop him. "Hey, I don't want to be left here alone."

"Nick is here." *He is?* Just the mention of his name forces a smile from my face. "Yeah, he is right over there. Nick!" My head spins in a direction I didn't think possible, but the moment I see him through the crowd, there is no pain from the awkward twist, only butterfly wings.

I fidget with my skirt and adjust my sweater as Nick comes near and kisses my cheek. "Hi, beautiful, glad to see you made it. Did you bring anyone else with you?" I point over to Brandi as she dives deeply into Elijah's mouth. Nick laughs. "Well she seems happily occupied. But I was actually wondering if you brought a date?"

"Oh, I was told he was coming here already, so I was hoping that I could talk to him here, and you know …"

"And make your move? Yeah not a bad idea. So… is he here?" he asks, and for some stupid reason, I nod. "He is huh? Where is he?" *Oh damn.* Carefully, I turn and search around for someone, anyone, until I see Parker Bruce look me over and nod my way with a smile. I only know him from when he played football for our high school a couple of years ago. He hasn't done much since he blew out his knee. I have only seen him lately because he delivers some of our inventory.

However, the only words spoken between us was when he grunted, "Have a nice day," past his grumbling lunch. He is still somewhat good looking and kind of believable so … I nod towards him to Nick.

"Bruce?" he asks, with furrowed brows.

"Yes, he is one of our delivery guys." I smile nervously.

"Did someone say my name?" Parker says, hovering behind me. Nick stands back with a glare towards Parker. *Is he jealous?* I turn around and wrap my arms around Parker and giggle like Brandi does with Elijah. "Hi Parker. I haven't seen you much this week."

He eagerly hugs me back. "Uhhh, no I have been doing other stuff. Wow, you look hot," Parker says, looking me over. Nick mumbles something away from me, but I choose to ignore him.

"Oh, thank you, Parker." I twist happily until my heel gets caught, and I stumble into Parker, giving him a little more hope than I wanted to give.

"Whoa! So how 'bout we take this to a quieter place." Parker takes my hand and quickly pulls me away from Nick. Weaving our way through the crowd, I look back for Nick only to see him shake his head and take hold of another girl who is more than happy to give him all the attention he wants. "Here we go," Parker says, pulling me into a nearly empty room and pushing me into a corner of the sofa. Immediately, he sticks his tongue down my throat. His abrupt approach is hard to take, but his wandering hands are even rougher. I have to push him away.

"Can you back off a little bit?" I ask.

"You're the one that came onto me. I think you need a drink." I nod, and he hurriedly takes off and is back, shoving a drink in my face before I can get comfortable. It is a nice fruit punch, so I keep drinking it to keep him out of my mouth, but his hands keep finding their way up my skirt. "What do you have under this skirt?" Parker breathes against my neck. My head begins to spin, and Parker pulls me underneath him. Positioning himself to his satisfaction, I begin feeling his erection digging into my thigh. "Take these panties off." *What?*

I force both my fists into his chest and struggle to get up. "No, I don't want to. Please leave me alone. I don't like you." Parker chooses to believe I mean for him to kiss me more and hold me tighter to him. "Parker, please. Parker! Get off of me."

"You need to keep drinking." He grabs his own glass and shoves it down my throat. "Is it because we are not alone? I can fix that." He drags me through another room and down a hall.

"No, stop. I don't want to go." I jerk my arm away from him and fall into Nick.

"Is there a problem?" Nick asks with a shapely blond attached to his hip. She looks down at me as she caresses Nick and kisses on his neck. *She is gorgeous, and I'm not.*

"No, we are just playing around." Parker winks at Nick, throws me over his shoulder, and runs down the hallway to a private bedroom. "This is perfect!" he yells after tossing me onto the bed. He climbs on top of me and goes back to kissing me. *Maybe I should just do this and be done. Then I will no longer be the only virgin. I don't know why I thought Nick would like me anyway.* Tears begin, and I try to embrace Parker, but I really want to go home. "What is wrong with you now?" he barks, huffing at me as I push him away and get up.

"I want to go home," I cry and storm out of the room with Parker trailing close behind. The moment we step out of the room, Parker's friends start laughing and teasing him.

"Shut up!" he yells at everyone. "She is a fucking frigid ass bitch!" Parker grabs my arm and snarls, "I thought you would be an easy lay. I would have never bothered with you if I had known you were useless." Gripping my arm, he begins to jerk me back and forth as he continues to yell at me. "The least you could do is get in that bedroom and suck my dick." I fall onto the floor from his forceful hand and am dragged by my hair back into the bedroom. My head continues to spin and spin until I begin to get sick. I try to crawl away from him, but he drags me back and forces his erection in my face. "Suck it, and I will leave you alone."

"I want to go home!" I cry out, pleading with him to let go of me.

"Just do it, and you can go home. It is not that big of a deal, Franky. You got all dressed up in your whore uniform and then came onto me. For what? To tease me? You fucking bitch. You owe me this much for teasing me like you did." He pushes my head back to his crotch. "Suck my dick, and you can go!"

"Franky? Franky!" Nick yells through the door. "Are you okay?"

"Go away, Jayzon. We are busy in here," Parker yells, gripping my hair tighter and causing me to cry out.

Boom!

Nick comes storming in and grabs Parker by the neck. Parker tries to fight back but has his head beat into the floor and then into the wall before he slides down it, cringing. Nick kicks him and then grabs him by the hair. "Apologize to my friend, or we are going to continue to have a problem," Nick growls. Rubbing my face, I try to see through my tears as Parker's bloodied face is brought up to my knees. Parker manages a mumbled sorry while I look up at Nick and begin to sway my way off the floor. "I don't feel so good."

"Come here, Kitten. I will take you home."

"Nick? What about me?" The gorgeous blond says, running up and grabbing hold of him.

"I need to take her home and make sure she is okay, Amanda."

"Are you coming back?" Amanda whines.

"I doubt it. I want to stay with Franky until she feels better."

"Can't she get someone else to take her home?" Nick turns to her and looks down at her with swirling eyes. "Okay, so call me later?" Amanda pleads and smiles happily once he nods.

I begin to sway again as everything begins to twist and turn around me. Taking my hand, Nick picks me up into his arms and lets me rest my head against his shoulder. "I am going to take you home now, Kitten. Don't worry about anything. Just hold onto me." I try to tell him that I left Brandi, but I am not sure he understands until after I say her name a few times. "Don't worry about her. Eli will make sure she gets home safely."

The sound of his voice calms me, but it is the security of his arms that I never want to leave. Nick slides me into a car, and I wrap around myself with left over tears trailing down my face. Then, I feel his hand take mine. "It's going to be okay. You will be home soon. You can get a hot shower and crawl into your bed where it is safe and warm." Seeing my house in the distance, I know my father is home, but I don't want to leave Nick. "Will you stay with me for a little while?"

"If you want me to, I will." He kisses the side of my head again and carries me up the steps, but he doesn't get much closer before my father walks out the front door.

"Get away from my daughter!" my father yells, pulling me from Nick and pushing him away from me. "What did you do to her? I will kill you if you hurt her!"

"Daddy, please! Nick helped me. It wasn't him. It was someone else."

I hold my father's arm, pulling him away from Nick. "I don't like you!" my father says, pointing at him. "I have seen you. You and your friends always up to no good. I know who you are. You stay away from my daughter."

"No, Daddy. I want him to stay. He helped me." I try to hold onto Nick's hand to keep him from leaving as he watches my father's fury come even stronger at him. "Nick please don't leave."

"I don't think I have a choice, Kitten. I will see you later, I promise."

"The hell you will!" My father jerks me away from Nick and gets right in his face. Fisting his hands, Nick immediately turns away from his glare. "You are nothing but a loser. You will never be anything, but a loser. If I ever catch you near my daughter, I will kill you and your loser friends." My father grabs Nick by his collar. "Do you understand me?"

Nick turns and looks into my father's eyes, "I understand you - perfectly." A sudden calmness comes over my father. He lets go of Nick and backs away. My father puts his arm around my shoulder and pushes me into the house.

"Daddy, why did you do that? I …"

"No, you stay away from him, Franky. He is dangerous. Trust me, baby. He is nothing, but bad news. You have to stay away from him for your own good."

My father wraps his arms around me and holds me, asking me what happened and telling me he will take care of it for me. I try to tell him that Nick has already handled everything, but he refuses to hear Nick's name.

After a long debate back and forth with my father about Nick, I finally decide to take a hot shower and wash the night completely off of me. My father checks on me a half a dozen times throughout the night, and every time I ignore him, refusing to speak another word to him until he agrees to listen to me about Nick. When he himself finally retires for the night, I crawl into bed and stop showing my stubbornness. As I try to fall asleep, I feel something strange and open my eyes to see a shadowy figure standing outside, watching me. Without thinking, I jump out of bed and raise my window. "Nick?" His weak smile becomes clearer and clearer until I finally feel his sweet breath on my face.

"Sorry, I know it's late, but I wanted to make sure that you're okay," he says, running his fingers down my cheek.

"I am, thank you." Overwhelmed, I reach out and pull him to me, kissing him like I want to. His soft warm lips are better than what I remembered. "Can you stay with me, at least until I fall asleep?"

"Whatever you want." Nick crawls through my window and into my bed with me.

It feels so good to lie against his chest and hold his hand, but the best part is feeling his sweet breath whisper, "Go to sleep, beautiful, I'm here as long as you need me to be."

"Stay all night. I need you to stay with me all night, Nick. I feel safer with you here. I feel … so much better when I am with you." I look into his eyes, and suddenly, I feel an overpowering awareness take over me. *I only want him.*

"I will stay with you all night then," he says as his weak smile becomes as strong as mine.

Chapter 13

Nick

Luke is already starting trouble when I walk up to meet him and Elijah. "What is he doing?" I ask Elijah.

"Being a dumbass as usual." We both watch as Luke taunts some high school kids playing basketball until he apparently manages to cross a line, and the irritated ballers decide to come after him. Elijah and I walk up to his side, and they back off immediately.

"Yeah, you better run!" Luke yells joyfully. Elijah smacks Luke in the back of the head before I get a chance to. "Hey, what was that for?"

"What is wrong with you? Can you not be calm for a second? You're like on a constant sugar high," Elijah rants as we take off to do our job.

Before the night is over, we fare to steal four cars and drive them to the exchange for our payment. The last one, I drove around a little longer than I should, but it was so sweet that I couldn't help myself. *One day. One day, I am going to buy whatever car I want.* I decide to drive the car by Franky's and check on her, but with her father home, I can do no more than knock on her window. She sits studying as I would have expected, but smiles wide when she sees me.

"Hi," she says looking me over. She has a wrap on her wrist and cuts and bruises all over her arms that make me cringe. Franky instantly hides them under her clothes as best she can.

"He hurt you pretty bad, huh?" She shakes her head, but I know better. "I can't believe you liked him; he treats people like shit, especially the girls he dates."

"I didn't know that. He seemed nice in the store." She looks down at her feet.

"I'm sorry. I should have said something, but I was …" My phone suddenly goes off, and being that it's Harvey, I can't ignore it. Before I can say much else, I have to go. "I have to go. I have a job I have to get to."

"This late?" she asks, and I nod. "It's not a normal job is it?" I don't respond. "Could you get hurt?" Again, I don't respond. Instead, I gently rub my thumb across the bruises on her wrist. "You should make sure you're warm at least." Franky unwraps the scarf from her neck and begins to wrap it around mine. "It's my lucky scarf. My mother gave it to me before she died. It will keep you warm … and safe."

I hate to leave Franky. There are so many questions I want to ask her, but Harvey has one last job he wants done. Something simple he says, but that something simple has us breaking into a competitor's warehouse and stealing a shipment that just came in. It's a test, a test to see how loyal we are to Harvey and how helpful we can be to him. It is going to determine our roles, who we will be under or who will be under us. I know that I will not be happy working for someone else, especially for anyone on Harvey's crew. Brilliant strategists they are not; they are more like beastly enforcers. Before we move in, I am handed my own gun for the first time. I have never had to handle one before. I don't know why it bothers me now;

it is not as if I didn't expect to have to use one at some point. I have been practicing with Elijah at the shooting range, but it is one thing to be aiming at a paper target and another to be aiming at a breathing someone.

Creeping in through the back, we make our way to the warehouse, waiting for the unexpected. My heart is racing, and my mind is going even faster. Then, it begins. The morons we are with rush in, and the three of us not being much smarter, follow after them. Elijah and I concentrate on the shipment, get it released, get it moved, get it out the door, and get it onto the truck. Luke watches our backs, having no problem taking out anyone that comes our way, even seeming to enjoy it.

"There is one more, boys! Go back and get it!" Matt, Harvey's right-hand man, yells at us.

"Are you crazy? There is no way we can go back in there now. All hell is breaking loose!" I yell back at him. "If you wanted more than this, then you should have told us so we could have planned for it ahead of time. It is too late now."

He simply smiles and shrugs his shoulders. "It is your job, and unless you want to be the ones to tell Harvey you failed…? But I don't think you will make it that far," he says, aiming his gun at us, with five others following his lead. *That fucker always hated us.*

"Come on, Nicky. We got this." Elijah grabs my arm, and we slide out the back and into a dark corner. We begin to analyze our next move, or really any move that won't get us killed. I spot the ladder to the roof and point it out to Elijah. He nods and motions for Luke to follow us. Once we get in, we watch the fighting below as it is slowly comes to an end. Our last men begin to flee, leaving us to die alone.

"The truck left us," Luke says as he sits down next to us. *Son of a bitch!*

"Let's just leave it and go," Elijah says.

"No, we are getting it, and we are going to prove to that motherfucker that he can't make a move without us from now on." Studying the area, I devise a plan to get us out of here in one piece and with the remaining container. It's simple, but patience is needed. All we have to do is wait. Wait until the calm, until the enemy relaxes. A two stage hit. No one ever expects that, *I hope.* We watch breathlessly as they clean up, inspect the damage, and report to their higher ups.

After things are quiet, and there is nothing more than a few guards sitting around a table playing cards, we make our move. Elijah and Luke move down to connect the last container to a truck that is sitting inside while I stay behind and watch their backs. Once they are secure and ready to go, all I have to do is create a diversion away from their escape route. I begin searching for just the right thing and end up finding a man checking on a large amount of cash within a safe, 22 … 33 … 19.

My attention is distracted for a moment, but only for a moment. I am not about to let my friends down for cash. Jumping to the front of the warehouse, I focus on the forklift and drive it straight through the front door. Security begins chasing after me, and thankfully, not recognizing the assault on the back door at the same time. I enjoy my ride, but jump off when sheltered by the darkness and run back inside. *That cash is mine.* The place is virtually empty now. The one man I have to get around is scared to death and hiding. I easily make it past him to the upstairs office and quickly take possession of the cash inside. I have only one armed obstacle on my way out, and with my gun raised, he pauses, but so do I. I have never shot anyone before, never had a reason to. I don't even know this man; he has never done anything to me except be in my way. Slowly, my gun starts to fall while the guard reaches for his and takes aim at me with no problem at all. I don't have a chance to run or even retake aim. All I can do is stare into the barrel of his gun.

Suddenly, the gun behind me fires, and the man in front of me falls. "What is wrong with you, Nick? Why didn't you shoot him? He was going to kill you. Damn, what are you doing back in here anyway? Let's go?" Luke screams at me, jarring me out of my trance. Gripping my neck, I fist Franky's scarf and smile.

"Did you have fun?" Elijah yells when I catch up to the car. I shrug, still smiling. "What is wrong with you? Are you crazy?"

"I'm fine. I got a lucky charm," I say, showing off my scarf. "Franky gave it to me, and it worked, too."

Elijah rolls his eyes. "Great, the girl in love saves the man she has always loved with a … scarf. How beautiful."

"Loves? Always loved?" I sit up looking at him as he nods. Elijah and Luke begin making fun of my scarf by wrapping up their necks with shirts and whatever else they can find. That doesn't bother me, but the flipping of their hair and sighing like little girls is ridiculous and annoying. "Enough already! If you don't stop, I won't share what I found," I say, pulling out the cash from the safe. My friends instantly change their tunes and begin singing my praises, and my scarf's too.

We report to Harvey with the remaining container, shocking but pleasing him. Matt is instantly scolded for leaving us, but only for appearances. Harvey won't let Matt go; he is still too valuable to him, and he doesn't trust us enough to take his place… yet. Harvey rewards each of us with some extra cash before sending us on our way. We never tell him about the safe I emptied, and instead, we split the cash equally. I stash my share into a safe place, a contribution to my future plans. I only hope I make it long enough to experience them.

The boys and I go out the next day and enjoy our rewards from the night before. I decide to take my portion and spend it on a girl who I have recently become fond of. I don't understand her hold on me, but I enjoy her smile and making her happy. Holding off Elijah and Luke briefly, I step inside the old store and walk right up to her as she sits with her book. I lean over the counter to her and toss her scarf around her neck. She looks up with a beautiful smile, sending an abundance of energy running through my body.

"Hi, what are you doing here?" Franky asks with a small bruise still on her cheek.

I sweep the tender area with my thumb, and she lays her head against my hand. "I wanted to check on you and give you your lucky charm back. I wanted to give you these, too," I say, handing over a bouquet of flowers and watching as her eyes light up like I have never seen them before. "Are you feeling better today?"

"Wow, these are beautiful! Thank you. You really didn't have to, Nick. I'm fine. I slept perfectly after you left, and my father and I are talking again for now."

"Oh, I definitely had to. I owe you now. The scarf helped me last night. You saved my life, Franky."

"Really?" she asks.

I nod, reaching across the counter to touch her hand. "So I guess you are not so much into your man anymore, huh?" She shakes her head. "Do you like anyone else?" She shrugs with an awkward nod. *She is a terrible liar.* "Oh, well, if you need any more help with your research for this new guy, let me know."

Franky, with her sweet, awkward smile, reaches out, touching my hand and taking hold of it with a joyful sigh. "I would like that, actually I like …" *Say it, Franky.*

"Nicky! The cops are looking for us. Harvey said we need to get back now," Elijah says, running in with Luke behind him. "We need to go. The cops turned down at the corner when they saw us." As Elijah finishes his sentence, the cops walk in behind him.

"You three need to come with us," one announces in a commanding voice.

"Why? We haven't done anything," I say.

"Oh, yes you have. All three of you were spotted by a witness down at a warehouse that was raided last night. You are wanted for criminal trespassing and murder."

Before I can say another word, Franky steps in front of us. "Last night? That is impossible. They were with me and my friend at the movies. They lost a bet, and had to pay for us to see the new documentary on how our environment effects our personal beliefs. It was quite amazing, but I am afraid these three fell asleep almost immediately. Very disappointing." She glances our way with a smirk and a shake of her head.

"Are you sure, Miss?"

"Franky, what is going on out here?" Her father walks out from the back, eyeing me briefly before putting his arm around his daughter's shoulder.

"We were talking to your daughter about where she was and with whom she was with last night, sir."

"She was at the movies," Franky's father says confidently. "I dropped her off there myself."

"And she was with these three?" the cop asks, gesturing our way in disbelief.

"She was with her friend, Brandi, and …" her father looks back at us, "and probably them too. They are always hanging around my daughter and her friend. These idiots have been trying to impress them for weeks. I guess they have never met girls who are of higher moral standard than they are. They are certainly annoying, but if my daughter said she was with them, then she was. I would hope that you are not calling her a liar. I know my daughter, officer, and she has never lied to me or anyone else." Franky's hand tenses, but both of the cops remain stiff in their stance.

"Sir, I don't believe that your daughter is lying, but I think it is still best that we take these three down to the station and have a talk with them."

"I assume you have a warrant to do that?" Both cops look down at their feet and shake their head. "Then I would suggest you go search for the real culprits," he says, showing them the door. Her father turns to us. "I owe you one for helping my daughter, and that was it. Don't expect anything else from me, and that includes my daughter. Stay away from her from now on." I nod and back away, following Luke and Elijah out the door. I look back only once at Franky's weak smile. *Why is it always the ones you shouldn't want, that you do want?*

Chapter 14

Franky

My flowers sit precisely in the center of my room so I can see them from everywhere. My father isn't too happy about them, but he is tolerant since they make me happy. I know how he feels about Nick, but I can't help how I feel about him either. I have to reassure my father a few times before he finally leaves for his girlfriend's house. I cannot think of anything other than Nick, so I decide to go to bed and let my imagination carry me away. Nick apparently has other ideas. He walks up the steps to my door before I can lay my head down. My excitement takes over, and I meet him at the door. "Hi," I say, pulling him inside with me.

"Did I wake you?" he asks so smoothly that my knees nearly give out from under me.

"No, I hadn't even gone to bed yet."

"Why did you help me, Franky? Why did your father help me and my friends?"

"He talked to the police, and they told him what you did. They said that Parker is going to press charges against you? You are going to get into trouble for that, aren't you?"

"Don't worry about it. The most important thing is that he won't be bothering you anymore," he says, looking down at me and brushing my hair out of my face.

"Nick, let me talk to them and explain. You shouldn't be …"

"Apparently, I broke his jaw, some ribs, and a few other bones, Franky. Nothing you say is going to change what I did to him." He smiles and continues to touch my face.

"Maybe my father …"

"Your father? I'm so sure he will be happy to help *me* out - again. Don't worry about it, Franky. I promise it is taken care of. Besides, if I had it to do all over again, I wouldn't change anything, except that I might have punched him one more time or two. I couldn't let him get away with hurting you." He leans in and kisses me gently along my swollen cheek.

"Are you hungry or something?" I ask nervously. I take his hand and try to lead him further into the house, but he stops me. "I wasn't planning on staying. I only wanted … well, I had to see you." I turn to him and force a smile, still worried about what he is here to tell me. "Your Dad made it hard on you, didn't he? For lying for us?"

"Yeah, but it will be okay. He didn't even ask me about it. He won't bring it up ever again. I am sure."

Nick shakes his head. "I'm sure he won't. Actually, now I am stalling. I really want to ask you about something else. About that night at the party? I was wondering what you were thinking with Parker. Why did you pretend to like someone you apparently can't stand? Why all the makeup and cheap clothes for someone that didn't even matter to you?"

"I told you. I was trying to impress the guy I like. It was Parker, even though I don't much care for him now." From his expression, I assume he doesn't believe me anymore.

"Parker, you are seriously telling me that Parker was the guy you liked? I don't think so Franky." He immediately sighs when I turn away and ignore him. "I don't understand Franky. Supposedly, this whole thing was about some questions you had to impress someone, and then I find out there isn't anyone … else. Your friend talks a lot. She told Eli a lot of things" *Damn he does know.* "Are you going to look at me, or you going to ignore me now?"

"I don't have any answers for you, Nick. Besides, you seem to think you have them all anyway."

"Oh, yes, you do. You just don't want to tell me. You know I don't like games. Tell me the truth. Tell me what is really going on. Why did you really pick me to help you?" I walk away from him, but he pulls me back.

"I … I really wanted to have sex, and I … kind of have a crush on … you. Have for awhile. I didn't know how to talk to you, so I thought maybe I could get you to talk to me with my story. I thought, maybe, I could feel special for a little while. Maybe I could be that girl that you pay attention to, even if it was only for one night."

"You lied to me, Franky?"

"Well, you wouldn't have talked to me otherwise," I force out with full power in my voice.

"I did talk to you otherwise," he mocks.

"No, you didn't. You wouldn't of had anything to do with me if it hadn't of been for your brother making a mess of my father's store. All those pretty girls, they swoon over you, all the time. What chance do I have to compete on their level? I had a better chance …"

"By provoking me, *up*, to your level. I guess I can understand that." Nick smiles, shaking his head. "I will give it to you. It was a good plan, up until you decided to go against your own plan." I look up at him, confused. "If you had stuck to your original plan, you would have had a better chance,

Franky. I was feeling something for you, but then you walked into that party with that dress and all that makeup shit. I was so mad at you that I couldn't even think straight. I was waiting for you, looking for you even. I was planning on trying to steal you away from the guy you liked. When I saw you come in, I purposely ignored you because it wasn't you. It was a lie. The truth suits you better, Franky, and I don't want you to lie for me ever again either." He glances down at me and sighs. I begin to fidget and feel uncomfortable. I want to say something, but I don't know what.

"Will it help if I do the banana thing again?" I ask, glancing up from my feet. Nick laughs, and I smile.

He gently brushes his thumb across my wide smile. "You are so beautiful when you smile." His eyes lure me in, and within seconds, I feel the smooth, soft touch of his lips caressing mine. He sucks on my bottom lip, and then the top, before taking them both in and pulling me against his chest. "I like your outfit," he says, not letting go of me and watching me closely. Looking down at his t-shirt, I realize all I have on is that, my scarf, and my underwear. Nick takes a fist full of his t-shirt and jerks me to him. "This looks good on you. Not as good as off though." His lips hypnotize me the moment they touch mine.

"Do you have to leave, Nick?"

"Why? Do you want me to stay here with you?"

"Yes." I nod. Taking in a deep breath, Nick picks me up and carries me to my bedroom. Laying me down in my bed, he kisses me once before taking off his shirt. My body starts to tingle and ache. The more he touches me, the more I want. He shouldn't feel this good. I should make him go like my father said, but instead, I pull his t-shirt from my body and climb into his lap. I kiss him in between wrapping my scarf around his neck. "Now I can pull you to me," I giggle, fisting my scarf and drawing him into me. I never thought I would get this chance again: feeling his hands on my bare skin, his lips on my breasts, his erection rubbing against me. Nick lays me down on my back while he takes off his pants. He pulls out a condom this time and places it next to me. His seductive eyes look deep into mine, causing my body to float to him. He trails his fingers along the edge of my underwear, with his lips following each tender touch. I breathe heavily as he slowly pulls them down my quivering legs.

Touching his lips with mine once again, I feel him against me. "Are you sure want to do this, Franky? With me?" Nick asks, caressing my legs with warm hands.

"Never been more sure of anything in my life. I never wanted anyone more." I wrap my arms around him with a soft exhale to make sure he doesn't leave me. Nick takes hold of my thighs, pushes them open, and leans down, kissing me in between, "OH! Oh Nick … what are you doing?"

"It's okay. Trust me." He looks up at me, settling my nerves. My toes curl and my body tenses in places I never thought possible. I scream out and quickly cover my mouth. I look down at him and meet his smiling eyes, watching as he kisses me, touches me, feels inside me, and sends moaning vibrations to my core the deeper he goes. Nick holds my legs out wide in front of him, enjoying himself immensely. Vulnerable, I grip the pillow underneath my head, fisting it tighter and tighter until he touches something inside of me that causes my body to burst into a quivering, building delight. The feeling continues to rush through me again, strengthening and heightening, again and again. I cry out his name, begging him until my eyes fall back and my body releases something deep inside me. My body shivers from the sweat dripping from my skin, but his sizzling hot, naked body quickly heats me up again.

"I assume that was your first orgasm?" *Oh… is that what that was … wow.* "I thought you were going to bring down the house, Kitten." He laughs with me. Nick kisses me and holds me, warming me up in his arms as he grabs the condom next to us. "You still want to do this?" I nod and watch him. His erection stands straight up between us, massive, strong, and hungry as it makes its way to what it seems to want. The pressure of it against me seems unreasonable, but Nick lifts my chin so I can see into his eyes. "This is going to hurt, are you sure?" I nod, and he moves against me, "Hold onto me. I'll move slow for you." His voice hums into the back of my mind as the pain surges. Gripping him tight, I call out to him. "It's okay, Franky. You're doing good… only a little further." Nick pushes into me, and suddenly, I feel him, feel him moving inside of me. I feel his lips touching my skin, his hands holding me tight as he moves. I rub my fingers across his glistening brow, kiss his lips softly, and feel down his muscles, rubbing each one with my hands. I exhale with a smile as Nick slides in and out of me. He groans deep into my lips as he moves my body into another position, comforting me every step of the way with his sensual voice.

There is pain, but there is also elation. *This is it. This is what I have been waiting for. The moment. The person. It is all happening.* His groans increase as he speeds up his pace. Nick kisses me hard until I feel the rumbling inside of me. I don't want him to move or leave. I hold him tight to me and beg him not to move away from me. With a smile, he kisses me gently. "Let's warm up together, okay?" Nick prepares a warm bath and takes my hand to help me slide into it. Sitting behind me, he pulls me to his chest and kisses my cheek. "Do you feel okay? It wasn't too painful, was it?" I shake my head. "You really are … not a very good liar at all," he says, rubbing my body with a warm cloth. "You are stiff and cringing."

"I don't care. I feel incredible." I lean into him and enjoy the moment. "You really are good at this," I say, causing him to laugh.

"Good at baths? I should hope so. I have been bathing myself since I was a child," he says, kissing the back of my neck.

"No, sexual things. Being so tempting."

"Hmm, is that what you heard? Is that why you wanted me?" he asks, nudging me and nibbling on my ear. "Is it?"

"Well it didn't hurt in my decision making process."

"Ah… your process. Only girl I know who wanted to fuck me because her mathematical equations worked out in my favor."

I look over my shoulder at him and shrug. "Well, you are kind of cute, too."

"You're a lot cute," he says with a crooked smile, erupting an incredible desire inside my body.

Chapter 15

Nick

Franky's father comes home a little quieter this morning, but luckily, we thought enough to lock her door.

"Franky, sweetheart, your door is locked. Are you okay?" He calls out through her door.

I look down at Franky lying across my chest, naked and out cold. "Franky," I whisper, shaking her gently and kissing her hand. She finally looks up with a goofy smile. "Hi. Your father is here." It takes a few seconds before her eyes go wild.

"Franky?" her father yells again. Franky panics, rushing around the room searching, before finally forcing me into her closet.

"Franky, I will just sneak out the window again," I reason, but she shakes her head, and closes me inside her closet.

"Hi, Daddy. Sorry, I was really tired."

"You're not getting sick are you, honey?"

"No, I stayed up late watching some scary movies, and then had a hard time falling asleep. I really should have learned my lesson by now, but you know me, always the stubborn one."

"Oh, you are stubborn for sure. I am surprised any movie monster would scare you awake." Her father laughs with her. "Well, I wanted to stop by, and check on you before I went into the store, sweetheart. Are you sure you're okay? You look flushed."

"I'm perfectly fine, Daddy. Do you need me to come in at all today?"

"No, honey. You enjoy your day. Your cousin is coming in to earn some extra money anyway." There is a sudden silence, which makes me nervous. "Francesca! Your room is atrocious. You might want to spend the day cleaning this mess," he says with a huff before seemingly walking away.

Franky opens up her closet and smiles at me. "Miss me?" I ask with a wink.

"Come here, you. You are too cute to be hiding in my closet."

"That's what I was thinking, too," I say, wrapping my arms around her. "So you are off today, huh?" She nods. "How about spending the day with me then?" Franky jumps into my arms, kissing me excitedly. "I'll take that as a yes."

It's the carnival, and it's the last few days before winter completely shuts it down. Franky holds my hand with both of hers, and I love it. She is so happy that she doesn't even seem to care what we do as long as we do it together. She's different from the other girls I have been with, content to be near me without making me feel as if I constantly have to prove myself to her. We walk up to a guy flipping cups, left and right, back and forth, all to confuse the onlookers to where the lost red ball may be hiding. One after the other, they pay their admission to compete against this man and his rapid hands, and one by one, they leave disappointed.

"What about you, stud? Do you think you can beat me?" he taunts. I step forward, and he smiles. "Be careful, my new friend. You might embarrass yourself in front of your girl." Franky doesn't hesitate. She unwraps her scarf from her neck and wraps it around mine.

I look up into my new friend's eyes and focus. "Play," I say, paying attention to the mirroring images in his eyes, listening to the ball as it rolls from one place to another. *Focus, focus, and …* "There," I say, never bothering to look down to verify my accuracy.

"Oh wow!" Franky screams while clapping for me. The man hands me my prize and moves to the next person before I can ask to try again. "Nick, that was amazing. How did you do that?"

"I don't know. I have always been able to focus perfectly on one thing, and memorize exactly what I see," I say, handing her the stuffed elephant I won. Franky cuddles it and allows me to keep her scarf wrapped around my neck. "I am keeping this now. It's my lucky scarf."

"Good. If it keeps you coming back to me safely, it's yours," she says with a kiss before gripping my arm tight. "So, focus and memorization, is that why you are so smart?"

"Me, smart? You're the smart one. You are the one getting the college scholarship and all."

"I am sure you could get one too if you would have shown up to school more than a few days a month. Although, it was rather enjoyable to watch you put Mr. Collins in his place. *Mr. Jayzon since you believe yourself to be too smart to bother to come to my class, then I am sure you must know the answer. As a matter of fact Mr. Collins the answer is …*"

"Yeah, he didn't like me too much, but at least after that day, he never bothered to try and embarrass me again."

School was such a long waste of my time. I would always read the textbooks the first few days after we got them, and then, I was done for the rest of the year. I showed up to class only to take the exams or if they started calling my father to check on my severe illnesses. I think they assumed I was scared of him. I wasn't; I simply got tired of him bitching at me all the time. Besides, sometimes it was fun screwing with the teachers. They were always shocked when this loser showed up to class and knew all the answers to their elementary questions.

"How did you always know the answers?"

"Let's not talk about school. I would rather go into the haunted house over there. You did say you like scary movies, so why not a haunted house?" Franky looks nervously at the creepy building, with all its ghosts and goblins hiding behind the corners. "Don't worry. I can take them all and kiss you at the same time." Holding hands, we walk in, and I do just that. Pulling her into a corner, I caress her face to my lips, warming her up while blocking the disguised pests from her sight. One goblin tries to scare my girl a little harder than the rest, but regrets it when he finds himself flying back into a wall. "See, it's not so scary, Kitten."

"Not when I am with you." She smiles.

"Let's go back to your place, and I can help you study for that exam of yours." I take Franky home and try to focus on helping her study, but it is not long before our clothes are off, and we are back in her bed. When her father comes home, I am holding his daughter in my arms and kissing her silently.

Franky holds me tighter. "Don't leave. I can't sleep without you."

"Whatever you want, Kitten."

"I love you, Nick," Franky whispers against my chest, shocking me.

"Yeah?" I ask, forcing her to look at me. She nods shyly, and I have to force her chin back up, "Don't be shy about that. It's the greatest thing I have ever heard. Especially since, I love you too." She giggles, almost too loud, but neither of us care. *She loves me? She loves me. Why?* I stare at her all night in amazement.

Chapter 16

Nick

I wake up early and realize I had better get out of Franky's house before her father wakes up. A quick kiss to Franky's lips, and I walk out of her bedroom door. Unfortunately, her Father begins coming in through the front door with the newspaper at the same time. *Fuck!* Looking around, I tiptoe through her house, dodging him at every corner until he finally takes his newspaper to the back of the house. I make a quick getaway out her back door, cross her backyard, and jump over her fence into her neighbor's yard. I feel good about my escape until I have to pass an older lady smiling a little too wide at me.

"Hi, are you the man I ordered?" she sings, jumping up and allowing her robe to open up too much. *Oh no, that is not pretty at all.*

"No, I am pretty sure I am not," I say, walking around her admiring eyes and just out of reach of her reaching hands.

"Come in. I made some breakfast muffins." She reaches out to grab me, but I manage to escape them and run.

I head to Elijah's, but he meets me at the door, "Nicky, what are you doing here?" He smiles nervously.

"I thought I would stop and see if you wanted to go get something to eat, but it smells like you already have something going. Is your dad feeling better?" I try to look around him, but he continues to block me. "What is wrong with you? What are you hiding?"

"Nothing, but I was heading out, so I will catch up with you later, alright?" Elijah says, still standing between me and whatever he is hiding from me.

I smile at him and fake a turn but fly around him and into his house in a flash to find Brandi, cooking away.

"Hi, Nick."

"Hi," I say while giving my friend a cocky smile. Brandi offers me some food, and I happily accept. She helps Elijah's father sit and makes him a plate, kissing him on the head as she sits his plate down for him. We sit around the table politely talking about our days until Brandi has to go to school. She quickly cleans up the kitchen before kissing Elijah and heading off. After she leaves, I stare at Elijah and wait. He tries to ignore me, but I know he can't. "What!" he snaps. "Yeah, so what, I had a girl stay over. What of it?"

"Stay over? You have a little domestic wife thing going on here, Eli."

"No, it is not like that all. She cooks well, and my dad really likes her. She is sweet and she …" He glances over at me. "She has the biggest tits. I am telling you, they are amazing." He holds his hands out to describe the size. "I just bury my head right in them and sleep like a baby."

"Whatever. You like her." He shakes his head, but I know better.

"So you fucked, Franky," he says, effectively changing my train of thought.

"How …?" *News travels fast, especially when your best friend is screwing your girl's best friend.* "Yeah, it was pretty great. I really like her. She's different than all those others."

"Hmm different, yeah I know what you mean, but different is only good for so long. I got a date with Leslie tonight."

"Oh no … no, I don't want to know anything about that. In fact, pretend I never heard a thing, and do me a favor please. Handle Brandi a little better than your usual *so babe we have had some fun but* routine, Eli."

"But that has worked well for me."

"It has not. You've been smacked, kicked, bit, chased, and that one girl, what was her name? She actually put a curse on you." I lean back in my chair, shaking my head at him, "Oh yeah, it works well for you." He shrugs with a laugh. "What was that curse anyway?" Elijah laughs.

"That my dick would shrivel up and fall off. That crazy bitch. My dick has got superpowers. It's immune to all that hibbety-jibbety voodoo stuff. I think it actually grew after that. You want to see?" he says, undoing his pants in front of me.

"Get the fuck away from me, dumbass. I don't want to see your dick. I have seen it more than I care to, as it is." I laugh and push him away from me.

"Hey, that was your own dumbass fault," he says, pointing back at me. "Oh, I know, Eli. Let's take the girls to a motel and go skinny dipping in their pool. It's late, and no one will ever know. Hey Nicky, next time don't leave our clothes in a bag with your dinner. *Fucking dog.*" I laugh, and he snarls me. "It's not funny. I had to walk home with nothing, but that stupid kids floaty around my waist and shoes."

"You had shoes! And I graciously let you have the floating panda. I had to take the swan," I remind him.

"The swan was better, Nicky!"

"How do you figure that?" I ask, holding my hands out.

"Oh shut up," he huffs, plopping back down in his seat. I laugh until he shakes his head and smiles.

"Hello Nick, how are you?" Elijah's father, Aaron, comes in and greets me. He always puts one hand on my head and one on my shoulder when he greets me, an encouraging gesture I have always appreciated.

"I am good, sir," I reply back to him.

"Tell your father, Nick, I have his machine working again." Glancing at Elijah, I wonder if he knew that my father visited his, and by his expression, it's apparent he didn't.

"His machine, sir?" I ask.

Aaron looks over at me with furrowed eyebrows. "Yes, I think it is something for a friend of his. Or, really, I think it is simply an excuse to visit. You know your father helped me save my business. I was sure I was going to lose everything until he stepped in. Ever since, I have promised to help him with his little machine projects. I am not sure what he uses them for exactly, but I have to say, it is nice to still have something to occupy my time that doesn't make me sick. Dante has so many projects for me, I accused him of building a small city underground." He smiles, patting me on the shoulder and returning to his room.

"What is your dad up to?" Elijah asks me.

"I don't know. I didn't even know they were still friends." My father has always had secrets, but I never cared enough to ask about any of them. Suddenly, I have hope that maybe this doesn't have anything to do with my father's secret. Maybe he simply cares about his friend. Considering my father has no other friends, it is nice to think that he does take care of the one person who considers him as so. Looking down at my hands, I begin to consider my friend, my best friend. "You know, Eli, you shouldn't go out with Leslie tonight. Stay with Brandi. You like her. I can tell, and that is a good thing. And your father likes her. It makes him happy to see you happy. Try a relationship for once. What's the worst that could happen?" I don't know if he will listen to me, but I want to make sure he knows that I prefer him happy opposed to trying to prove he is a bigger player than I am… or was.

"Yeah you too. It's nice that you like Franky. She's a nice girl. Maybe we could double date or something?" I nod for a second before looking back up at him oddly. "I mean, maybe we could split the cost of a nice hotel and both have sex all night. Lots of dirty sex with the girls, while watching porn. Did I tell you she has big … ?" I nod and change the subject.

I could hardly wait to finish up work and get back to Franky's. I carefully scope out her house to verify that her father has left already before knocking on her door. Opening, her door, she stands in front of me in nothing but her underwear. "Oooh, I was going to see what you made for dinner, but maybe … hmmm." Picking her up, I kick the door closed behind me and growl my appreciation in her ear.

"I will make you whatever you want," Franky says.

"Right now, I only want you." Kissing my face, she makes me feel more loved than I have ever felt before. Her innocence makes me feel the same, like a kid again, a chance for normality that I never thought possible.

The next night, Franky decides she has to study and has a plate of food waiting to distract me. I finish my food quickly and move closer to her while she studies. I don't make it easy for her. I kiss her neck and feel under her shirt.

"Nick, I am trying to study, and you know I can't resist you, so please, allow me a little while longer," she asks, trying to resist me but failing miserably. "Why don't you help me with this so I can finish quicker? You are so smart." I ignore her request, shaking my head and turning her back around so we can get back to what I want to do. "Nick, please, you never studied for anything, and you knew the answers all the time. You can't fool me. You are so smart, way smarter than I ever could be, and you quit … why?"

"I didn't quit. I got my diploma. I just didn't go to class to do it. It was boring. School was a nuisance. I didn't belong there, and you know that."

"Nick, you can do anything you want to. I bet any college in the world would give you a full scholarship. You just have to …"

"Franky, what the hell are you talking about? No one is going to give me a scholarship. They don't want me anywhere near their campus. They would get one look at me and call the cops immediately."

"No they wouldn't, not if they saw what I see. You can do anything Nick. You shouldn't spend your life working for someone else. You're too smart for that. You should be working for yourself, working with what you have. I believe in you, Nick." She takes hold of my face and looks right into my eyes. "Don't waste your life earning for others when you can do better. I know you are better than that. I know you can do anything you want to." Grabbing her hands, I look into her sincere eyes and smile.

"Thank you, but no. College isn't for me, Kitten. I appreciate the support though. I will support you. I will visit you at school every chance I get. And if you need anything, I will be right there." I kiss her, holding her tight to remove the pout from her face. "I will be right there whenever things get hard, and I won't let anyone hurt you ever. I will sleep outside your window if I have to, anything to make sure you sleep well at night. I will take care of you forever. Besides, I make good money now, in fact." I reach over to my coat and pull out a box and hand it to her.

"What is this?" She turns the box around and admires it entirely.

"A gift. So open it." Franky opens the box and pulls out the charm bracelet with the ruby heart dangling from it. "Do you like it?" I ask, enjoying her smile.

"Yes, very much, but Nick this expensive. How did you?"

"Don't worry about it. Just put it on." She pauses, looking at me with questioning eyes. "Please. I really wanted to get you something nice." She puts it on and smiles. Franky crawls into my lap and allows me to kiss down her neck. "I love you, Franky," I say, watching her closely as she looks up at me.

"I love you. I love you so much, Nick that it hurts."

She looks into my eyes with a look that makes me groan with happiness. I tear off our clothes and make love to her the best way I know how. I will protect her forever. That is all I want to do. Sleeping next to her at night is rough in her tiny bed, but when she turns her face towards me and grins, I don't care about the damn bed. She simply smiles beautifully and trusts me for no reason other than she loves me. My world changes at that moment. I want nothing more than to protect her, to love her, and to make sure *she* is happy. Something my father would never understand.

Chapter 17

Nick

Elijah and I have spent the last few days goofing off, while Luke is promoted up into Harvey's crew. Elijah and I both decided a long time ago we wanted to hold out for better, but after Luke was promoted, I couldn't convince Elijah to wait any longer. Luke is now considered our boss, and if we don't agree to Harvey's terms, we will be behind him, not something Elijah is comfortable with. Harvey knows he has me now, and he is being overly friendly to Elijah to show how much better off I could be. The only problem with that is, no one else understands that several people on Harvey's crew are already talking in Harvey's ear, *that Elijah will fail.*

They want him to fail. "No kid should be allowed to come in and take over my position," Matt Drake said the other night while we were working a party for Harvey. Matt, Harvey's once right hand man and the man Elijah replaced, hates us all but especially Elijah. No matter what Elijah has against him, Luke and I have his back, and with us, there is no way he will fail.

My job for the day is to be Elijah's and Luke's lackey. I have to drive them around while they make pickups, my punishment for fighting for something more than I apparently have a right to. Harvey is pushing us to our limits. We spend all day and into the night running for him. Eli and Luke are both beyond exhausted and beginning to make stupid mistakes, and as only their driver, there is little I can do to help them. By the end of the night, we are nearly ready to head back to Harvey when Elijah begins to panic. He searches the car, frantically. "What's wrong?" I ask.

"I can't find the cash from the last run. I know I had it in my coat, but it's gone." We both tear up the car, his coat, Luke's coat and mine, searching for the missing money. Luke stalls for us by making a call that we are on our way. "Oh fuck. Fuck!" Elijah sits back with his hands on his head. "I'm dead. He is going to kill me."

"Don't worry. We'll figure it out," I say.

"Harvey said not to move. He is sending someone to come get the money from us. I think he suspects something is wrong," Luke says, climbing back into the car.

"They are going to be here any minute, Nicky. What am I going to say?" Sinking down into his palms, Elijah begins to shake in fear. "I was so tired. I must have dropped it, or … left it."

"We need to go back and look for it," Luke says.

"You know as well as I do that it is gone now. No way has it gone unnoticed this long," Elijah sighs.

"Harvey is going to kill us all if we come back even a dollar short." Luke slams his head into the seat in front of him.

"They're pulling up behind us," Luke says, watching the headlights coming in closer.

"Give me all the money," I say, holding my hand out. "You two leave as soon as I reach their car." Neither of them speak. They simply stare at me as if I have lost my mind. I stuff the money into my coat and jump out of the car without thinking any further. Someone is going to have to take the blame, and with Harvey wanting me to agree to join the team, I am hoping I have a better chance of survival. We can get him the rest of the money if he gives us some time, but Harvey has never been one for negotiation. My only hope is a miracle.

Squished between two of his goons, I am taken back to Harvey for my sentencing. They throw me in front of my judge, and I wait for the puff of smoke to pass from in front of his face before I attempt to speak. "Harvey, if you will give me a day, I can get the rest of the money for you, and I agree to your terms. I will be a part of your crew, in whatever manner you want me to be," I plead.

"Shut up, Jayzon. You know damn well that I don't give second chances, or extra time, but lucky for you, it wasn't *your* responsibility." Elijah is pushed into the room and thrown down in front of Harvey. He has already taken a bad beating, but he is surely about to receive a lot more. "Your friend here left the envelope behind at one of his meetings. Luckily, Matt was following along and prevented a complete disaster."

"He was following us?" I ask looking over at Matt and his smug attitude. "Bullshit," I say, causing everyone to snap his head in my direction. "Eli would never leave money behind. He didn't leave any money behind."

"He obviously did, Jayzon," Matt says with a smile. "Too bad for him, but once he is gone, that opens up an opportunity for you." He moves towards Elijah and begins to beat him in front of me. Elijah lies on the ground, bleeding and waiting to die while I am held back from stepping in. Matt looks over at me and takes out his gun. "Your punishment is … you have to clean up the mess." Matt grabs Elijah by the back of his head, and pulls him to the point of the gun. "You should have been more careful, Elijah."

The anger that has built up in me is too much. I have no control over myself and neither do my restraints. Reaching out, I grab Matt's neck and stare deeply into his eyes. "You set him up," I accuse him. Matt begins to sweat and struggles to breathe. Two more guards take hold of me and pull me away from him, but I stay focused on my target. I don't even realize what I am doing or do the others in the room. Matt falls to the ground, clutching his chest, gasping for breath, and looking up at me with pleading eyes, but he finds no mercy. The scrambling around me does nothing to break my focus. It is not until Elijah stands up and forces me out of the room that I begin to then hear the yelling and commotion. "What happened?" I ask him.

"You were right, Nicky. He set me up … and then you killed him. Harvey thinks you slipped him something." Elijah looks back at Matt's body through the open doors of Harvey's office. "Take me home, Nicky. I think we both need to call it a night," Elijah says, holding his ribs and still bleeding from his mouth. I only look back once at Harvey as we leave. He nods silently, but I have no idea what that means for me exactly.

Elijah glances back at me for the hundredth time as I drive him home. "What was that, Nicky?"

"Like Harvey said, I slipped him a drug and caused him to have a heart attack, or something. Knowing Matt, he probably does enough drugs that his heart was already weak," I say, concentrating on the road.

"No, no, I know you, and I saw you. No one was looking at you. They were all watching Matt. You don't carry drugs, Nicky, and you didn't have a weapon of any kind." I keep silent because I don't know what I can tell him, or even if I know the answers myself. "I don't understand what happened, Nicky, but whatever it was - thank you. Although, I am not sure that Harvey isn't going to still try and kill me anyway."

"He doesn't trust me any more than he trusts you, Eli. I agreed to his terms too easily when I thought you were in trouble. He might keep us close for now, but only to find our weaknesses and use them against us."

"If he goes after my father, I will have to kill him."

"We are going to have to get him before he can get us. All we need to do is be patient and wait for the right moment," I say, avoiding his eyes.

"And Luke? We are going to need help getting to Harvey, and we will need to use Luke to do it," Elijah says, glancing my way as I nod in agreement.

"And what about us, are we still ...?" I ask nervously.

He is silent for a time, but finally exhales with a nod. "Brothers for life, Nicky. No matter what crazy alien eye thing you have going on," he laughs.

We agree to talk in more detail another day, after we both get some sleep. I hope Elijah begins to believe his lack of sleep caused his delusions about me so we don't actually have to talk about anything.

They found the missing money in Matt's coat and release Elijah with no apology, but he is alive and will continue to stay that way while I am Harvey's right hand man. I accepted Harvey's offer to save my friend, and Harvey offered me the better position since, apparently he needed a new one. His old one died suddenly.

Chapter 18

Nick

Harvey is one disgusting individual. Following him around all day is enough to make me want to go back to school. He loves to talk to me in French and then laugh when I clearly don't understand what he is saying. "Jayzon, wait here for me, and here, read this while you wait." He laughs, tossing me a French newspaper. *Fucking bastard.* To have to wait for him while he fucks one of his many whores has got to be one of the worst jobs I have ever had to do. I only have to wait a few minutes before I hear her screaming, and he comes out, straightening his tie. "Clean that up for me and meet me back at the restaurant for lunch," he says, sticking that nasty cigar back in his mouth. Stepping inside, I find the woman naked and severely beaten. I should shoot her and put her out of her misery, as she is begging me to do. Thankfully, she dies before I can even pull my gun. She apparently wasn't a whore after all. *Damn, I hate him.* I wrap her up in the bed cover and put her in another car. I have Luke meet me at a place I know she will never be found. He helps me make her disappear, something I learn how to do well working for Harvey. Neither of us speaks. We simply do our job and try to get through the day.

At the end of the day, the only thing I want to do is see Franky. She is gracious enough to meet me since her father would not dare allow me to pick her up at home. Her smile is a welcoming part of my day. She is dressed in a simple red dress, and I wear a suit and her lucky scarf, of course. "You look beautiful," I say with a kiss. Taking her hand, I lead her to dinner. "How was your day?"

"It was good. And you? What did you do today?" she asks, clearly not understanding who I really am.

"Oh, you know, follow my boss around and kiss his ass from sunrise to sundown."

"I can't imagine you kissing anyone's ass."

"I don't want to talk about work. Let's talk about you. Actually, let's not talk at all. Let's dance instead." I kiss her hand and escort her to the dance floor.

"I am really not that good at dancing, Nick."

"Don't worry, Beautiful. Just wrap your arms around me and let me show you the way." Franky rests her head on my shoulder and allows me to hold her through song after song. I feel amazing until a sudden eerie feeling washes over me. *Someone is watching us.* I search the room casually so as not to alarm Franky, but I cannot make out anyone suspicious. Still, I feel him, even if I can't see him. "You know what, Kitten, I am really tired. Do you mind if we call it an early night?" Franky nods and follows me back to our table where I immediately try to pay for our meal, but apparently someone has already done that for me.

"Good evening, Nicholas," I turn to face Mr. Savage, Mr. Dennis Savage. I haven't seen him in some time, but I will never forget him. He has aged only slightly and still a man who gets plenty of attention from the females in the room. Young or old, he easily attracts them. I assume his obvious wealth helps his prowess with the women some too. Although that cane, that ruby-eyed dragon he carries, can make anyone feel uncomfortable; it certainly sends chills down my spine. "If I had known you were going to be here tonight, I would have offered one of my tables where the view is much better. Instead, all I could do is pay for your dinner," he says, leaning on that damn serpent, like he is a weak old man.

"Why would you do that?" I ask.

"You're a young man, Nicholas. You should not be spending money on a restaurant like this. Let me take care of it for you, I am, after all, an old family friend."

"From what I understand, my father doesn't consider you a friend at all," I say.

"Your father is temporarily angry with me, but there is no reason for you and me to quarrel. In fact, I would love to have you and your lovely girl over for dinner one night. Or even better, come to my party next week. I would love to introduce you to some of my associates."

"Thank you, but I don't think my boss would like me socializing with his competitor."

With an amused cock of his head, "Rice is not my competitor. He barely qualifies as a man. The disgust is a nuisance at times, but he falls vastly short of competing with me. You would be better off working for me. I can teach you things that Rice can't even dream up in the faux-French head of his. I can turn you into a real man," he says, looking me over as if I am a prized possession of his.

"Thank you, but I am good. I have plans of my own. I won't be working for Harvey much longer anyway. I will have my own …"

"Oh really, that's good to hear. I knew, the first moment I saw you, that you were going to be something special. Your father must be proud, and if not, I certainly am for him." Glancing over at Franky, he smiles, "Planning to get married? A family maybe? Children are a blessing."

"No, no kids for me. A woman, maybe, but no kids…ever. It isn't in my blood to be a father."

"Hmmm, too bad," he sings in a rough tone that makes me uneasy. "You should stay, Nicholas, and enjoy your dinner. You have barely touched it. I need to go take care of some business, but I am sure we will see each other again soon." The glimmer in his eyes sparks something within me that I don't understand.

Franky and I leave soon after Mr. Savage. I am curious to watch him leave, to see where he goes, and with whom. I am curious about him like my brother is curious about me. I spot his car but have no idea where he is. I try to drag Franky to a safer place, but Conner and his boys corner us and back us into an alleyway. "Stay behind me," I say as she tightly hugs me from behind. I back up, carefully searching for my best … her best escape. Connor knows he has me. His smile is haunting. Franky whimpers my name in my ear. I hold tight to her hand to comfort her as best I can, but Connor's threats to my life scare her, angering me.

The first man comes flying at me with threats and fists that not only threaten me but Franky too. Reaching out, I find myself easily pushing him away from us and into the brick wall. The next slows his pace in shock, but with encouragement from my brother, he continues on, and again, I am able to push him aside with little effort. Again and again, they come, but each time, I eliminate them. Connor's rage becomes evident, and I can do no more than back up and conceal Franky from him. Connor commands his men to shoot me instead, but before I can prepare, Savage returns. Connor's men instantly pause, curiously eyeing the strange old man walking into their fight.

He casually walks up, ruby-eyed dragon in tow. He looks vulnerable. I see no one backing him, no hired guns, no bodyguards, no one at all. I begin to wonder how he expects to deal with Connor and his men, all on his own. However, I am hoping whatever he has planned allows me to get Franky out of here safely.

"Good evening, gentlemen," Savage says in a low bellow. A lion, a king announcing his presence, expecting everyone to bow without question. "I don't think any of you belong here. This is my restaurant, and therefore, my alleyway. I didn't invite any of you here. Leave, now," Savage orders calmly. Connor's men straighten, and one after the other, walk away.

Connor angrily yells at his men, but they continue to mindlessly walk away. His anger escalates, and he rages at Savage. "Who are you?" Connor demands in his Jayzon tone. Savage pauses his casual pace and glares at Connor for some time, in silence. I swear, I see that dragon's eyes glow for a second just before Savage's calm demeanor acutely changes. He faces Connor with squared shoulders and stares him down. It seems like a smile that crosses his face, but it isn't. It is something potent, something sinister, and something that causes us all to take a step backwards. "I said …" Connor mumbles before clearing his tight throat. "Who are you?"

Savage snarls his detest for him. "I am … what *you* will never be." I struggle to see the exchange more clearly through the darkness when suddenly, Connor runs. *He runs? An older man, and Connor runs rather than face off with him?* I see no other guards or guns following behind Savage, but still, his presence forces Connor and all of his men *to run away?* Meeting Savage's eyes, I exhale and match his nod of appreciation.

"Have a good night, Nicholas," he sings into the darkness.

"Nick," Franky murmurs behind me.

"It's okay. Let me take you home now." She doesn't let go of me and seems too scared to look away from the depths of my coat. "It's okay. I won't let anything happen to you," I whisper and kiss her on the head.

Once we arrive at her house, she won't leave my side. "Will you stay with me? I will worry about you otherwise," she asks, increasing her grip on me.

"Oh, Kitten, there is no reason to worry about me. I'm immortal," I say, laughing along with her, but quietly, I follow her into her house. Franky smiles innocently at me after I shut her bedroom door, and that's all I need. Ripping my shirt off over my head, I look down at her, licking my lips, tempting her closer to my body. Feeling up her body while she kisses down my neck, I try to keep my moaning down, but it is difficult. Her father is surely going to wake up before we are done, but I am not stopping until I feel her come on me and she feels me come inside her.

We fall asleep, we forget, and he wakes up while we sleep. "Motherfucker!" he screams, waking us both. "Get the fuck away from my daughter!"

Franky holds tightly to me, crying, "Daddy, please, I love him!"

"It's okay, Franky." I wrap my arms around her, angering her father even more.

"No! You get the fuck out of my house!" he screams, raging towards us both.

"You are upsetting her. Calm down, leave her room, and I will leave, but only if you promise not to hurt her," I say, still keeping a protective hold over her.

"I would never hurt my daughter, you scum. Not like you." He leans down with fisted hands. "What have you done to her?"

"I love her, and she loves me. Nothing more and nothing less." He backs off in shock. Sinking his head into his hands, he walks out of the room, weeping his pain. Looking into Franky's eyes, I get up and get dressed. "Come here, Franky." I hold her tightly in my arms. "I will talk to you later, okay?" I kiss her gently and caress her cheek before leaving her and her devastated father.

"The devil has my daughter," her father begins repeating in tears.

I can't help but replay his cries in my head as I leave for home.

Elijah meets me at his door with his still curious eyes. "You look better," I say to him.

"Well, I'm still alive, thanks to you," he says, cocking his head in his usual smartass way.

"Don't do that, Eli. Don't look at me like I am some kind of …"

"Some kind of what? What exactly are you? Are you like Superman from an alien planet or something?"

"No! I told you. I didn't do anything. The guy obviously panicked that Harvey was going to find out and had a heart attack. It's that simple," I insist, tired of talking about this already.

"It's that simple? Alright, so you are Harvey's new whipping boy, huh?" He nods towards me.

"It's temporary. I can't stand him. Sick fuck. I know he is doing these disgusting things to push me."

"Well, he bumped me back down to his errand boy. I get to pick up his dry cleaning." Elijah fists his hands and growls his anger. "I have to get away from him Nicky. We have to figure out something so we make enough money to destroy that bastard." Elijah sinks his head into his hands with a heavy sigh. "Anyway, until then, we are going to have to stick to the small extra jobs. Luke found out there is a huge party tonight at that fancy club. I think we can pick up some extra cash taking possession of a few cars for Ruge. If we are going to battle Harvey, we are going to need all the extra cash we can get."

"Okay. I can meet you after Franky falls asleep, but I don't want to leave her until then."

"After she falls asleep? Oh come on, Nicky. We need you to get this done."

"I will be there. Don't worry, but I need to see her tonight. Her dad found out about us, and he isn't too happy about it to say the least."

"Great. You know, you really need to back off this girl. Her father hates you. There is no way he is going to let you two be. I mean, what do you think you are going to do, move in, with her and her father? Work for him at his store while she is away at college? If she is anything like her friend, she is just going to end up screwing some other guy while you're gone."

"Brandi cheated on you?"

"Wasn't like we were serious. I really only liked her because my father liked her so much." Elijah shrugs, but I know him. He would have never introduced her to his father if he didn't like her. He wants to have the life his father wanted for him, before his father isn't around to enjoy it. Brandi seemed to fit that, but apparently, Elijah only awoke an inner sex addict. "I am never introducing a girl to my father again," he says, slamming his fist into a wall. "And to think, I actually thought because she was a virgin and me being her first, that maybe, just maybe, she would be more interested in being with me forever. Only, I am nothing but a hood rat to her and her new uptown boyfriend. We are just a joke to them, Nicky."

"I'm sorry about Brandi, but Franky loves me. She said so, and I love her. It's different."

"Oh yeah. I'm sure it is real different, especially when she goes off to that big college of hers. Everything is going to be real different, Nick."

Elijah sits, sulking over his broken heart, and I have little to offer him but my own happiness. “You know what, Nicky? I hope things do work out for you, but don’t forget that we had a deal, to break away from Harvey and build our own. I am not going to be living for someone else much longer, with or without your help.”

Before I can respond to him, I get a call about Ryan. The dumbass got picked up trying to steal a car. I leave Elijah with a promise to meet him later, to help us all build our own dreams. I have no time to convince him; I have to bail my baby brother out of jail.

Ryan looks defeated, and embarrassed, to have to call me to come get him. “Thanks, Nick. I tried to call Dad, but apparently I don’t exist to him.”

“He said that?” Ryan nods. “Why were you stealing a car anyway?” He doesn’t respond, seeming content to ignore me and continue steaming over our father’s indifference to him, which answers my question. Ryan will do anything to get our father’s attention, especially now that he is assured he is losing his mother. I could give him hell for his stupidity, but I spare him that heartache for now. Instead, I drop him off to see to his mother while I go see to my father.

Chapter 19

Nick

This day has not gone well, at all. The last thing I want to do is face off with my father right now, but I have little choice if I want to keep my brother from falling into a bad life. The man needs to at least make an effort to be there for Ryan, and he needs to go see Rianne before it's too late. As soon as I arrive home, I see Franky racing out my front door crying.

"Franky!" When I catch up to her, she buries her head in my coat, to hide her tears. "What's wrong? What happened?" She shakes her head, still sobbing uncontrollably. Looking back, I see my father standing in the door. "Did my father say something to you?" She nods. My body tenses, and my anger towards my father only builds. "What did he say?" I ask through my teeth.

"He said I was wrong for you, and that I should leave and never come back." My blood begins to boil even more than it already was. "I was only coming to invite you to dinner. My father said he is willing to give you a chance for me. But ..."

Forcing her face up to me, I look into her eyes. "Listen to me. You are perfect for me, and I will be happy to have dinner with you and your father. Don't listen to my father. He doesn't know what love is, but I do, and I love you, Franky. No one is going to change my mind about that. Do you hear me? No one. I love you."

"I love you too," she says sweetly, allowing me to kiss her tears away.

I comfort Franky until she stops crying, and then, I send her home with a promise to see her later. After she is gone, I turn towards my house to face off with my father. Stepping inside, I watch him, scrambling around the house like a crazy person. "What is wrong with you? First, you ignore your own son, and then you tell my girlfriend she isn't good enough for me."

"I didn't say she wasn't good enough. I said she isn't the right one for you," he says, still gathering and making notes of some sort.

"And how do you know? You don't even know her. You don't even know me," I yell as he begins to pack a bag full of my clothes. I snatch it away from him, "What are you doing? Are you kicking me out now? I have been paying the rent and the bills to help Mom out. Are you going to do that now?" He shakes his head with a groan.

"I know you, but you don't know you." My father approaches me and hands me the key he gave me once before. "You need to learn who you are, before it is too late. I am going to take you away and hide you until you learn everything."

Tossing the key aside, I step away from his grip and stare him down. "What are you talking about? I need you to understand that this is my life. I am in love with Franky, and you need to take a bigger interest in your other children." He waves me off, gathering the key again from the floor. "Are you listening to me? I want you to apologize to my girlfriend, to your son and …"

"No, you're not listening, Nicholas," he says, shaking his finger in my face. "I need you to understand and stop blowing off your responsibilities. I need you to take this key and go to a place I have set up for us. You are not like everyone else, son. You need to understand the power you have before it takes you over and turns you into someone you don't want to be." I sigh, rolling my eyes away from him. My clear frustration with him only angers him. "Nicholas!" he snaps, getting my attention. "That girl is not truly in love with you. She only thinks she is. She is not strong enough to fight your power over her. You need to find someone who can fight that power, your Sophia."

"Sophia? Who the fuck is Sophia?" I yell at him.

"Sophia was the one that helped me, and you need to find someone just like her. And when you do, you need to keep her away from that man or he will kill her, just like he did with my Sophia. Your Sophia, that is the person for you, if she exists. Franky is nothing more than another girl. You will forget about her, eventually. There will always be another one like her coming along, and another, and …"

"Another? Shut Up! Franky is the right one! I don't know what you are talking about."

"I'm trying to tell you! If you would just listen to me for once, Nicholas. She does not love you. No one truly loves you! Most don't have the ability to overcome you to love you. Do you hear me? Only a select few are strong enough, and the chance of you ever meeting someone like that … well, it is not likely. It is likely though, son, that no woman will ever truly love you, so you need to learn to deal with your anger and the world around you another way." All his words begin to swarm around me, brewing like a dark storm. "Nicholas! Listen to me. She doesn't love you! I don't want her back in this house. I don't want you seeing her anymore. You need to pack up the rest of your things and come with me. Do as I say, Nicholas, and stop fighting me on this."

"No! I am sick of you. I am sick of this. I am leaving, but not with you, and I am not coming back. I am going to marry Franky, and I am going to leave this damn city. For good. I don't want to know you or my horrible mother."

"That woman loves you too much."

"Since when? She ignores me every chance she gets. I am sure she would have preferred that I never existed. Hell, as long as she has you, she doesn't need anyone else."

"That is the disease. She has no idea how to express her emotions properly."

"She expresses them just fine for you. She is nothing but a bitch to me and everyone else she comes in contact with, and you…you're nothing but a disappointment," I say, meeting him face to face.

My father rages at me with his eyes swirling, "Nicholas! You do not understand anything that you are talking about and that is why you need to listen to me now. You will do what I say, and you *will* come with me! It is for your own good. You have no choice in this, Nicholas. No choice!" He comes at me, gripping me and trying to control me. He sets me off to a place I haven't been in a long time.

I know he is speaking to me, and I know I am yelling just as much back at him, but things begin to blur. My heart begins to race, and all I can feel is the boiling of my blood, steaming up to the edges of my breaking point. I notice nothing more than my father backing away from me with fear, halting the churning of his own eyes. He grips me, grips his chest, and calls out to me, but as much as I try to calm enough to understand, I can't. I can't control my emotions, or my torrid blood until… it is too late.

"Well done, Nicholas." I turn quickly to see Savage watching me with a calm smile. I have no idea what he is referring to until I look down and see my father's motionless body sprawled out in front of me. My body begins to cool as I reach out with a shaky hand to feel of him.

"Oh no! No! I have to call for help," I say, reaching for my phone.

"He is dead. What's the urgency?" Savage asks. Falling to my knees, I hang my head over my father's body, and I begin vibrating with a sudden understanding. "Yes, it is sad, but it was necessary. Even your father knew it. You are much too powerful for even him." My eyes begin to fill with the pain that is cutting through me. Savage sits down casually with his ruby-eyed dragon sparkling within my shadow and across my father's lifeless body.

"What are you doing here?" I manage to say, gripping my father's hand.

"I told your father I was coming to talk about you. I want you to join my organization, Nicholas. Your father worked for me, and I think it is time that you begin your life right and join me. It is in your best interest. No one else knows how to teach you what you need to know like I do. Rice is …" he sighs with a growl, "… a pathetic piece of trash." He continues talking as if nothing is amiss, as if he was invited to dinner on a Sunday afternoon and is waiting to be served.

"Do you know who I am? What I am?" I ask.

Savage sits back with a growing smile, "He taught you nothing? You managed to do this without even knowing? Hmmm. Well, that is something." Leaning forward, Savage whispers into my ear to follow him, to work for him, and he will promise to show me all that I can be.

The more he speaks, the louder my father's voice gets, *"Nicholas, I want you to listen to me, and never forget what I am about to say to you. That man, Dennis Savage, do not ever go near him. He is not to be trusted. He only wants bad things for you. Promise me, son, that you will never go near that man?"* I promised, and I can't go back on that now. In fact, I don't want to know who I am. I don't ever want to know who I am if this is any indication of what I can do.

I leave my knees and my father and look down at Savage. "My father is dead, and I killed him. Why would you want me, unless it is for something worse than I have already done? I don't want to work for you. I don't work for anyone." His sinister eyes do nothing to sway my decision. He can kill me for all I care. I'd almost prefer it.

"Nicholas, you are clearly not ready like I had hoped you would be." He sighs and stands in front of me. "You will soon understand on your own. I was going to take care of that … brother of yours, but I think I will leave him for you to handle. It will be a good learning experience. Don't let him live too long though. He will only become a bigger issue for you. Not to mention, he annoys the hell out of me." Savage inhales deeply, glancing down at my father. "Pity. I had hopes for him at one point, but now, I will work with someone else until you are ready." Savage walks out the door and nods towards the man waiting for him at his car. He leaves me to deal with my life alone. Rushing into my room, I gather the bag my father had begun to pack for me and fill it with the rest of my things. When I finish, I dig out my stash of cash and give my father nothing more than a glance before I run out the door. I never look back. Maybe I am too scared to, but all I care about now is getting the hell out of this city for good.

My mind screams at me while the rest of my body feels numb. I am still planning my next move when I spot Connor and his boys coming my way. Seeing him only reignites me, so instead of hiding, I stop my car and get out to face him. He smiles and sends in one of his biggest goons, but the fool attacks me face up, and therefore, he dies face down. Connor's eyes widen, but none of his men can get close enough to throw any bags over my head this time. I fight like never before, provoking Connor to anxiously rush to his car. He doesn't even look back before screeching his tires down the road. I get back in my car and breathe, trying to focus on calming down before I go to see Franky.

Instead of facing off with her father one more time, I wait for him to leave. She answers the door with a smile that rapidly disappears when she catches sight of me. "Oh, Nick, what happened?" I look down at myself and realize my brother's men didn't die completely in vain. My clothes are torn and covered in blood, and the pain in my head is not just from my horrible day but also from the dry, bloodied gash someone managed to inflict.

"It's nothing," I say, dismissing her worry with a smile. "I was wearing your scarf, so I am fine," I say, fisting her scarf around my neck. "Franky, I need to ask you something." Looking down at her, I stare into her eyes with the voice of my father still floating in the back of my head. "Do you love me, Franky?"

"Yes, I love you very much," she says.

"Good, because I love you more than anything. In fact, I want to marry you." Her smile turns into shock. "Seriously, I want to run away with you tonight, get married, and leave all of this behind." She doesn't return my happiness. "You said you love me, and would do anything for me, and I want to get out of here, Franky. I don't want to work for Harvey anymore. Hell, I will even try and go to college for you … with you even. We can go together, Franky." Her interest begins to peak, giving me hope. "Yeah, we can go together and be together. Help each other. But we have to leave tonight or I may not ever be able to leave."

"Why Nick? What happened? Is it your brother?" she asks, worrying rather than focusing on what I want her to.

"Yes, I have to get away and hide from him before things get worse. If you don't come with me tonight, I may never be able to see you again, and I don't want that. Do you?"

"No, of course not. I want to be with you." Hugging her tightly, I smile and begin packing her bags for her. She doesn't move. She stands, dumbfounded, watching me frantically gather her things as I ask what is important and what isn't. I choose to ignore her solemn demeanor, but the longer she stands, still and silent, the angrier I become. "Nick, what about my father?"

"What about him?" I snap.

"I need to tell him where we are going, I need to make sure he can contact me," she says, fidgeting.

"No. You can't contact him, Franky, otherwise, my brother will be able to find us. Don't worry. I will love you enough."

"Nick, I can't leave my father. I'm all he's got," she pleads, sitting down and curling over herself.

"You're all I have. Do I not matter?" I stare at her in amazement. The girl who did everything to get my attention, who says she loves me, is now, willing to let me go.

"That's not what I said. Maybe we should talk to my father, and he can help with your brother. He is very smart. He will know what to do to help you." She grasps me, smiling with hope.

"He can't help me, Franky. No one can. The only thing I can do is leave, and I want you to leave with me." Her silence screams. Dropping my hands from her, I back away "You don't love me."

"Yes, I do, Nick, but I think we need to think this through before …"

"I have thought it through! I thought you trusted me. Aren't you the one that said I am too smart? Suddenly, I am not that smart after all? I guess when it comes time to prove your love for me, I am nothing to you."

"That is not true, Nick. I do love you, but I don't understand."

"No, you don't. I don't know why I thought someone like you would think I was worth anything." Franky grips my coat, shaking her head and trying to convince me of her allegedly true feelings. "I have to go. I have one last job I need to do before I can leave town. You stay here with your father, Franky. He needs you." I leave her screaming for me to stay, but her pleas do nothing to sway me.

I meet up with the boys at our regular place, trying to forget about Franky and my father. "Nicky, are you paying attention?" Elijah asks me. "Hey, what is wrong with you? First you're late, and now you have no opinion on how we should do this job? Did you have a fight with Franky or something?"

"We aren't together anymore," I say setting Elijah and Luke back on their heels. "And I don't want to talk about it. In fact, this is my last job. I am leaving town tonight for good."

"What? Nick! You can't be serious. You have it made right now …" Elijah interrupts Luke's rant and pushes me off to the side.

"What is going on, Nicky? You say you broke up with Franky, but yet you are still wearing that damn scarf." I look down and fist the damn scarf around my neck, as an overwhelming pain rushes through me. "Nicky, what is wrong with you? No bullshit. This is not like you at all. And if you think for one second that I am going to let my best friend just run off with no explanation, then you are too crazy to be allowed to do so. So talk." Elijah grips my arm, making sure I don't walk away before he hears some kind of explanation.

"My father … he's dead." Elijah steps back with wide eyes. "I … he had a heart attack," I say, not looking up from my feet.

"Damn. I'm sorry, Nicky."

Shaking my head, I say, "No big deal. It's not like we got along anyway."

"It is a big deal, and I don't think it is a good idea that you run away because of it. You have people here that need you and depend on you. And what about your mother? You're upset about your girl and your father. I get that, but don't make decisions based on your emotions right now."

"Can we just get this job done?" I walk away from him and towards the corner with Luke. I grip my head as the entire day begins to multiply in it. The idea of leaving is all I can think about, but Elijah is right. I can't leave Ryan, Lena, or even my mother, but I don't want to face Franky ever again. I am tired of dealing with my brother, Harvey, and everyone else who wants something from me. Of all the faces in my head, Franky's suddenly appears accompanied by a huge amount of guilt for putting her in a position I should have known she couldn't handle. I turn, gripping my head and wanting to scream, but instead, I look up and see my brother's smile and his gun. Looking down the barrel, the world begins to decelerate and blur. Nothing but the metallic sheen of the gun in is focus.

"Nick, get down!" Luke yells, but all I can do is feel numb, standing frozen and facing death.

"Nick!" Franky yells. I suddenly feel her jump into my arms and hold tightly to me. I look down into her eyes and see nothing but fear. Elijah grabs me and pulls us down on the ground.

I hover over Franky, trying to hide us both from the oncoming gunfire, while Luke and Elijah return fire in an attempt to push back my brother's attack. Franky grips my shirt. "I do love you, Nick. We can leave together. I want to. I do," she says, struggling to breathe but continuing to hold tight. I look down at my bloody hands and then at her. *No! No, it was supposed to be me!*

"It's okay. We don't have to leave, Kitten. We can stay here, and you can be with your father too. Okay? Talk to me. Tell me that you are okay?" I scream, peering at all the blood trailing down the walkway. "I love you, Franky. I do."

"Don't let me go, Nick. Don't leave me. I can't live without you," she says, shivering.

"I won't. I won't ever leave you," I say, wrapping her lucky scarf around her neck and holding her closer to me. Franky smiles and releases my shirt as her eyes roll back and her head falls. "No, it was supposed to be me!"

"Francesca!" her father yells and races towards us. He pushes me away from her, taking her limp body into his arms. "What did he do to you?" he cries out. Looking at me, his pain becomes clear "You killed my daughter. She left to be with *you*, and now look. *You* killed her! You have no soul," he screams at me.

"Nicky, come on. You need to get out of here. The cops won't believe you had nothing to do with this," Elijah says as he and Luke take hold of me and drag me away. The sirens begin to echo as they near us.

From the corner of my eye, I catch sight of Connor driving away. I twist away from my friends and watch him leave with a smile, giving me a reason to stay. "I'm going to kill him."

"Another day, Nicky. Save that for another day."

I will kill Connor one day.

Chapter 20

Nick

Nightmares. That was all I had last night. I spend most of the night hiding out at Luke's. No one would think to look for me here. No one would think anyone would even live in this shit hole. Stumbling my way through his … what seems to be a kitchen, I find nothing more than a half a bottle of beer and an open box of cereal. *What the hell am I supposed to do with this?* Looking into Luke's room, I can find no walking space, only a mattress and Luke laid out with his mouth open and his bare ass sticking up in the air. I decide it better to go look for breakfast on my own. No way am I getting near that mess to ask him anything. I grab my coat, walk out the door, and run right into Elijah.

"Where are you going?" he asks like he is preventing me from trouble.

"I'm hungry, so I thought I would go eat something. What are you doing here?" I ask in a mocking tone.

"I brought breakfast, and I want to talk," he says as I sigh. "You're in trouble, Nicky. Your brother is not just out to knock you around anymore. He wants to kill you. Any ideas on why he has suddenly changed his mind?" I shrug. "No? No idea at all? Hmm – well, I find that hard to believe."

"I assume he heard I am working with Harvey now, and he wants to take me out before I move up any further," I reply, confessing the first thing that comes to my mind.

"I guess that makes sense, but now what? You can't protect Harvey if you are having to watch your own back."

"Connor won't come after me when I am with Harvey, so I will stay with Harvey full time now. It's what he wants anyway," I say, stuffing a bite of warm, fresh food into my mouth, something Luke needs to learn about. Elijah reminds me of our own plans, and I assure him that I haven't changed my mind. The only way I can get Connor is if I build my own crew to attack him with. Harvey is nothing more than a stepping stone to get to what I want, but before I can commit to Harvey, I have to take care of a few things.

My house looks desperately different right now. I am surprised not to see police looking for me, but maybe they believed my father's death to be some kind of accident. *I wish that were true.* I take one step inside my house and cringe. "Mother?" I yell. The woman walks past the kitchen doorway with a slight acknowledgment to my presence. Stomping forward, I force my mother to stop cleaning and pay attention to me. "Mother, what are you doing?" I can tell by her expression that she is clueless to the world around her. It is all I can do to hold back tears of frustration.

"Nicholas, you look tired. You should go to bed and get some sleep," she says, patting me on the arm before she goes back to cleaning.

At least she acknowledged me. I look around the house that is barely hanging on. It needs painting, the wiring needs to be redone, the floors are buckling, and to top it off, the roof is leaking. There is nothing about this house that means anything to me, and it would take more money to fix it than it could ever be worth in this neighborhood. I know what I need to do, and I know what I want to do, so I am going to compromise between the two. Though my father was wrong about a lot of things, I can't dismiss my mother forever. I see the sickness in her eyes, and that alone gives me reason to try and forgive her. Taking in a deep breath, I stop my mother and look down into her eyes. "We are going to take a trip, Mom. A special vacation, and you don't have to worry about anything ever again."

She seems excited at first. "But we can't leave your father here by himself."

"We aren't. He is going to meet us there. He has to take care of some business first, but he will visit you often. He told me to make sure you were well taken care of so you won't have to work anymore." She smiles wide with a gasp. "Yes, he only wants you to be happy."

Kissing my cheek, she vibrates with happiness. "I knew he loved me. I did. I knew it. So when do we leave?"

"Right now. Pack your bags, Mom. Take everything you treasure and leave what you don't." My mother races to her room while I cover my father. He is sitting up in his chair with the plate of food my mother prepared for him after she picked him up off the floor. I don't know what is wrong with my mother, but she clearly isn't capable of living on her own, and she needs more help than I can give her.

After I load my mother and her things into the car, I call my sister and ask her to help me take care of our father. I will meet her later, but first, I have to take care of my mother. Skyland Mental Facility is more than an hour out of town, and nowhere near cheap. It's worth the money to keep my mother safe and, hopefully, healed someday. I kiss her goodbye once I believe she is happily settled in her new place. Before the end of my day, I am called to clean up another mess for Harvey and end up using this new body for my own purpose. Clearing out my home of anything important to me, which is little to nothing, I strike a match and set the place ablaze, leaving my supposed dead mother hanging inside. Nothing is going to be the same from this point on, and I am going to leave no trace of anyone close to me. If I have nothing to lose, then there is nothing anyone can take from me.

Now. Now is the time to build my own power and become Nicholas Jayzon.

Chapter 21

Nick

I was forbidden to be at Franky's funeral, so I watch from afar with every part of me aching to hold her again and to apologize for being me. Her father's cries tear me up from the inside out. It's all my fault. It is *all* … my fault. After everyone leaves, I take the flowers I bought for her and throw them onto her casket, wanting to dive in after them.

"I'm sorry, Franky. I should have never made you choose. I should have never cursed you with my presence. Your father is right. I am the devil, and you deserved better than me. Far better. I will spend the rest of my life missing you, aching to hold you again. I would do anything to see your smile again. I would do anything to change what happened, what I did to you. As I am sure you are in heaven, be assured I am in hell. Goodbye, Franky."

The tears forming in my eyes are concealed behind my sunglasses, and I will give no one the opportunity to know of them. I decide to leave before someone catches sight of me and protests that I am here. I walk back towards Elijah who is waiting for me by the car. I watch his eyes dart around the area, and I follow. There is something about this funeral. There are way too many men in suits standing around, and all of them seem to be watching me. I never got to see Franky in the hospital or after. The word of her death came via community talk and was verified when her father approached me out of nowhere to say, "*Do me, and my daughter, a favor by not showing your face anywhere near her funeral.* He said that I don't deserve to grieve properly for her. I agreed, but I couldn't completely abide by his wishes. She does deserve to know of my pain for her, the pain I reasoned to myself late last night.

"Who are they?" Elijah asks, motioning towards the men watching us.

"I don't know, but they aren't here for her." The moment I step into the car, I see my brother's car leave in the other direction. The suits must think he is here watching her funeral. Fools. He is here watching me. I have become my brother's growing obsession, and he isn't going to stop until he finds a way to destroy me.

I have decided to become someone new and forget who I was. The first step to that is learning how to control my anger and learning another way to fight. My brother is constantly searching for me. Anytime I leave Harvey's side, I have to make sure no one sees me come or go, and I only retreat to places no one would expect me to be. There is only one place I can safely learn what I need to know. This is the place, and I am not even sure if I should be here, but I thought if anyone can help me, it would be him. I walk into Whittaker Street Center, and Bo Sirra, the guy who appears and disappears in a blink is nowhere to be found. With a hunch of his pending presence, I wait.

"Jayzon, right?" Sirra says, walking up behind me. *Ha! I didn't even have to blink this time.* I nod and hold out my hand to him which he immediately takes with a smile. "So, I take this to mean you actually want to learn how to fight, and not continue to do that desperate, pathetic shit you were doing?"

Exhaling fully to his cocky smile, I nod, despite my urge to leave and tell him to go fuck himself. "Something like that. I was actually more interested in what you said about control, about being able to control my anger and other crap."

Sirra rolls his eyes. "And other crap? Umm yeah, you can learn to control your anger and all your other crap, and after seeing you fight, I am sure there is a lot of crap. I am happy to help you, but first, tell me why you want to know?" I shake my head with a shrug. "Unless you tell me why, all of a sudden, you sought me out, I can't help you."

Sighing, I stand silent until he throws his hands up and begins to leave. "Fine! I feel like I have some anger issues, that I would like to learn how to control," I say.

Sirra motions for me to follow him into a private room where he promptly shuts the door behind us. "Talk, Jayzon. I know enough about you to know that you don't usually fight with your fists. Not to mention, fighting rarely matters in your line of work, unless Harvey Rice has decided to conduct business without guns."

"I don't know you. Why I would tell you anything? I only want to know what you said you could teach me."

"I can't teach you with partial information. There is a reason you are here, and I can't help you unless I know what it is." He sits down, picks up a magazine, and begins reading. I huff for a few seconds before walking out. I end up pacing around the block a few times before returning to him and his stupid smile. "Yes?" he asks.

"I need help with something … I don't even understand it, so I don't know how I can explain it to someone who certainly won't!" I snap as he silently waits for me to continue. "I get angry, and I feel things happening inside me, and then …"

"And then you lose focus, and everything becomes a dream that you have no control in. You're a spectator of your own actions."

"Yes!" I say, wondering if he does understand who I am.

"It's common, Nick," he says, as if he assumes I am no different than anyone else with anger issues. "Come with me, and we will get started."

Sirra lines me up in front of a mirror and teaches me how to breathe. It is a slow start, but eventually, we pass the breathing exercises and move on to balancing, focusing, and understanding what is actually around me - seeing what is beyond the obvious. I meet with him several times a week for months, and slowly, I develop a fighting technique that is more powerful than I have ever had. But it is the balance, the control, and the patience that change me for the better.

I am with Harvey at his favorite restaurant one night when, from out of nowhere, a waiter catches my attention. I am unsure what it is about him that is so off, but his mannerisms are strange. I breathe while watching him. Harvey is oblivious, stuffing his face and laughing it up with some associate of his. When the waiter comes near, he watches us all, and I wait. The moment he steps closer, he stops and exhales. I dig into his gut with my fist, and he is down on the ground, gasping, with his gun spiraling into the air and into my hand. Another swift kick, and he is out cold. Harvey looks up, and I simply nod. The man is quietly escorted out by another guard and never heard from again. I begin to enjoy my extra sense of perception. It is something I use to ignore, but now, it is at the forefront of everything I am.

Chapter 22

Nick

All I do is work. My focus is to gain the knowledge I need from Harvey, build on it, break from him, and become my own power. I want a power bigger than Connor, one that will make him pay and give me what I need to take care of the rest of my family, like my father should have done. My determination and goals are taking over, and my friends begin to worry that I may not be enjoying life enough. Elijah and Luke both think it is best for me to get out and get laid. I don't know if it is what I need, but I humor them and join them at a local strip club they have been raving about. It is disgusting, and the women are desperate, mostly drug addicts who will do anything for some extra cash. The back, private area is well-used, and it is barely concealed. The last thing I care about seeing is other men having sex; however, my friends seem to enjoy the completely nude women doing anything they want to get extra cash. I can't take it any longer and leave.

I am shocked that they even noticed me enough to follow me out. Their sighs continue until I finally agree to go into a nearby bar with them. For once, Elijah is more interested in finding a girl for me than one for himself, which is humorous to Luke and me both. Elijah hits on them and then, halfway through, remembers he is supposed to be helping me. He tries to ugly himself up, or says something stupid, but he ends up turning to me and shrugging his shoulders because he obviously is too handsome to be unappealing. Night after night, I go out with them, and night after night, Elijah is the only one that ends up having sex of any sort.

On some nights, I try to talk to a few girls, but Franky is always in the back of my mind. Why bother getting to know someone that isn't going to love me, or is going to end up dead when she thinks she does. I visit her grave often and talk to her about everything. She is the only one I can talk to. It is has been enough so far. I can't imagine any woman making me feel better, but maybe getting laid would be good for me. I fight the urge until Elijah brings me a package.

"Someone sent this to my house for you. I guess they didn't know where else to send it. I didn't open it, but it has her last name on it for the return address. You might think about throwing it out instead of opening it, Nicky," Elijah says, leaving me to be alone.

I assume it is from Franky's father, and I hesitate opening it for a time, but after a few days, I get the courage to tear through it and pull out her lucky scarf. *That bastard!*

"You deserve to be happy, Nicky," Elijah says to me as I ignore his huffs and persistent questions about the package that was sent to me. "Her father doesn't understand what was going on between you two, and he certainly doesn't understand that it wasn't your fault. Maybe you don't understand that either. It wasn't your fault, Nicky. It was one of the worst days of your life. You had a bad day, and she got caught in the middle. Not because of you, but because of Connor. If not for him, you two would still be happy together or maybe broken up, but she would be happy somewhere and you would still be Nicky. You're not the same lately. You're getting more and more distant and becoming something I don't think you want. When was the last time you talked to Ryan, and I don't mean sending him money? Do you even visit your parents' graves?" I glance his way with a snarl. "Be angry at me, but you're avoiding too much, and forgetting even more, all because you blame yourself. You are never going to find that happiness again, Nicky, if you keep blaming yourself. Despite what you think, you deserve to be happy. Hell, we all do. And you, being my brother for life, are making me unhappy. So, you owe it to me to come out and get laid. I cannot feel good about having sex every night if I am worried about you. You are ruining my fucks, Nicky. Don't do that to me. Come out and get your dick sucked at least. For me, Nicky. What do you say? Will you please let someone suck your dick?" he says with a slight smile. I try to hide mine, but it is no use. *Idiot.*

We arrive at a new bar with wall-to-wall women, many of which are dressed to get laid. For the sake of Elijah's sex life, I look around, searching for one who will suffice. My efforts are cut short when a tall brunette slides up to my side and inhales my scent. I take a drink and then sit back, putting my arm behind her chair. I start at her toes and look slowly up her body before concentrating on her eyes. She smiles, and I lick my lips. "You want to fuck me?" She nods. "What will you do for me?"

"You can come all over me."

"I can come on anyone. What makes you different?" She pauses and sits back in shock.

"Isn't it enough just to let you do whatever you want to me?" she asks, sliding her hand down to my dick. "And I am more than willing to do everything you want me to."

"That might get most men sweetheart, but if you want me, then prove you're worth it."

"I also have friends, for your friends," she says, motioning for two other girls to walk up and take hold of Luke and Elijah, both of which are nowhere near us or each other.

"How long have you been watching me?"

"Since the moment you walked through the door, and I haven't been able to take my eyes off you since," she hums.

"Is that right?" She nods, but I am not convinced just yet. I hold her off for a second and talk to my friends. If they want to leave, I will leave. Neither have to say a word. Their wide smiles are all I need to grab my girl's hand and walk out the door. Thankfully, the girls have their own place, so we don't have to go to Luke's.

I don't bother to worry about my friends for the moment. I take my girl to her room and strip her down to nothing. Feeling her bare skin against my hands and against my mouth, I begin to enjoy the sensation of a woman again. "You smell like someone I know," I whisper, gripping her hair and pulling her head back to look down into her eyes. "How bad do you want me?"

She instantly drops to her knees, pulls out my dick, and sucks me hard. My body heats up the more I look at her, and the more I focus on her, the more I know I can't take it anymore. I pull her up off the floor and spread her legs out wide in front of me. Pushing my hardened dick inside of her, I glare at her and read every emotion on her face. She moans abruptly, cries out, and tries to regain her control. Every time she makes a move, I deepen my thrust and fondle her with more pressure, sending her gasping backwards.

"Stop fighting it. You know you want to relax and enjoy it. Besides, you might as well know what a good fuck is before you finish the job and have to go back to him?" She looks up at me and begins to realize that I know who she is.

"You know?" she moans, losing more and more control with each thrust I make into her.

"Of course I know." Pushing her head to the side, I lean down and enjoy the moans coming from her mouth even more. "Are you going to come? Are you going to let me come all over you like you said? You can't help yourself, can you? I can feel you tightening, craving more of me. I can feel you losing control, so do it." Lifting her, I let her watch my dick slide in and out of her wetness, and she begins to breathe my name with a heavy breath. "Is this what you wanted, or did you expect it to end before it got this far? Did you expect to end it before I made you come, before you felt me release on your body?" Jerking her back up to look me in the eyes, I continue. "Or, would you prefer for me to come in your mouth so you can taste what real man is?" Her head falls back as she grips the bed around her, tightening on my dick so hard that I know she has nothing left, and I have her completely under my control. I pull out and come on her as she tries to recover from her own orgasm. I grip her back to me. "I bet my brother never fucked you like that!" I stand up and open the bedroom door. "Do it boys before it is too late." The moment I yell, their girls scramble, and before I know it, there is gunfire. Luke is kind enough to walk out in his boxers while Elijah slowly emerges, pissed off and with his dick still hanging out. "You good?" I ask and they nod. "Good. Let's clean it and go."

My girl begins to move again. "Oh yeah." I turn back to her as she begins reaching for her nightstand drawer. Her phone begins to ring from within it, so I hold her back and reach in to take the gun out first and then answer her call.

"Is it done?" Connor asks.

I feel nothing for her. All I see is my hate, my pain, and every frustration that has built up inside me, and I shoot. My first shot. My first kill, with a gun at least, and I feel nothing, but satisfaction. "It is now," I seethe. I would do anything to see Connor's face right now. It is lucky for him that he doesn't have to wait to know the answer he wanted. I wonder how long he would have waited for her, if he would have sent someone out to look for her, or if he would have known the moment I got him, before he got me.

Chapter 23

Nick

Harvey gladly gives me more responsibility after I save his life a few times. I make every effort to make him believe I am completely loyal to him, and I am … for now. Luke is moved near me, and Elijah is given a second chance but is not allowed close to Harvey. Harvey will never fully trust Elijah. I stick to our routines until one day when Harvey trusts me too much. He knows I am smart, but he thinks he is smarter, and I let him continue to think that. If I give him any reason to believe otherwise, he will slit my throat in a heartbeat.

Harvey keeps his money in many different places, but he keeps his drug money in one place. He exchanges it to be laundered by simply exchanging keys. Only he knows where the money is being stored during the time before the exchange. It is a small window he allows for it to be vulnerable, but still he keeps it to himself. Harvey has never had problems with his routine, that is, until me. I figured out his routine fairly quick, but it is the place where he keeps the key that I am unsure about. Harvey has me at his side all day today. He is tired and, unfortunately for him, drank way too much to think clearly when he approaches his safe. He stops suddenly, looking me over with suspicious eyes. With a twirl of his hand, he huffs until I turn around. He doesn't realize that it takes me less than a second to memorize numbers or that I can block out everything and focus completely on counting the clicks to figure them out. Thanks to his foolish trust, I now know how to get his money. This is the opportunity we have been waiting for. Now, we only have to figure out how to take advantage.

At the end of my day, I sit down at Franky's grave. Taking her scarf from inside my coat, I wrap it around my neck and begin to tell her everything. "There has to be way to get that money, Franky. We only have so many days to get to it before it is gone and he moves on to the next place. I don't know how much it is, but it should be enough. I am going to get it all, but I wish you were here to enjoy it with me." I sit, breathing in her scent from her scarf and talking through everything I need to do. "I need to let you go, Franky. I need to move on, but I just don't know how. I don't know how to find someone else. Is there even anyone out there that will love me, *actually* love me? I guess not."

I sigh, realizing my father was right. Franky was never really in love with me. We were nothing alike and had no reason to be together except that I bumped into her one day and stared too deeply into her eyes.

I leave Franky and find myself gazing down at my father's grave. "You said she might exist. Well if she does, help me find her. Otherwise, Dad, I am not sure I am going to be able to avoid becoming what you don't want me to be."

We get few opportunities to meet up without outside ears listening in, so when we do, Elijah, Luke, and I take full advantage. "Where are we going?" I ask Luke as he drives us farther out of town.

"It's this little diner I found the other day when I was running for Harvey. The food is great. You are going to love it."

One look around the old, overly simple diner, and I eye Luke with a sigh. I can't imagine this food is any good, and sure enough, when our plates are set in front of us, I immediately have to push it away. "So listen. I know Harvey's safe combination where he keeps one of his money keys. All we need to do is buy me enough time to get in there to replace the key with a fake and then get out without being detected. I don't know how much money is in this one, but considering how much he checks on it, there is enough that we have to cash in on this opportunity."

"If Harvey finds out we stole his key, he will immediately sign our death warrants," Luke says, vibrating with uneasiness.

"We need to make sure to replace the key with a phony and act as if nothing is amiss until we can get to that money and clean him out," I say with happiness. "We have four days to clean him out. He goes to check on his money every Tuesday and Friday, but this next week, he can't go until Wednesday at the earliest. We have to move now."

"I don't know, Nick. I think if we stay with Harvey, then we are good forever. He has a lot of connections, and his power is growing every day. Why not stick with him and grow with him?" Luke remarks with a blind optimism.

I watch Elijah as he rolls his eyes. He is miserable and wants more than anything to stick it to Harvey. Not to mention, his father needs even more care than what Elijah can afford right now. Luke rambles on with his usual abundant energy, barely paying attention to us as he watches the waitress pass by us. "Luke. Luke!" I snap until he looks at me. "Listen to me. We are going to do this, and it is going to be better. Trust me, and I will take care of you better than Harvey ever will." Once Luke calms and nods, I sit back and glance Elijah's way, noticing his quick look away from me.

"I want to go my own way, Nicky. I would love to work together, but I think, for the sake of our friendship, it would be best that we aren't both trying to be the boss. We can help each other if need be, but … I need to go my own way," Elijah says.

Despite his avoidance of my eyes, I trust Elijah more than anyone else, so I nod in agreement. "Okay, so let's get this plan worked out." Luke immediately dives in with his thoughts, aggravating Elijah to the point that he can no longer let it go. The two bicker while I block them out and think of my own strategy. I concentrate on Harvey and become angry. I think of Connor, and my entire body tightens into a heated rage. I want him dead, and I want Harvey dead. In fact, I want to take them both down completely and take over. I daydream my revenge until something distracts me, or rather someone. She walks in with little to no body shape at all. Her glasses are huge and beyond horrible, but the moment her eyes meet mine, I tremble. *I tremble?*

I try to ignore her and get back into the conversation at my table, but she sits down at the table beside us, and I can think of nothing else. She won't even look at me. She just buries herself within her book and ignores the world around her. Pulling my plate towards me, I begin to pick at my food. *I need salt.*

"Excuse me, can I borrow your salt?" I ask the girl at the table next to us, smiling my best smile of course. She grabs the salt and hands it to me without removing her book from her nose. *Okay?* "Thank you." *Pepper!* Leaning over again. "Sorry to bother you again, but can I borrow your pepper too?" She grabs the pepper and hands it to me, only this time, I graze her hand with my thumb. A smile instantly rushes to my face, and I can do nothing to stop it. "Thank you," I say, looking back up at her and her complete indifference to me. Sliding back into my seat and stuffing a fork full of food into my mouth, I stare at her. Frustrated, I lean back towards her. "If you don't mind …"

She looks up and takes the whole carousel of condiments and puts it in my hands. "There. You should be set now. Right?"

"It seems that way," I say, cocking my head as I stare into her eyes with no reaction from her at all.

"Good. So then I guess you will be leaving me alone now?" She holds up her book. "I only have five chapters left. Please."

"Sure. Enjoy it," I say, sitting back in my seat while she goes back to reading like I don't exist at all. I look back at Elijah as he holds his hands out. "What?"

"What? We are trying to figure out our next move, and you are collecting condiments. Nicky, if you don't like your food, you can get something else after we leave," Elijah says with an exhausted frustration.

"Kayla, will you put that damn book down and eat your food before it gets cold," our waitress says to the girl next to us.

"I would, but I don't have any salt or anything. Oh well, I guess I will continue reading," Kayla remarks with a smile, giving me a quick glance before returning to her book.

I quickly stand up and stare down at the beautiful blond waitress, causing her to giggle. "My fault. I'm sorry. I am finished with it all. Thank you for your kindness, Kayla, is it?"

"Oh, don't worry about it. She will use any excuse to keep her nose in her books," the waitress gushes as I glance down at her name tag. *Braylin.*

"You two are related, sisters?" Braylin nods. "I should have guessed the two most beautiful women in the place are related."

"Oh please, go back and eat your waffles, Mr. Smooth," Kayla huffs in disgust.

"It's Nick actually," I say, staring down at Kayla as she rolls her eyes away from me. *She is really starting to get on my nerves.*

Kayla waves her hand and sticks her nose right back into her book. Before I can say something back to her, Braylin giggles again. "I am so sorry. She is … well, she is not very social. If there is anything you need though, Nick, I would be happy to get it for you."

Smiling at the blushing blond, I say, "Thank you, Braylin, I think I am good for now, but don't go too far. I may need you."

"Oh, okay," Braylin gushes, touching my arm and sighing.

"Oh my God. *I may need you. Oh, I am so desperate to get into your pants before you figure out I am a complete loser,*" Kayla mocks before rolling her eyes again. I look down into her eyes, her beautiful eyes, and try to change the annoyance's mind about me, but she ridicules my stare and turns away. "Do you mind? I have to hurry up and eat this crap so I can finish my book." *She is really annoying!*

Sitting back down, I look over at Elijah and his crossed arms. "Are you done now? Can we get back to business, or do you need to get laid first?"

"What? I'm here. I'm listening." After they both huff at me a few times, I try to get my head back into the plans. It is difficult, but they manage to come up with some solid ideas that I agree to. Now, all we have to do is execute them. Before I leave, I lean over Kayla and try again. "Goodbye Kayla," I whisper, only to have a hand shoved in my face. *I really do not like this girl at all.* Her sister, however, is much more reasonable. I give her a wink as we leave, and she curls into a gooey mush. *Yeah, she is much more reasonable.* Even through the window, Kayla ignores me. Never in my life has anyone aggravated me so much.

Harvey's party is crowded with disgusting animals, all pawing the prostitutes that he brought in for the night. It is the perfect time to make our move. My job for the evening is to keep people in order. Luke's is to keep people out, and Elijah wasn't invited to do anything. All I have to do is find a way to get into Harvey's office while he is occupied and hand the key off to Luke who will hand it off to Elijah. Seems simple enough, except I have to go unseen. Everyone needs to believe that I never left my post. I didn't tell Luke or Elijah that I have chosen to alter our previously discussed plan, in hopes of preventing them from getting the wrong impression of my approach or my sanity. *Crazy does run in the family.*

Hours into the party, Harvey moves to his bedroom with three women. Others pass out or leave with women of their own. We are supposed to stand guard over the few left, watch them, make sure they are not up to anything that Harvey would not approve of, and if necessary, escort them to a room and stand guard. Eventually, all but one guard leaves with his charges. I don't know how much time I have before someone comes back, so I take advantage of the situation while I can.

"George?" I say slowly to the lone guard, making eye contact with him. Damn, I hope I know how to do this right. Focusing, I tune out the world around me, concentrate on him, and speak directly to his inner awareness. Once his eyes begin to focus and his pupils grow, I know I have him. "Stay right here and watch over everything, and I will be with you the whole time." He nods, and I slide my gloves on. Grabbing Luke's pack on my way, I move quickly to Harvey's office, taking care of the combination within seconds, removing the key, and replacing it with the phony even faster. I place Luke's pack in its original place and take my position next to George. "George, are you okay? You look a little dazed?"

"I'm fine. Do you have to stand so close to me the whole time we are here?" I take a step away from him with a mocking smile. "I hate working with this jackass," he mumbles.

Luke comes in after the last guest leaves. "I am going to grab my pack and change clothes?" he says.

"Make sure you do it in the guards' quarters. You know Harvey doesn't like people using his house for anything other than work," Shane, the head guard for the house, exclaims with an attitude.

"Oh, come on," Luke whines.

"Norton, don't start with me. Just go do what you have to do and be back here to help clean up."

"Fine," Luke huffs, making eye contact with me briefly.

Luke returns, and we all help clean up like servants. Before we can leave, we are all searched thoroughly. We are searched mostly to make sure we didn't take any of Harvey's tacky artwork but also in case something bigger happens to go missing. That way, they can immediately eliminate us. This exact scenario is happening tonight, only no one knows it. They ask each of us if we saw anyone do anything out of the ordinary. I vouched for George and then they asked George.

"Jayzon was here by me the whole time," he says with a shrug. Harvey knows the man detests me and would jump at the opportunity to accuse me. "Unless he is superman, he couldn't have got by me and back again." George laughs, but Harvey simply puffs cigar smoke in his face. After more interrogation and searching, we are allowed to leave with everyone feeling at ease.

I return to Luke's and find Elijah and Luke drunk, singing, and what seems to be dancing, but it is hard to tell with them. There is little I can do but shake my head at them while I make myself a drink. I would hate to be left out of the joy. "Don't get too excited, boys. We still have to move the money out in less than four days."

Chapter 24

Nick

We wait until the early hours of the morning, when we know the watch manager is asleep. It helped that we spiked his coffee too. Moving in, we notice Harvey is not that careless. He has hidden guards posted around the area. We have to be careful and, somehow, get in and get out without anyone noticing. What better way to be unseen than to be the unimportant. We pay off the regular cleaning crew, borrow their van, and promise to clean up for them. We decide to dress for the parts, even adding in our own individual touches for entertainment's sake. We look like three of the biggest morons in the world, and best of all, we are completely forgettable.

We take out the security cameras and then try to figure out which one of the three of us has to do the actual cleaning while the other two clean Harvey out. I come up with the short straws competition. Luke draws first and pulls the short straw from the start. He is disappointed, but Elijah and I are grateful that his dad taught us never to draw first, especially when all three straws are the short straw. We wave goodbye to our friend and his broom before we go searching for the money. I know where Harvey's storage facility is, and I know which bay, but he wouldn't allow me any closer than that. We stop at the edge of the long hall and stare down at all the square, drab, green units.

"Okay, so now what?" Elijah says with a long sigh.

"Well, Harvey and his lazy ass aren't going to walk far, and so it isn't going to be in the front." I walk slowly down the long stretch of bays, closing my eyes and waiting until it hits me. "Here." I say, turning to him with a smile. I hold out my arms as he looks at me with suspicious eyes. "It's Harvey. He leaves his stench wherever he goes, and the smell can't be mistaken for anything else."

Elijah smiles, taking out the key, pushing it into the lock, and twisting with a wide smile. "Damn, Nicky, you're like a bloodhound." We raise the door, and our jaws drop. "And with this, I will happily buy you all the treats you want."

We spend until dawn carrying out cash, and we still don't get it all. We briefly consider leaving some, but after returning to work for a day, we change our minds. The next night, Luke again draws first, and Elijah and I are the ones to move the cash. Exhausted, we move out as much as we can, but without sleep, we have trouble seeing straight to finish the job. The next night, we call someone in to help.

Ryan shows up the next day with a large truck and parks it in an empty storage unit we rent out. He closes it up, and saves it for later that night. When evening falls, we dress him up to match us.

"What the hell is this shit? I look like an idiot. I am not wearing this," he growls.

"You are going to wear it, and you're going to like it," I say as he crosses his arms with a scowl. I fight to keep from laughing at his dorky appearance.

Elijah doesn't bother to hide his laughter, "You know, Little Bite, I think you have found the perfect look for yourself." Elijah pushes him around as he adjusts his clothes for him, trying to make them fit his skinny body, frustrating Ryan even more.

"Okay that's enough. Now, show me this truck you got," I say, pushing Elijah off Ryan who, holding up his oversized pants, leads us to the storage unit. I have to continuously punch Elijah to keep him from laughing and saying something that will upset my brother anymore than he already is.

"He looks like a giant, grey penguin with glasses," Luke says, forcing Elijah to dive into his arm to conceal his laughter.

Ryan raises the door, and I look into the unit and see a truck with a giant furniture logo on the side. I don't bother to ask how he got it, I simply shake my head. "What? You said find something huge to move big items, so I found something," Ryan says. "Don't worry, Nick, I didn't steal it. A friend of mine works at the furniture store. He is supposed to get this washed for them, so make sure you give me a few bucks to clean it up with when we are done," he says as we round the corner to Harvey's storage unit. Ryan's jaw drops to the ground.

"I think we have enough to get it spotless," I say, with a smile.

"This is nothing, Ryan. You should see what we cleared out yesterday," Luke laughs.

"Alright, let's go!" Ryan claps his hands and yells.

"Oh no. You are not going to be helping us clean out the cash. You're going to be cleaning up everything else," I say as Luke smiles wide and hands him his cleaning supplies.

"That's not fair, Nick! I just got here. Let me enjoy this too."

"You will enjoy it…after we get it moved out. Now, go get to work," I say, shoving him on his way.

"And don't forget to clean up the extra trash I hid behind bay six," Luke yells at him. "I spent the last two days building that up."

We work nearly until dawn, yet we still barely finish in time, and by dawn we are downing caffeine and praying we don't fall asleep at some point during the day.

"I think I will call and say I have the flu," Luke whines.

"No! We have to all go in so he doesn't suspect anything. Drink your damn coffee," Elijah says, smacking Luke in the back of the head to wake him up. "You know what, Nicky?" I lift my head off my warm cup and do my best to open my eyes to look at him. "For a rich guy, you look like shit," he laughs.

"Get up and let's go. We still have to figure out how to get this key back," I say, pushing them both back onto their feet.

I manage a shower and dress properly, for my day with Harvey, but I can barely hide my yawns or my heavy eyes.

Harvey eyes me a couple of times and always with a grunt following. "What's wrong with you, Jayzon? Did you find a woman you couldn't stop fucking last night?" he says, walking away from me.

"Three … sir," I say. Harvey turns to me, fighting a smile. We move forward, and I catch Luke leaning against a wall with his sunglasses on, so I smack him awake again, causing him to jump. "Wake the fuck up," I whisper to him.

"I am so tired, Nick. I think I am starting to see things."

"Oh yeah, do you see that naked girl over there?" He stands up straight, wide-eyed and searching hard. "You look fine to me."

"That was cruel, Nick." Luke shuffles his way back to Harvey as we follow him around for a good part of the day, hoping to replace the key while he is with one of his whores tonight. The only problem: Harvey changes plans and decides he needs to make a drop at his storage unit. Luke and I exchange glances a few times on our way back to the unit. It takes some balls to steal the amount of cash we did, but it takes some really huge balls to accompany him to the crime scene with his key in your pocket. Luke begins to sweat, and I am afraid that, even if I figure a way out of this mess, he is going to give us away by the amount of guilt etched into his face. Once we get there, I pull him to the side and say, "Stop sweating."

"How the hell am I supposed to do that? He is going to know, and he is going to kill us, and leave our bodies to rot in storage so he can laugh at us forever."

"Stop over dramatizing." Looking around, I decide I only have one option. "Distract Bryan for two minutes, and I will take care of the rest. And don't ask me how."

"Okay." Luke straightens himself back up and smoothly walks up to Bryan. "Hey Bry, you will never believe what happened to me last night. I got a call from my ex-girlfriend, Deanna, and she said she wanted to get back together. I haven't seen this bitch in years, and she calls and wants to get back together. Can you believe that? I thought what the fuck is wrong with this bitch, but then, I remembered she did have big tits, some great legs, and an ass I could fuck all night, so I thought … maybe. But then I thought …" He continues while I approach Harvey straight on and wait for him to look up. *All I have to do is exchange the keys, simple … concentrate … focus … breathe …* 'So I said, 'Deanna, you know it would be great to see you again baby, but I am not as young as I used to be.' And she said, 'I know and that's okay.' I mean that is incredible right? So I said, 'But, baby, I am kind of losing my hair now,' and she said, 'that's okay. I will love you even if you go bald.' I mean what a fucking great woman, right?! So I said, 'well, baby, to be honest, I have kind of put on a few pounds since you saw me last,' and she said, 'that's okay. I have put on a little weight too.' So I said, 'fuck off, bitch!'" Luke laughs hard jumping around with his usual enthusiasm as Bryan shakes his head, fighting a smile of his own.

"You're an idiot," Bryan says.

Luke continues to laugh as Harvey grunts. "Norton, shut the fuck up! You're getting on my damn nerves," Harvey says, puffing on his cigar and looking up at me with crunched eyebrows, "…and what the fuck are you doing, Jayzon?"

"Nothing sir, just standing here," I say straightening my smile.

"Open the fucking door for me!" he says, puffing smoke in my face. "*Just standing here*, morons, all of them," he mumbles. "Wait here idiots." Luke eyes me carefully, but before I can say anything, Harvey storms out with a flaming red face and screaming at all of us. I don't think he even realizes what he is saying. I probably wouldn't even understand him if I didn't know already. We all stare at him in confusion just angering him more. "You idiots!" Harvey holds his fists up in the air, staring at his guards standing around the area before kicking the door and bashing his fists down into his car. "Shoot those fucks up there!" he yells at us. "Don't just stand there, you idiots! Someone stole everything! Find them now!" As we all stand around staring at him, I see Ryan driving out of the facility with the large furniture truck containing Harvey's cash.

Harvey is driven back home while Luke and I are ordered to figure out who stole his money. We stare at the empty unit eating Twizzlers when Elijah walks up behind us.

"What are you guys doing?" he asks.

"Trying to figure out who stole Harvey's money," I say.

"How's that going?"

"Pretty good. I think we are nearly on to something," I say, handing him a Twizzler. "How about you? What are you doing here?"

"I was told to check through this mess and see if there is anything left, but since I did that this morning after we stole all his money, I guess I have some free time. You guys want to go get a drink?" We nod and leave the empty unit with wide smiles. "You know, Nicky, he really should launder money the old fashion way and not keep it all stored up and hidden like that. It makes it easy for someone to steal his key and just come along and take it all. How much you say he lost?"

"I would say enough to build our own enterprises and never work for that dickhead again."

We each stash our money in safe places of our own while we slowly launder it clean. I move mine into several different areas, making sure to not duplicate Harvey's stupidity. For now, we stay on with Harvey as if nothing is different, and we plan to stay that way until we can have enough power to intimidate him to stay clear of us. Harvey has been suspicious, but he can find no reason to believe I, or anyone of us, had anything to do with his missing money.

We continue to seek out information leading to the supposed culprits, coming up with evidence that my brother, Connor, had something to do with it. At least, that is what we tell Harvey. We point the finger at a whore Harvey had over one night and never saw again. She worked for Connor and must have helped him get the key. We never bother to tell him she overdosed on heroin the day after he slept with her. His suspicion of my brother only intensifies when he runs into my him at his usual eating spot. Harvey watches my brother, who is pretending not to watch me. Luke and I found it to be quite comical, and neither of us hesitates to add comments to the tense situation.

"What's he looking at?" Harvey snarls.

"I think he is trying to see if you noticed his new watch. Wow, and is his wife wearing a new ring too? I knew he got that new car, but he is really showing off today," I say, as Harvey sits back in his seat with a grunt. "I have never liked that guy. He actually tried to recruit me."

"He did?" Harvey asks.

"Oh yeah. He has been after Nick forever. Connor has gone out of his way to tell Nick they have a special kinship, even considers Nick his brother he said. The man is delusional. I guess he took it as a huge slap in the face when Nick turned him down to work for you," Luke says.

Harvey smiles and manages to enjoy his meal again, and for some reason, he decides to move me to a new position, one in which I am able to be more of a part of his dealings and meetings with his associates. The opportunity also allows me to have more free time, so I accept and use my off time to take advantage of exploring my own needs.

Chapter 25

Nick

She walks alone and is not deterred in the least by the boys harassing her. I watch everything and everyone around her. The moment I feel she is in trouble, I am ready to move, but that moment never arrives. Her nose is always in those books as if she refuses to live beyond reality, in some world she created as an escape. *I have to know why.* Sliding into a seat nearby, I casually watch as some boys approach her with obvious intentions. They take her book and kick her. They do everything they can to provoke her into tears, but she never budges. She never engages them until they lean in to grope her, then, and only then, does she move towards them. A flip of her hand and she penetrates the oncoming hand with her fork, spearing it into the seat beside her. The boy's scream encourages his friends to move, but they don't get far. She has her hands full, and I make sure she gets no other trouble from anyone else. It's enjoyable watching her. She argues with the boy before her sister has him kicked out, and then, she argues with her. She never backs down. She never is shaken, and she never bothers to look my way before she returns to her book.

"You came back?" Braylin asks me.

"I did." Leaning towards her, I take her hand and smile. "And I promise it wasn't because I liked the food." Braylin smiles wide. Taking out her notepad, she writes her number down and hands it to me with a sexy lean. She says nothing as she turns and walks away, allowing me to admire her firm ass. It brings a smile to my face, but someone else is not so happy. It's the first time I think she has actually looked up from her book. The moment is short lived though; she immediately retreats back to the pages in her book. I start to say something, but I am halted by her hand reaching out, grabbing her condiment bin, and pushing it to the edge of the table towards me. No need to ask her for anything I suppose, but damn, I have a lot of questions. I fight my smile and my laughter. The girl is absolutely … amazing.

Harvey has invited me into his small network of trust. I begin making deals on my own and even arrangements for my own needs, but I still report good news back to Harvey. He still believes my brother stole his money, but when I take it upon myself to arrange an interception of one Connor's shipments, Harvey becomes enraged. I have no idea why until he calls me in to see him. Like a child, I stand in front of him as he yells at the top of his blackened lungs, demanding me to tell him who is in charge and who makes the decisions around here. I have trouble seeing the problem, which only angers Harvey more. It was the smart thing to do I insist, and I can't have my hands tied waiting for him to okay everything or we will miss opportunities. My entrepreneurial mind only continues to make things worse between Harvey and me until he finally decides I need to be reminded who is in charge. I had assumed I was beyond his demeaning tactics, but something provokes him to call me out in front of his associates. Maybe he wants to prove himself in front of some possible doubting associates, maybe he is drunk and wants to have some fun at my expense, or maybe he just doesn't trust me as much as I thought. Then again, maybe it's because Elijah left and started his own business. Harvey never warmed back up to Elijah, and when he needed someone to take the fall for one of his many bad ideas, he offered up Elijah to the police. Elijah decided not to do as told and denied knowing anything, putting Harvey back in the hot-seat. Elijah hired an attorney and escaped to his own safe haven before Harvey could have him killed. Harvey has had to scramble to remove himself from the police's focus and ends up losing even more money to pay off some officials to help him out. His grumpy mood increases as the days go by, and so does mine. I can't take much more of his bullshit. I have to get away from him soon.

I stand at Harvey's side, trying not to suck in anymore of his toxic smoke into my lungs than necessary while I wait impatiently for the night to be over. "Jayzon, entertain us," Harvey suddenly demands. I ignore him. "Jayzon, dance!" he says, taking out a gun and shooting at my feet, laughing hysterically when I jump. A few more times and my blood reaches its boiling point, my raging point. I haven't lost control in a long time, but he has pushed me too far. I don't even recognize it until the whole room steps backwards, and I look down to find my hands wrapped around his throat. Instantly, I have guns from every direction pointed at my head. Harvey swallows hard. "Leave. You are not needed anymore tonight."

My mind is still racing and heated when I leave, so I hit the nearest bar, trying to calm my nerves with alcohol. It doesn't work. "Hi," a young blond says, sliding in next to me. I try to ignore her, but she is determined to get my attention. "What, are you shy? I can cure you of that," she says with an innocent laugh, but I continue to ignore her. Huffing, she slams her drink down and fully turns to me. "Or, maybe you just don't think you could satisfy me."

I turn to her instantly and look her over. "I can fuck you so hard that every time you think of me, you will come all over your panties, but I am not sure you can handle that." She tries to huff, but I stand up to her. With a downward gaze, I lean down and graze her lips softly. "Come with me, if you are interested in me proving it to you."

I take the girl back to Luke's, where I have continued to stay while I build my own place. Before she has a chance to judge the place, I turn her to me and suck on her lips. I bring her ass in closer and let her feel my dick hardening, raising her expectations. Her moan is a clear sign to move forward. Her eyes look feebly up at me while I stare strongly down into hers, bringing her to her knees.

Deep into her mouth, my dick grows and hardens. I pull her off the ground and listen to her gasps as I pull her clothes off and suck her breasts into my mouth. My want becomes unbearable. Gazing down at her, she lies back into the bed, breathless. I spread her legs out in front of me. I feel her wetness with my fingers and remind myself how bad I need this. As I push deep into her, her head falls back, and she grips me tighter, begging me for more. My frustrations for the entire day run through my head with each thrust. Then, something else takes me over - my rage. This nameless woman lies out in front of me with her breasts bouncing freely, her moans filling the room around me. Taking a fist full of her hair, I pull her in close and demand, "Come hard on my dick." The moment the words leave my mouth, she does as I ask, and I am able to finish, satisfied and back under control.

I put my pants back on and leave the girl passed out in Luke's bed. His expression when I leave his room is that of confusion and frustration. "Rough day, Nick?"

"You could say that. I think we need to move now. I am tired of simply stealing from him. I want to be done with him." Luke immediately shivers.

"Do we have to do it tonight?" he asks, avoiding looking my way.

"No. It can wait until tomorrow. You don't mind if I borrow your room for the night, do you? I haven't finished with her yet." I don't give him a chance to answer before I return to the sleeping girl and wake her for my own pleasure.

I am requested by Harvey first thing in the morning. No surprise, and I intend to watch my back every step of the way. Men surround me, including Luke, the moment I step out of the car. They don't have to guide me. I know where I am going. Harvey greets me by moving his cigar from the center of his mouth to the side, with his usual *you're finished* grunt.

"Sit," he says bluntly. "I have always known you're smart, Jayzon, but your desires and motivations are puzzling, and that scares me. I don't feel your dedication to me is as strong as it should be, especially considering all I have done for you and taught you. I would have thought you would be willing to do whatever I asked without question and do everything you can to please me."

"I don't enjoy being treated like a puppet. I told you I can be of better value than a simple guard to your whores and the person that displaces your bodies." Leaning forward, I force him to sit back. "I can either be your partner or your enemy, Harvey. I suggest the latter is not favorable to you."

"Damn you! How dare you speak to me as if you are my equal. You are nothing, Jayzon. You have nothing, and without me, you will never have anything. Unless you get down on your knees right now and beg for my forgiveness, we are done, and you are no longer going to have my protection from Connor."

I laugh harshly at him while Luke becomes uncomfortable with the escalating emotion within the room. Taking notice of the nearest gun to me, I begin to speak freely. "Connor is not scared of you. That much is clear. He stole your money, yet you chastise me like a child when I repay the favor. You're scared of him. You can't protect me from him. I protect me from him. The only chance I have against Connor is running my own game."

"Il l'a assassiné!" Harvey yells in French, but before the last syllable leaves his mouth, I am up and dashing for the gun of the moron standing next to me. Harvey dives behind his desk and one of his other guards before I can shoot him. I shoot his guard while Luke surprises the other two in the room. The two of us take off out the door. "Jayzon!" Harvey yells firing his gun from behind us. We jump into one of Harvey's cars, and Luke drives us away before we are killed by the oncoming army of guards.

Grimacing, I feel my side and come up with a handful blood. "Luke, we need to make a stop before we go anywhere else." He looks over at me and his eyes go wide. I have him take me to my sister without telling him who she is. Luke simply believes she is a girlfriend of mine. Lena has yet to become a doctor, but she is close enough for me, and the only one I can trust.

"Dumbass! What do you want me to do? You should go to the hospital, Nick," she yells at me while she scrambles to make some sort of space for me in her tiny apartment.

"Are you going to argue with me and let me bleed to death, or are you going to help me?" Lena continues to curse me while she helps me. The good news is the bullet went right through my side, but my sister's sewing skills need more work. Thankfully, my growing tattoo camouflages her student efforts. Lena fits me with a tight wrap to my side but never ceases to hide her frustration with me.

"Now what are you going to do? He is going to come after you now and kill you," Lena says with tears forming in her eyes.

"Don't cry, Le. I will be fine. I have a plan."

"Oh yeah, what is that?"

Smiling, I kiss her cheek. "Don't worry. I am going to become bigger than him. He won't want to come anywhere near me, Ma soeur." I call her in French. She suddenly looks up at me in shock. Harvey's French newspapers weren't a complete waste of my time. "Now, you concentrate on finishing school. With that new scholarship you just got, you shouldn't have to worry about anything else." She smiles, but then slowly looks up at me.

"How did you know about my scholarship, Nick?" she asks.

"I told you not to worry. I already have a plan in place." Luke and I hide out at Elijah's new place for a few days until my own house is completed. We agree to work together for a little longer, build up new territories, and divide them equally between us. Luke wants no part of being on his own. He prefers to work with me and not have to deal with making the decisions. I think nothing about it, but Elijah remarks as if it is no surprise to him. I ignore his comments, and we proceed with our plans.

Chapter 26

Nick

Over the next few weeks, Elijah, Luke, and I spend our days building our enterprises while hiding from Harvey. It is not ideal, but we are free to do as we please. We start to feel good about our growth until we meet Hugh Bonnie, a fast talking machine that is more energetic than twelve Lukes put together. He has managed to gain a hold on some key businesses that I want; however Bonnie is not our problem. His guard, Dwayne Dobbins, the biggest man I have ever seen, is. The three of us eye him from across the street as we eat our lunch.

"What do you think he eats? Like whole cows at a time or something?" Elijah asks.

"Let's follow him and find out. Maybe we can sway him to help us," I say optimistically.

"Okay, fine, but just make sure he *sways* in your direction," Elijah jokes.

Dwayne rarely speaks, and his life outside of work is fairly simple. There is little routine that we can force our way into to meet our expectant new friend. I eventually become impatient and decide to force him to listen to us. We wait for the right time, and I run up to him, blatantly taking his wallet. After he starts chasing me, I run into the nearby alley into which he follows. "Dwayne, I am happy to give this back to you, but I would like for you to listen to me first," I say, backing up as he comes forward. His only response is a groan of displeasure, and I assume from its tone that he is not in agreement to my terms. I glance towards Luke and Elijah as they follow behind him and motion for them to do something.

"Oh this is not good," Elijah says, looking the large man over.

"Maybe we should shoot him in the leg or something," Luke suggests.

"And what, anger it more?" Elijah rebuts.

"Dwayne, seriously, I have a great offer for you," I say as the bull moves forward, focusing only on the wallet in my hand.

"Give me my wallet …" He grumbles until Elijah and Luke both jump onto his back. Dwayne still moves forward, carrying my friends like an amusement park ride. "Get off me you fools." Dwayne throws them from side to side like a bucking bull. I nearly start laughing at them trying to hold on until they finally trip him up and get him on the ground. I jump in, thinking I can help, but all I do is make a bigger mess. Dwayne has us all in a bear hug before we can get any kind of advantage. "Give me my wallet," he growls.

"Oh, this worked out beautifully, Nick. Now I am going to die by an elephant," Luke yells.

"Are you calling me fat?" Dwayne asks, dropping us and bearing down on Luke.

"No, I only meant your height." Dwayne snarls louder as Luke backs away from him. "What? You are in great shape. You are quite … appealing?" Luke shrugs. Elijah and I glance at each other, unsure of how to proceed. "Are you guys going to help me out?"

"No, I don't think so," Elijah says, shaking his head.

Luke decides to run full force into Dwayne, but ends up upside down and screaming as Dwayne spins him. Thankfully, Luke somehow throws Dwayne off balance, and sends them both to the ground. While the giant bear is tired, I take my opportunity to talk to him.

I stare down into Dwayne's bulging eyes. "We need your help, so listen to me, and I will make sure you will be taken care of for the rest of your life."

"I don't like him," Dwayne says, in regards to Luke.

"None of us really do," Elijah says, earning a glare from Luke as he cleans the trash off himself, "...but he does grow on you." And that was the beginning of a new friendship for us all - except Luke.

I feel great about my new ally. Dwayne allows us into Bonnie's office to transfer funds and information at will. We take over his strongholds and kill him with his own hired guns. We are quickly able to build and become strong enough that Harvey backs off and minds his own business. I concentrate on destroying Connor, while Elijah decides it's time we go our separate ways. My long time best friend leaves me with a handshake and a final promise, "Brothers for life, Nicky."

Chapter 27

Nick

My home is finally complete, and feeling incredible pride, I tour the grounds with my new guards. The interior of my house is done to perfection, elegant with a comforting warmth. I don't want to feel like a prisoner in my own home, but I want it secure, and most of all, I want my secrets secure. I have been adding in extras to my home for business sake.

"Nick, I think you are really going to love it. I have been working on it ever since I got out of rehab," Tanner says, bubbling over with excitement.

"You didn't have to work all day and night, Tanner. It would have gotten done eventually," I say, happy to see him happy.

"No, no I owe you everything and wanted to prove to you that I can finish something now. I am a changed man, and I can do any task you will have me do. You are my nephew, and I want to make sure you of all people are proud of me."

"I am proud of you, and I will hire you on, but no one is to ever know we are related." He nods with a defeated expression. "It is not because I am embarrassed about you, Tanner. It's so you won't become a target. Now, show me this hidden room you have been working on." Tanner leads me upstairs to one of my guest rooms and shows me the beautiful new cabinet he made that conceals all my secrets and everything I want no one to find. My computer, notes, transactions, clients, workers, and a key. In a hidden slide out within the cabinet, I place my father's key and promise myself never to look back. I close it all up and wander my new home with ideas and expectations of what I want most in my life. I want to know how she can see all of me and not be affected at all.

Everything I could ever want is now going to be mine, but will my life ever include her? The only thought that rings through my head is the words of my father, "No will ever truly love you." *So why bother trying?* I ask myself. It's because I am curious. How does she make me feel for her the way other women feel for me? She has captured me, the awkward girl with no fear is the angel I have long awaited, and she has to be the one my father told me didn't exist. I have to know for sure. Can she overcome me and still love me?

She walks down the street to the same window that she explored the day before. Only today, the shop owner comes out, yells at her to go away, and then quickly wipes her hand prints off his glass. Kayla walks away, looking back with a sadness that penetrates me to the core. Once she is long out of sight, I try to breathe calmly before stepping out of my new car. I walk up to the sparkling clean window and to the old book being displayed upon its golden stand. In my new, expensive wares, the shop owner greets me with respect. I wish he had done that for her. Maybe then I would be a little more forgiving of him. "I want that book in the window. No need to wrap it."

"Oh no, sir that book is not for sale. It is an expensive addition to my own collection," he says, moving away to show me some other books for sale.

"Did I ask if it was for sale? I said I want that book and that book only." I move to the counter to wait to pay for my purchase and turn to look at him. "No need to wrap it." I leave the store and head straight to someone who I know will appreciate the book.

Braylin always has a bright smile on her face when I visit her. "Hi," she says, running up and hugging me. "Wow, you look so handsome."

"Thank you. You look beautiful today." I grasp her waist, keeping her close to me so I can take full control of her lips. "I found something for you today." I hand her a bag. "A friend of mine was throwing out some books. This one looked interesting, so I pulled it from his trash. I thought maybe you could give it to that moody sister of yours." Braylin happily pulls the book out. "Be careful it is old."

"Wow, it really is. Hey, maybe you stumbled upon something valuable. Whether it is or not, Kayla is going to want to thank you herself for sure," Braylin says, kissing me.

"No, don't tell her I gave it to you. Tell her a customer left it as a tip for you. That would be more believable. I get the feeling she doesn't think that much of me."

"Kayla isn't too fond of most men, but I like you."

"Well, then maybe you can thank me for her," I say, earning a gleeful smile from her. I want to ask her a million questions, but I don't. Instead, I take Braylin to dinner and then home. Kayla's sweet gaze, briefly eyes us both before she rushes back into her room. Focusing on Braylin, I reach for her, kissing her before I pick her up and carry her to her bed. I don't need her on her knees. I only need her to resemble someone else for the night. It isn't perfect, but it eases my frustrations all the same, and that is all I can ask for now.

Business is good. I sit back in my chair, feeling like I am exactly where I need to be. There is a battle coming our way, but I am confident.

"Jayzon, I suspect since you are here that you will be accepting my offer," Perry says with a twinge of excitement. Perry Bilson is a long time crook who, for the longest time, thought I was beneath him and not worth his time to talk to. I have tried to work with him, but I was always met with a closed door. Now things have changed, and he calls me with an offer. He wants to take down Joseph Estrella and split the rewards with me, sixty/forty in his favor. Not exactly a fair deal considering he wants me to lead the attack while he stands in the shadows, waiting for it to be over. For his part, he promises weapons to do the job. It seems like a good opportunity for me; Luke was even excited to have the chance to work with the great Perry Bilson. I, however, believe we can do better.

I take a moment to look around the area, verifying the placement of my men and then I smile. "Actually, Perry, I have decided to go a different way," I say, causing his smile to fade. I hold up one finger and give the signal to round them up.

"What is this?" Perry demands.

"This, this is me taking you over," I say, staring him down and waiting for it. A win like this is a lifetime in the making. This will set me up as the main power hold for this city. I already control Estrella, unbeknownst to Perry, and now, I am going to use Estrella to own Perry's large hold. However, I know it is not going to be that easy. Perry will never go down without a major fight, so I prepare to do something I promised myself I would never do again.

Perry furrows his brows and opens his mouth, "You are going to die, Jayzon. Kill him!" he yells out, as I focus on meeting his eyes perfectly.

The fire shooting through my veins feels amazing. The control over my enemy only increases my desire and surges my strength. I walk to my enemy as he fights for breath from his knees and look down upon him. The whole room is silenced by his struggle.

"I now own all that was yours. Do you want to know why?" He grips his collar with burning eyes. "Because you're dead," I say, walking away from his lifeless body.

I meet Braylin for dinner later that night to celebrate. She doesn't understand, but it doesn't matter. I have what I want, and now, I get to spend the evening with a beautiful woman. Braylin sits, smiling uncontrollably in the beautiful new dress and jewelry I bought for her. I enjoy being around her and spoiling her terribly. Today especially, I feel like no one can stop me. I agree to take Braylin back home so she can check on her sister. I have nearly put Kayla out of my mind the last few weeks. Braylin is so perfect for me that there is no reason for me to be distracted by her sister. It must be her attitude towards me that makes me crazy. She's the one girl who seems to dismiss me, but I am sure she is no different. She just hides it better. We arrive back at their place, and I feel incredible until I hear Kayla screaming. I rush in, expecting to kill some intruder that is hurting her, but instead, I find her asleep. Kayla grips me and cries for me to help her, and for a brief moment, she looks right at me with her bright beautiful green eyes. Once again, I tremble.

Braylin pushes me and my gun out of the way, immediately takes hold of her sister, and wakes her. Kayla cries and cries but finally calms enough to go back to asleep.

My heart is still racing when Braylin returns to me. "She's okay now. I'm sorry. She has nightmares sometimes. Usually she only needs her blanket wrapped back around her, but I guess it laid in the floor too long. That ruined the mood, didn't it?" she asks, wrapping her arms around me. She's right; it did ruin my mood, and not only the sexual desires but the controlling, powerful ones too. I have never felt so calm before.

After I leave Braylin, I meet up with Luke to talk to a guy who has been giving us trouble. He is a pain in the ass, but Luke feels that if I talk to him myself, I may be able to resolve the issues much faster. I stand back, watching Luke argue and argue with this man, waiting for me to jump in. "Listen, asshole, we don't need you. We can just as easily get someone else to do it. So either you help us or you can disappear, and we will get someone else to take your place," Luke says, glancing back at me.

"Alright, I have had enough of this. What do you want to get this done?" I ask the man to Luke's surprise. I negotiate a deal I can live with and walk away.

"What the hell was that about? Why didn't you beat the fuck out of him?"

"What good would that have done?"

"It would have showed we meant business," Luke says.

"I think we have made ourselves clear to people by now. There is no need for violence every time we leave the house."

"No need for violence? Nick, we can control everything if people continue to fear you. All you have to do …"

"Is what, Luke? Continue killing with no feeling at all?" He looks at me strangely. "I don't want to become a killer. That was not my goal. My goal is to build up a business, businesses, and not have to worry about money ever again."

"And your brother?"

"My brother's time will come, but right now, we need to concentrate on business."

"I don't know. What is wrong with you? Yesterday you were ready to take down the world, and now you want to be some typical suit?" He continues to rant. "Nick!"

"What, Luke? I already told you what I want. If you don't want that, then go off on your own and do your own thing. No one is stopping you," I yell back at him. He forces Tanner to stop the car, and he gets out, refusing to speak to me any longer. Tanner looks my way within the rearview mirror and smiles with obvious approval.

I have spent a lot of time with Braylin lately. I keep telling myself it's because I like spending time with her, but I am always eager to take her home at the end of the night, only so I can see Kayla. Their house is even worse than the one I grew up in, but it is loved and comfortable, despite the springs poking me in the back. Braylin lies next to me, motionless, when Kayla begins crying out. I have heard her a several times over the last few weeks, and I have gone to see to her on my own, only if Braylin doesn't. Tonight, Braylin isn't moving, so I do. Dressing myself more appropriately, I ease Kayla's door open and look over her as the moonlight hits her pain filled face. I pick her blanket up off the floor and wrap it around her, quieting her terror. The cure is simple. Except tonight, she grabs my hand and pulls me in. I haven't touched her since I thought there was an intruder attacking her, but the feeling rushing through my veins is even better than the day at the diner when she first touched me. Kayla's touch instantly puts my whole body at ease. She won't let go. She believes me to be someone else, someone more deserving of her. Her lively dream sucks me in, and before I know it, I find myself laying next to her, telling her a story, and pretending to be hers. My smile is so wide it hurts. I wish to kiss her, to carry her away from her pain. I wish … to be by her side forever.

Kayla sits up against me, and I run my fingers through her hair, stroke her cheek, and breathe her in when she suddenly opens her eyes and looks deeply into my heart. "I love you," she says. "Do you love me?"

My mind races, my heart pounds, and everything within me comes alive like never before. "Yes," I say without any doubt. My confession is instantly rewarded with a kiss. The touch of her lips is intoxicating. I open my eyes, wanting to take her into my arms, but reality becomes real. Kayla begins talking of her castles, kings, and all the other fantasies within her dream world, and I again, become nothing but a participant in her imaginary world. *Yes, I love you. I love you so much it pains me like no other, but you, will never love me.*

I have tried everything to get Kayla out of my head, but nothing works. Her hold on me is paralyzing. I have to push Braylin away to prevent seeing Kayla anymore. I concentrate on work, on building up my businesses, and on taking down my brother, piece by piece, every chance I get. Still, at times, I find myself watching Kayla from afar, dreaming of her saying to me what she did that night, running up to me with that sweet smile, and looking up at me like she does no one else. I have tried every woman I can to erase her from my memory, but no other compares.

Chapter 28

Nick

After a long day, it ends with me discussing business with a new client. He is no more than a new political disgust, a bundle of greed that is anxious to rise to power, which makes it easy for me to negotiate with him. All he asks for is more money and access to his opponents' private information. I am thankful to finish our meeting early and walk back out to my car; however, when I step outside, I notice Luke speaking to someone I haven't seen in some time.

"Nicholas." Savage speaks with an eager tone. "Did your dinner meeting go well?"

"It was wonderful, but now I have other business to take care of, if you don't mind," I say, nodding in his direction.

"Of course. I wouldn't want to stand in the way of a growing entrepreneur. It is nice to see you again, Nicholas. I hope that, perhaps, we can meet again for a social dinner soon. I am curious to see how you are doing since our last meeting."

"Perhaps …" I say, glancing towards Luke as he smiles widely. "It was nice to see you again, Mr. Savage." I crash into the car, meeting

Tanner's eyes and telling him all my fears with one look. When Luke sits down across from me, I eye him until he looks up at me. "What did you talk to him about?"

"Who? That old man? Nothing. He only wanted to know how you are doing. Why? Who is he?" he says, as I sit back and continue to look him over for any sign of deception. "Damn, Nick! Why are you looking at me that way? I swear, I am still loyal to you and only you. The old man wanted nothing more than to ask me if you are happy."

"And what did you say?" I ask.

"I don't know. I didn't say much of anything to him," he yells back at me.

"You don't know, or you don't remember?" I ask him, but all he can do is huff and shake his head. I realize he doesn't remember which worries me even more.

As if that night wasn't disturbing enough, it was only a few days later that I got even worse news.

The day Braylin died, I was busy working. I didn't even know until Kayla had already been taken away, but no one knew to where. Maybe I overreacted at first, but I felt I had to find her. I have to bring her to my home and take care of her, before she is hurt any more than she already has been. After I scream at anyone who is not giving me the information I want, I begin my search for her, on my own and with complete dedication.

I manage to call in a favor to one of my new political friends, and he helps me locate Kayla at her mother's house. I keep my next moves to myself so no one can talk me out of going after her. Pulling up to the trash heap of a house, I immediately get an overwhelming, horrific feeling through my veins. Then, I hear her. Her screams, her painful cries to anyone who can hear her. I scream out to her, and to *him,* until his lewd eyes meet mine with anger. I interrupt his attack on Kayla, but he is not about to let her go now. The fisted hold he has on her and the tears streaming from her eyes, are all it takes to bring my blood to a boil. He opens his mouth, ready to make his threats towards me, but before he can, I capture his heart and squeeze. His soul is mine, and he has no choice but to release her. His desperation for life does nothing to ease my grip. Concentrating hard on his eyes, I reach in and release the blood from his suffocating heart. One gasp is all I allow from his dried mouth before plunging my knife into him. He deserves to die in pain, to die like the disgust he inflicts. When I look up, she is gone, and I realize she is never going to run back to me.

I spend days trying to find her, but there is no sign of her anywhere. The only person I thought who would know where she might have run to was her mother. As it turns out, the drunken bitch is more upset about her lover than her own daughter. I want to kill her. The more and more I scream at her, the more she laughs, telling me stories that won't help me at all in finding Kayla. The woman's drunken, disgusting manner works me into such a rage that I hold her up against the wall and stare deeply into her eyes, and she laughs at me. *She laughed?* "I'll kill you," I say to her as I let her slide back down the wall.

She stumbles away from me. "Kill me then. You would only be doing me a favor." She turns and looks into my eyes. "There is something different about you. You remind of that man that came by yesterday."

"What man?" I ask her.

"The one that bought me this bottle. Nice man. I liked him. He asked a bunch of questions too, but I refused to tell him anything, that is, until he bought me the bottle," she says, smiling wide at me.

"And what did you tell him?"

"I told him that, for a price, I would tell him whatever he wanted to know."

Grabbing her by the neck, I growl my impatience, "What did you tell him?"

Her eyes widen, but there is no sign that I have any control of her. "Calm down, handsome. I only told him my daughter died. I have no other family in my life."

"What about Kayla?"

"That little bitch is nothing but a nuisance, and she is nothing to me. No one would ever care to ask about her. Braylin was the one all the men loved. Kayla is too ugly to love."

I slam her against the wall. "Where is Kayla? Where would she go?"

"I might know if you do me a favor." She smiles wide. This woman has no clue about Kayla. She never told her who her father was, and she never cared to pay enough attention to have any idea where she might have run to.

"I am not buying you any more alcohol. You can shiver and die in your own filth. Enjoy sobering up," I say, gathering Kayla's things and carrying them out the door with me as the evil witch chases after me, begging for her loving bottle.

With Franky's scarf wrapped around my neck, I sit down at her grave and try to understand my emotions. "I ruined her life. I selfishly interrupted her life and destroyed it, kind of the way I did yours. I am a menace, Franky. Your father was right. I spent days waiting for word from the man I sent out to find her. That's his only job: to find Kayla, protect her, and never to tell me where she is so I can't cause her anymore pain. I only hope, for her sake, she stays away from me." I lay the flowers down on Franky's grave and leave for home.

I'm standing with a drink in hand when Luke comes in and crashes into the seat near me. "How did things go?" I ask, trying to hide my original concern.

"It went great. You were right. Everything worked out just like you thought it would. You have come so far, Nick. The things you can do, you are unstoppable. No one can battle you. I can't imagine how far you can climb, and I am going to be with you every step of the way," Luke says. Glancing his way, I try to feel encouraged by his dedication, but something inside me feels broken. "I know what you need. You know those two girls we met last night at the club? They really want to meet you, so I brought them both here." Luke walks in with one blond and one brunette. "Girls, Nicholas Jayzon," he says, smiling. Both girls instantly take a seductive stance in front of me.

I take a drink and look them over from the top of my glass. "I'll take them both." Sitting my glass down, I walk in between them and look down at each of them. "I want to fuck someone tonight. Which one of you is interested?" Promptly, they both warm up to me. "Oh honey, take me. I am sure I can please you," the brunette says, finding my dick in my pants.

Turning to the blond, I ask, "So what about you? Do you want to please me too?"

She nods. "I want to do nothing but please you," she says stripping off her clothes.

They both take turns sucking on my dick, feeling it penetrate deep inside of them, and allowing me to taste their wetness. It was a long night of fucking and trying to forget. Unfortunately, none of it does anything to diminish my thoughts of Kayla.

I spend years working and fucking, fucking and working, but nothing and no one helps me forget her. My heart continues to search for Kayla, despite my protests.

It was years before my search came to an end, when Kayla decided to look for me. I couldn't sleep at all. I couldn't stop thinking about her. I was so happy to see her again, despite the fact that she wanted to kill me. I debated on whether I should protect her from me, or protect her from everyone else. Connor forces my hand, and once I decided that I couldn't live without her, there was no turning back. I saved her from Connor, and she returned to me with love in her eyes. Her heart finally wanting me as much mine wanted her. It was all a sign, a sign that she was meant for me, and I am not about to let her go, no matter what.

Chapter 29

Nick

"I'm Nicky Jayzon!" I round the corner as the teenager walks up to my six-year-old son and grabs him, forcing him to watch the dog being beaten. Before I can stop him, the punk releases my son and crashes to the ground, wreathing in pain.

His friends turn in shock, "What did you do? You want a beating too, kid?" Nicky fists his hands and stiffens, standing his ground despite being outnumbered. He doesn't know his abilities yet, and I am not sure I do either, but I won't allow him to be tested here and certainly not in this way. I approach Nicky's back and stare down the punks before they get the notion to try and battle me.

"I suggest you run and run fast before I decide to ruin your day any further," I growl, fighting a smile when they don't hesitate to run in the opposite direction. Nicky runs to the dog's side, petting him to a calmer state. "Nicky, I thought I told you …"

"But Daddy, I was only bringing him my sandwich. He was hungry. Then, they told me not to feed him, but I wasn't going to listen to them.

They came over and started hitting him with that stick. We need to take him to the doctor," Nicky says, still trying to comfort the dog.

Leaning down at the bloodied dog's side, I realize this dog is not going to live much longer no matter what doctor we take him too. "Nicky, I don't …" My son's face is heartbreaking, and like his mother, I am unable to say no to him. "We will take him to the doctor, and let them take care of him."

"Can we take him home with us afterwards?" Nicky joyfully asks.

I consider the dog's condition with a long sigh. "If the doctor says it's okay, we can." I take a blanket from the car and wrap the large dog up to carry him. Placing him in the back seat with my son, I drive to a nearby vet's office. The whole way there, Nicky is determined to get me to pet this dog with him while I try and drive. I manage a few rubs of the dog's ears by the time we arrive, but I am more concerned about how I am going to explain to my son about this dog dying, or, even worse, why we have to put him to sleep. Once we arrive, I carry the broken dog in and hand him over to the pessimistic crew, who don't seem to be aware of my son's concern for the creature. They all stare at me as if they are unsure of what I want them to do.

"Sir, this dog is …" the doctor says.

"I know, but my son wants to do everything we can for him, even if it means that we need to find a way to let him rest peacefully and pain free," I emphasize.

"Okay, we will see what we can do and then call you back here shortly," the doctor says, escorting the nurses back with the dog.

"He has big floppy ears. I think we should name him Eeyore, okay Daddy?" I nod, and Nicky leans against me, obviously worried about the dog and making it even harder for me to figure out what to say to him when the dog dies. As I sit back, I notice the doctor flirting with one of the nurses and clearly not paying any attention to the dog. I stare at him until he notices. He smiles and disappears for a time before motioning for me to come near.

"I think you're aware that there is not much we can do for this dog. I think the only thing we need to do at this point is decide if you want us to handle his body or if you want to have him cremated and keep his ashes. There is a great deal on that right now. It comes with a decorative box where you can put a picture of the dog. It will be a wonderful way for your son to remember his childhood pet." He continues to bring out pamphlets and pictures, trying to sell me everything under the sun. I turn away from him to check on Nicky, but he has disappeared again.

"Nicky!" I yell.

He comes running out from the back with the dog running at his side. "I'm here Daddy. Eey is all better now. Can we stop by the pet store on the way home so we can get him some toys?" Nicky asks, looking up at me innocently as the dog sits patiently, waiting by his side.

I glare back at the doctor who is now staring at the dog in amazement. "Ummm, I think maybe we should check your dog over once more, sir."

"You think?" I snap. *Unbelievable.*

"Mr. Jayzon, your dog is ready to go now." *My dog? No. No, we just found him dying in the alley.* "We cleaned him up, and gave him his shots, so he should be good for awhile. You will want to bring him back for his second set of shots in a few months. We will call …"

"This is unbelievable. The dog was broken and near death. You had cremation papers out for me to sign, and now you are telling me he is fine?" I say, looking for an answer that no one apparently has here.

"But he is fine. The dog is in perfect health. He must have looked worse than he was?" The doctor shrugs as they bring the now clean, tail wagging giant towards us. "Much worse." Nicky jumps for joy, running at the dog as if we have had him for years. *Oh great! Now we have a dog. Kayla is going to love this. I am just not sure how I am going to explain it.*

My new dog gets out of my car, happily following after my son. I barely step foot in the house before my wife approaches me. Her eyes are curious, but her concern is more about my brother approaching with his arms crossed. All I can do is sigh. Kayla kisses my cheek. "A dog, Nick?"

"It is a long story Princess," I say, noticing Elijah approaching as well. "What are you doing here?"

"What? A guy can't stop by for a visit anymore?" he says with a drink already in his hand.

Nicky runs up to me with his new dog right at his side. "Daddy, I gave him some water, but he is still hungry. Can I give him dinner now, too?"

"Wait Son, and I will help you. For now, take him outside to play for awhile." Nicky turns and waves at Elijah in a ridiculously cute way, causing his mother to gush.

Elijah smiles, "Hi little Nick. How are you?"

"Oh, you know, it's hard keeping the ladies off my jewels, but I manage to keep them under control," my son says causing, a puzzled expression to Elijah's face and sending my wife into a rage at my now hysterically laughing brother.

"I am going to hurt you!" she yells at Ryan as he runs away from her.

"See you tomorrow Nick. Talk to you later Kayla," Ryan laughs, running out the door while I try to restrain Kayla.

"Did I miss something?" Elijah asks.

I laugh, looking down at my frustrated wife. "No, my son is a little bit Kayla and a lot me, right Princess?" Kayla smiles up at me, and I happily take hold of her lips.

"I missed you today," she says, kissing me again with a long, inviting sigh. "But I will let you talk business while I go see to our new dog, which I expect for you to explain to me later," she says, gripping my ass and reminding of my earlier promise.

With a wide smile, I look up at Elijah and him shaking his head. "I didn't need to see that," he says.

"Well, then, what are you doing here? This is my house," I say, leading him to my office.

"Business Nicky. Always business. Why else would I be here?" Elijah sits down, already hinting at me to offer him a drink. I hand him one more with concern, but he smiles nonetheless. "Cheer up, Nicky. You got it all now, at least let me have my little source of happiness."

"So what is this business you want to talk about?" I ask.

"I have decided to move out west, and I was hoping you could look after my interests here until I get myself established in the new place."

"Why are you leaving? Your whole life is here."

"My whole life? What life, Nicky? There is nothing for me here anymore. I need a change. All there is here are old memories that I need to move on from," he says as Kayla comes in and whispers something dirty in my ear. She leaves me with my favorite drink and a sinful kiss. Elijah eyes her completely. "Where is my drink Kayla?"

"It looks as if you already have one Eli."

"It isn't the same without your … special touch." He smiles.

"I am surprised you haven't had enough special touching from your own women," Kayla says before winking at me and walking out.

"None of them are like you Kayla," Elijah yells after her. I watch him carefully as he follows her every move. "You know, Nicky, you are one lucky man, and when I grow up, I want to be just like you."

"Are you in love with my wife Eli?"

He laughs, "I am in love with love, that's all. Don't worry Nicky. Your wife is nowhere near my type. Besides, we can't stand each other." Elijah continues to discuss business, but all I can do is wonder about why he is really leaving.

I try to ignore her eyes on me because I know what she wants. "Just say it."

"What baby? What is it you would like me to say?" Kayla nuzzles in under my arm, kissing up my neck to nibble on my ear. "Huh baby, what does my perfect husband want from me?"

"Oh, I am perfect now? All because I allowed my son to have a dog? Please, do me a favor, and don't ask how he duped me into that one. I am positive my son has too much of his mother in him." I smile into her sexually inspired eyes.

"I won't ask if you give me a reason to think of something else," she hisses, forcing me to take hold of her ass with one hand and push her lacy bra to one side with the other. Her breasts taste incredible and always fill my mouth perfectly. Lifting her further, I drag her panties down her legs and feel for what I want. Kayla bites her bottom lip and straddles me, letting me in. I caress her ass and tongue my way deep inside her, allowing my fingers to trail along and into her body. Her head falls back as she moans and shifts her body into my mouth even more. Her orgasm shakes her whole body and tastes better than her breasts. Licking her come off my lips, I move her down onto the bed and slide my hardened dick past the wetness I created and into the soft, tight warmth of my wife. Her legs wrap around my waist while her hands grip my ass, enjoying every movement into her.

"You feel so good, Princess." Kayla shifts her hips up into mine and smiles with a moan. Her lips play with mine while I enjoy feeling her naked body against mine. I play with her and feel her gasp against my neck. I pick her up and hold her against the wall, pulling her legs up around me. Her breasts playfully bounce in front of my lips, giving me ample availability to her nipples. Kayla fists my hair, calling out to me and encouraging my dick to grow even tighter inside of her. Her softness becomes so wet and tight around my dick that she releases, breathing her praises with a blissful sigh. Finding her lips, I gently kiss her with satisfaction. "I love you," I hum, leaning up and twisting her body into a new position which surprises her, but she doesn't protest. "I told you I was going to make it up to you. How does it feel?" While I control her body, Kayla looks down at my erection sliding in and out of her and smiles up at me. "I will take that to mean you like it." She tightens again with wide eyes and a smile while I also slip away into ecstasy. I groan my pleasure to her while coming strong. "Damn, I love you," I exhale deeply.

Kayla reaches up and grabs my lips. "Oh Nick, I love you too." She continues kissing me while I try to recover.

"If you love me, then will you please back off of Ryan so he can get his job done and stop whining to me every day?"

Kayla sighs, smiling and caressing my face, but I know better than to believe she is going to do as I ask. "I wish I could baby, but your brother has crossed a line. I did warn him, but he ignored it, and now, I have to make him pay." Frustrated, I look up into her eyes and try another way to persuade her into my way of thinking. "Nick, you know I love when you do that, but you also know …" She squeezes out from under my arms, smiling and laughing as I try to bring her back. "You have no power over me, Nick." Kayla gets dressed and leans back to me for another kiss. "But I do love you, and I will be happy to come back to your incredible naked body after I check on your sons."

"Would you like some help, Princess?" Her smile is enough to get me up and following after her. While Kayla looks in on Brayden, I see to Nicky. I open his door and find him sound asleep, and Eey lifts his head. I am not sure how my son fits in his bed with that big ass dog next to him, but somehow, he has managed to squeeze in close to him with one arm wrapped around his dog and a huge smile on his face. Eey watches me closely as I run my fingers through my son's hair and kiss him on his head. "Watch over my son, Eey. Someone wants to take him from me." Brushing my hand across the dogs head, he whimpers with acknowledgment. "If anyone can protect him, it should be a dog that has come back from the dead. Right?"

Chapter 30

Nick

Kayla and I sit near the back of the ceremony, invited guests rather than invited family. Kayla, being a friend of Brady's, is the perfect excuse for me to be at my sister's wedding. It is slightly irritating to be treated as an unwelcome guest at my own sister's wedding, especially with all these fat cops stuffing their faces with the food I paid for. Kayla keeps reminding me that this is about my sister and her happiness, but I still have to hide away in the corner in order to keep myself under control.

"Jayzon, nice of you to come despite all the cops in attendance. You must feel terribly uncomfortable?" Brady remarks as he approaches my side.

"Not in the least. What do I have to worry about? I do own this hotel. I will simply kick them out when I get tired of their disgusting asses." I smile.

"Always so cocky. Still can't believe we are related now. That makes me uncomfortable," he sighs.

"Now, *that* is something that we both can agree on."

"Thank you, by the way, for paying for all of this, making Lena's day the perfect dream for her. I have never seen her look so happy," he says as we both gaze over at my sister who is laughing with joy. "You have given her the perfect wedding gift. Now how about mine?" he asks, giving me a look of determination.

"I told you, Savage is not someone you want to deal with, and for my sister's sake, I suggest you keep your distance from him. Be satisfied with the wins you have gotten lately," I insist, fisting my drink.

"Satisfied? How can I be satisfied when my parents' murderer is still out there, still free to do as he pleases, to kill who he pleases. I am supposed to be satisfied with that Jayzon?" Brady asks with a tone containing every ounce of anger he has built up over the years.

"I don't think you understand who he is and what he is capable of. He is too strong for you. He is too strong for anyone to try and take down. I find it better to stay out of his path," I say, trying to avoid looking at him any more than I have to.

"Are you kidding me? You mean there is actually someone out there that Nicholas Jayzon is afraid of?" he asks, obviously not believing it to be true.

Slamming my drink down, I face him head on. "You're damn right I am, and you should be too," I say, walking away from his shocked expression.

With Brady gone on his honeymoon, I decide to visit Savage once more to thank him and let him know he will have no further trouble from Simone. I hope, by treating him with respect, I can safely distance myself from the man once again. This time, I am a little more comfortable meeting him because it is at a downtown restaurant and not as his home. I go alone, but he arrives with his usual entourage of people, plus one more, a man near my age and someone who instantly annoys me with his smug, white smile. He dresses affluently and holds his head high above his broad shoulders. He wears his hair long and has his facial hair tailored to perfection, but it is his dark, burning eyes that tell me everything I need to know about him.

"Nicholas, how nice to you again. I have to say, I was quite excited to hear from you again." Savage greets me respectfully, as he always has, but he turns and motions towards the gentleman dressed in nothing but attitude. "I hope you don't mind, Nicholas, but I invited Adair, my first in command. Adair has worked his way to the top. He is quite impressive in his abilities."

"No, I don't mind at all. Nice to meet you, Adair," I say, shaking his hand and immediately feeling as if I made an agreement to battle.

"Nicholas, I have been told so much about you. I hope you don't mind that I am joining the meeting, but after what I have heard about you, I had to see the man of such great accomplishment for myself," Adair says, looking me over as if I am three feet tall and five years old.

"Thank you," I say simply before sitting and hoping to get this meal over with. "Mr. Savage, I wanted to let you know that Chief Simone has agreed to back off and should no longer be a problem. I want to thank you for your patience and assistance with that matter."

"Of course, it was no problem. Like I said, we are old family friends. We might as well be family, and there is nothing I wouldn't do for family," he says, sipping his wine like nobility. "Speaking of family affairs." Savage motions for his man Rabbie who instantly appears at our table and hands me an envelope before disappearing again. "We will be celebrating Adair's new position in a few months, and I would love for you to join us.

There will be many influential people there, and I would be happy to introduce you to them."

"I assume these influential people will be in their usual political masks, kind to anyone that makes large donations to their campaigns," I say smartly.

Savage laughs, "Masks, yes, I assume they will be. Actually, that is a good idea - a masquerade ball. Too bad we didn't think of that before, but I assure you, Nicholas, it will be an extravagant affair all the same. You and your beautiful wife will be a wonderful addition to our celebration."

"Personally, I would love to be introduced to your wife. I know a dance with her would make the celebration complete for me," Adair says with a lick of his lips.

I begin to twirl my glass, pushing my fire back down to a minimum before I speak. "If you need a date, Adair, I can hire a whore for you, a gift for you on your big night. I will make sure she stays the night even. Maybe it will be an even bigger night for you. It will be a first time for you. No? I know someone that could teach you how to do it right."

Adair leans back in his seat and watches my mocking smile. "I assure you, my skills in bed have been polished to perfection, better than you I would think considering your frail appearance," he says, causing me to laugh. "If you would like to know for sure, I am willing to let your wife decide, Nicholas," Adair says.

"Mr. Savage, thank you for dinner and the invitation. I will talk with my wife and let you know as soon as I can," I say to Savage who is nodding in agreement. Turning towards Adair's cocky smile, I lean forward and say, "I assure you, Adair, that if you speak of my wife again as if she is some kind of property that can be traded for pleasure, you will not be smiling so handsomely ever again." I nod at Savage's wide smile and adjust my jacket back to perfection before leaving with heated hands.

Chapter 31

Nick

I love my quiet and calm days at home. Kayla and Ryan have finally called a truce thanks to Sam. Kayla broke out the big guns and told Ryan's girl, Sam, everything that Ryan taught Nicky. Ryan met a cold silence for two days before he finally broke and begged forgiveness. I have to give it to him, I can't believe he held out without sex for that long.

For the first time in a while, everything is quiet, actually too quiet. I sit up listening and begin to wonder what my son is up to. Kayla left him with me, and if he and that dog break something else in this house, I may be meeting her cold silence. Before I become too worried, I hear the dog barking outside and look to see Nicky running and playing with him. I lean down to look over some numbers once again but am quickly interrupted by Eey's growls. Deep, daring growls which escalate into barking madness. I race out to see Nicky standing behind his dog as Adair approaches him. "Nicky, go in the house, son," I say, getting between him and Adair. "What are you doing here?"

"I was in the neighborhood, and I thought I would drop by and say hello." I watch him carefully as he glances back at my son who is peeking around the doorway. "Your son is something. I heard a lot about him, so I couldn't help but come out here and talk to him."

"I don't want you here, and I certainly don't want you anywhere near my son. I don't know how you got in here, but I want you to leave, now," I say adamantly.

"I only came here to try and become friends. I feel bad for the way we started. I admit, I started it, but we both acted childishly, don't you think?" I stand silent. "Oh, Nicholas, we really should find a way to be civil to each other. It would be in both of our best interests."

"I don't trust you. I don't like you, and I want you to leave my home before I force you to, "I say, heating up and feeling his excitement intensify. Adair steps forward, and suddenly, Eey comes running at him in a rage.

"I think there is something wrong with your dog, Nicholas."

"Get out before I allow him to tear you apart." I watch him back away and leave the way he came. I spot the guard who seems to be in a daze and immediately replace him before sending him home. I warn Nicky to stay away from Adair and talk to Kayla about watching over our sons more closely, since our guards are not exactly trustworthy with everyone. She doesn't completely understand, but all I can ask is that she trust me for now. I don't want to worry her until I, myself, understand more.

I had hoped I would never see Adair again, but when I show up with Kayla to a benefit dinner, there he is with a woman on each side of him and a smile I want to knock off his face. Kayla notices my emotions instantly but is unclear why. I spend most of our night avoiding him and steering Kayla away from his direction. I thought I had made it clear that I didn't want to speak to him, but he goes out of his way to be in my face.

"Good evening, Nicholas," Adair says with a chipper tone. "This must be your lovely wife. Kayla, correct?" he says reaching out for her hand.

"Yes, and you are?" she says, gazing at him and obviously impressed.

"My name is Adair, Adair Savage. Nicholas's father and mine were old friends from what my grandfather tells me. Which makes us …?"

"Absolutely nothing," I say bluntly.

"Nick," Kayla says, looking up at me.

"Oh, it is okay. It is probably my fault. I was a little rude when we first met, and I guess I owe you both an apology for showing up at your home unannounced. I saw your son playing, and he was so innocent that I couldn't help myself. I simply had to meet him."

"You talked to my son?" Kayla asks. "You came to our home and scared my son." Kayla steps into his face and looks him dead in his eyes before smacking him hard across the face. "Don't *ever* come near my son again."

Adair looks up in shock as I pull Kayla back away from him. He slowly smiles as he looks her over. "I am truly sorry for my behavior. You are right. I should have never gone near your son. I certainly didn't mean to scare him or harm him in any way. My grandfather speaks so highly of you, Nicholas, that my curiosity got the best of me, but I promise that it will never happen again. Despite our differences, Kayla, I hope you and Nicholas will be able to make it to my celebration. I would hate for my grandfather to be disappointed just because of something I did."

"Your celebration? And what are you celebrating?" Kayla asks.

"Well, it is the night my grandfather announces me as his next in line, something I have been waiting for for a very long time," he says, glancing my way for some reason.

"Good for you, but unfortunately, we are already obligated to be somewhere else that night," I say, pulling Kayla closer to me and away from him. Kayla looks up at me suddenly, wide eyed.

"Nicholas, I really wish we could be friends. I think it would be good for both of us. Let me introduce you to my dates, Taylor and Hillary. Ladies, Mr. Nicholas Jayzon. They're dancers. You should let them show you what they can do. Ladies." The two women drag me to the dance floor surrounding me like vultures. I turn away from them, only to find Adair has disappeared with my wife.

"Get off me!" I demand as the two women paw at me as if I am going to fuck them any second. I immediately search for Kayla, pushing my way through the crowd until I see her. Adair has a grip on both of her arms as he looks down at her. She tries to jerk away from him, but he is determined to hold onto her. "Kayla!" I yell, snapping his concentration on her. Taking hold of my wife, I push her behind me and look deep into his eyes. "You are crossing one line after the other, Adair. Out of respect for your grandfather, I will allow you to walk out of here on your own, but don't tempt me any further."

"Why, what are you going to do about it, Nicholas?" he asks.

"You don't want to go there with me," I say, feeling Kayla grip my jacket, reminding of her presence and calming my boiling blood.

"Oh, I think I do. She is something special, your wife. I think she is worth fighting for, and it seems that you do too."

I stand back with Kayla slipping her hands into mine and holding tight. "Nick, let's go. He is not worth your time," she says.

I stay focused on him, shielding my suddenly trembling wife from his sight. "You don't want to fight me, Adair. Trust me. You have nothing to gain from it and a lot to lose."

"I have seen your son, and now I have seen your wife, and I want her. I am willing to do whatever it takes to get her. How far will you go for her, Nicholas? It is clear that you will fight for her, but to what extent?" The clarity in his eyes makes his intentions clear to me.

My body begins to heat, my blood boils, and a low thundering growl erupts from my lungs, "To the death."

When we arrive back home, I pace the room, going over the night in my head, going through every moment of my life, searching for the missing pieces to this puzzle. "Nick?" Kayla whispers from behind me. She stands against the doorway of my office, dressed in the sensuous silk robe I bought for her not that long ago and her beautiful body highlighted underneath by the light. The moment I look into her eyes, she smiles and reaches out for me. "Are you okay?"

I take her hand and pull her into my arms, holding her so tight against me that I exhale deeply. "As long as I have you I am." My hands feel over her body, lifting her up and sitting her on my desk. She sheds the robe from her bare body and welcomes my lips to her warm skin. Every part of her reminds me why I fell in love with her. Kayla gasps as I push deep inside her, but her eyes stay focused on me as I look into them. "You're still mine? You're still Kayla?" Thrusting hard into her, I breathe her in with every moan she makes.

"I am yours because I love you, Nick. No one can ever change that." She grasps the back of my head and forces me to stay focused on her.

"He tried, but he didn't succeed." I bring her to me, burying my face into her hair. "Nick, you have to tell me … why I saw the swirling shadows in his eyes that I have seen in yours?"

Chapter 32

Nick

The idealistic cloud of buildings sits high on the hill, daring me to move forward. It always does this to me when I come here. I hate coming here, but I can't bear the thought of leaving her alone forever either, no matter how little I mean to her. This is the first time that I am bringing Nicky with me, and he is obviously as curious as am I to her response to him.

I check in and take Nicky's hand to lead him down to her room. Before I open the door, I look down at him. "Remember what I told you?" He nods. "She is very sick, and she doesn't know who you are."

"Okay, Daddy. I'll be good."

"I know you will, Son." I am hoping that having Nicky around may jog her memory, as I resemble my father, Nicky resembles me. Walking into her room, I see her, sitting in the rocking chair, rocking and humming her favorite tune, "Gillian." She turns, instantly greeting us with a wide smile.

"Oh, how wonderful. I had a feeling you would come today." Kissing my cheek, she hugs me, tighter than she ever did when I was a child. "Oh, Dante, I have so much to tell you ..." She rambles for some time about all the people in the home. Some women she finds repulsive as well as some men who don't understand she is in love with another.

I finally have to interrupt her nonsense. "Is your health okay? Are you still happy here?"

"Yes, but I wish you could visit more often. Are you taking care of the house? I can't imagine the mess it must be in. I haven't heard anything from my office. Will you call them for me? I could go in this week for awhile if they need me to."

"I told you that you don't work there anymore. You don't need to work anymore. I am taking care of everything." It is always the same when I come to see her. Her mind has no sense of time. Pulling out the key my father once gave me, I hold it up to her, hoping she will somehow recall it. "Do you remember this key?"

"Your work?" I nod. "Do you want me to help you again, Dante?"

"Yes, and I want to take Nicky … Nicholas there. Can you remind me where it is?" I ask. She steps back from me, looking confused and scared.

"You said you would not take him there until he was older. He is still much too young, Dante," she says, finally noticing Nicky, "…don't you think?"

"Hello," Nicky says, startling my mother and forcing me to steady her legs for her. "How are you today, Gillian?" Nicky asks, taking her hand.

My mother stands, speechless for some time, before finally looking up at me and then back down at Nicky, "Who are you?" she asks, looking back up at me and shaking her head. "Nicholas?" I nod, following her eyes down to Nicky. "Who is this? Why are you here? Why am I …"

"Mom, do you remember me?"

"You are my son," she says, looking away from me. "Dante's son, Nicholas."

"Yes, and do you remember what happened to him?" She looks up at me with tears in her eyes. I give her some time to deal with her sudden understanding before I speak again.

"Nicholas?" she says again, looking me over more closely. I nod, speechless myself. "Oh, you have grown so much. And this is your … your son? He looks so much like you. Oh my, how much time has gone?" Looking brutally saddened, she returns to her chair.

I sit down in front of her as she looks upon Nicky and me. "Mom, I need your help. I need to know where Dad's place was, where it is that this key fits." I hold up my father's key again, and she instantly reaches for it.

"Dante, my love, always the secret one. Always determined to find a way," she says, gazing off into nowhere.

"Find a way to do what, Mom?" I ask, wondering if she knows more than I thought.

"Do you know he would sit with me for hours, working out numbers and formulas and even more formulas? I am good at that you know? Dante, he is gone now?"

I am not sure what to say to her. I am unsure if she is finally grieving or grieving for him again. "Yes, he is, but Mom, about the key?"

"He only took me there until he was ready to endure that machine. He didn't want me to see." My confusion only grows, but I stay quiet, feeling as if she is trying to tell me something more. Reaching out, she grabs my hand and smiles. "We conceived you there one night. He was so irresistible, but he was a man on a mission, determined especially when you were born. He was so protective of you. He knew *he* would find you. I hated that man. The others were safe, but you, you were too strong. Scared me, I was sure you were going to be taken and killed. So sure." She tears up.

Nicky gets up and hugs her before I can stop him, and shockingly, she hugs him back.

"Where is this place, Mom? I have to find it because he did. He found me. He wants me to work with him."

She looks at me straight away and then stares up at the ceiling humming, "It was outside of the city, a bunker of some sort, in a farmhouse. I don't remember exactly the road names, but I remember the scenery." Shivering, she searches around her.

"Are you cold? Let me get you a sweater." Rummaging through her drawer, I finally find something for her, but in the process, I pull out a scarf I know well. "Mom, where did you get this scarf?"

"That's mine," she says defensively as she grabs it out of my hand.

"Okay, it's yours, but who gave it to you?" I ask, looking it over to be sure.

Wrapping the scarf around herself, she sits much calmer. "My doctor. I told her how much I liked it, and she said I could have it."

"Okay." I put her sweater around her shoulders and kiss the top of her head. The scarf is odd, but it has to be a duplicate somehow. Shaking off the strange coincidence, I put the damn scarf to the back of my mind. I have more important things to worry about right now. "I am going to take you out of here for the day, Mom." She instantly smiles again. "Help me find Dad's workplace, and then, I will take you wherever you want to go. I will even take you to my home to meet the rest of my family if you'd like."

My mother somehow shows life like I have never seen from her. I am not sure how that is possible. Perhaps a jog in her memory jumped her forward again. Whatever the reason, I am going to take advantage of it as much as I can before she reverts back. Before I leave the facility, I search for her doctor to make sure I get permission to take my mother out of care for awhile and to see where this doctor got Franky's scarf I left on her grave. One nurse after another tries to direct me to find this doctor until I get a feeling and rush into an empty patient's room. The moment the door swings open, my jaw drops. "Franky?"

"Hi, Nick." She sets her iPad down, walks towards me, and attempts to hug me.

"What are you doing here?" I ask, standing back from her, trying to comprehend what is going on.

"Working," she says, trying to smile while all I can do is stare at her in amazement.

"What? How? I …" I stumble over my words, not believing what I am seeing.

I start to leave, but Franky grabs my arm and pulls me back to her. "It was all to keep your brother from coming after me again. Who would have thought I could testify against him at some point? But, they wanted more than just my testimony. Unfortunately, they could never get anything else on him until … well, you know. Once Connor was killed, they let me move closer and do as I please. I would have contacted you, but I was so nervous to see you again."

"Now you are running from me?" I ask, shaking my head.

"No! Oh, no. I am still so very nervous. I am dressed in this horrible mess, and my hair, and I only wanted everything to be perfect when I saw you again. I have missed you so much."

"Franky, why here, how did you … did you know she is my mother?" I ask watching her carefully.

She looks down at her feet and back up again. "My father followed you that night you put her in here. He wanted to kill you."

"So why didn't he?"

"He said he saw how much pain you were in and preferred you to live with that rather than to put you out of your misery."

I can't help but laugh about that bastard wanting me to suffer. "That sounds like him."

"Oh, Nick. I have missed you so much." She tears up and wraps her arms around my neck.

"Daddy, can we go now?" Nicky asks, gripping my hand a little harder to get my attention.

Franky lets go of my neck and looks down at him, "Your son?" I nod and pick him up. "Wow, I had no idea. Your mother only has pictures of you as a child; she doesn't have any of her, grandchildren."

"She wouldn't know my family, anyway, so why confuse her. I am married with another son at home." Franky takes several step back from me with a heartbreaking expression. Nicky lays his head on my shoulder with heavy eyes. "I need to get my son home. It has been a long day for him."

"He is adorable. He looks so much like you," she says, admiring Nicky. "So, will you be coming back soon?"

"Yes, I need to get permission to take my mother out for the day."

"I don't think that is a good idea, Nick. She is making some progress, but …"

"It isn't really your choice. I put her in here, and I can easily take her out. I am only asking to make things simpler for everyone."

"She doesn't even know you, Nick. She still thinks her husband is alive," Franky insists.

"She did today. She knew who I was and remembered things."

Franky looks me over in disbelief. "Well, I will look her over, and if that is true, then maybe I will release her for a few hours."

"I will be back here to pick her up in the morning, no matter what your decision is." I am not sure what else to say to her right now. "It was good … I'm glad you are doing well, Franky."

"Nick." She grabs me with pleading eyes. "Please don't be mad at me. I have missed you so much." She looks into my eyes and crashes into my chest, crying. "I have wanted nothing more than to get back to you again." Reaching out, I put an arm around her, and she instantly sighs in relief and looks up at me with a smile. A feeling rushes through me that forces a sigh from my own lips.

Seeing her again reminds of so many memories of my past, good and bad. "I am not mad at you. I understand that you did what was best. My brother would have, otherwise, killed you eventually." She nods, looking at me with her weepy eyes, reminding me of more than memories. "I have to go, Franky. I will talk to you tomorrow."

Kayla was nervous when I left her. Having to explain to her about my mother being alive was not easy, especially when I was supposed to have no hidden secrets from her. She yells at me for hours, but it wasn't about not trusting her to know, it was about the embarrassment of my mother. She was mentally gone. She had no idea about her life or who I was. How can I explain that to my wife, to anyone? How can I explain that my mother seemed to want to forget me? So, I remind her of her mother, and I didn't need to say anything else. Kayla understood perfectly. Once I finally calmed her down, I told her why I hid my mother and how I kept her from being found. I explain to her that I need to know who I am, and for the sake of our family, she needs to know too. Kayla wraps her arms around me and tells me she loves me, and then, I tell her the rest. *Franky is alive.* The questions become more demanding, and I have even less answers. Franky was my first love, but Kayla is the one that truly loves me. My heart beats in rhythm with hers and hers alone. She doesn't want to let me go alone, but I don't know where we are going to end up, and I am not putting her at risk.

My mother is dressed and ready to go when I show up to take her out for the day. She is so excited and eager to leave with Franky's scarf wrapped around her neck. We don't get two steps out of her room before Franky greets us with her own coat on. I eye her carefully. "Going somewhere?" I ask.

"I am going with you. If you want your mother to leave here, then you are going to have to take me with you so I can be assured she will be okay. I don't want you pushing her too hard, Nick. If she is starting to remember things, she could be at a fragile state right now. She is not as young as she used to be," Franky says, standing her ground with me.

I search her over before looking back at my mother. "Fine, but you're only going to go where I say, and you are only going to do as I say. No arguments or I will bring you right back here and check my mother right out," I demand, receiving a timid nod in response.

With everyone in agreement, I escort them both to my car. "Nice car, Nick. You really have moved up since we were together," Franky says.

"You were together?" my mother asks with a hopeful tone.

"A long time ago, Mom. I am married now, happily married," I emphasize to Franky who smiles for some reason. My mother sits up front while Franky, who exchanges uncomfortable glances with me the entire trip, sits in back.

My mother directs me to take the interstate, and it seems like forever before she directs me to turn off an exit.

"It was a small road, named … Shadow Mark." We search and search, but the road never appears, and my mother cannot recall any of the area around us. It's the middle of nowhere, there are only a few gas stations, and even less that I feel comfortable stopping at, but I have little choice if I want to find this place.

"Stay in the car," I say, stepping out and locking it behind me. Walking into the store, I am immediately sized up by the clerk and two others sitting near the counter. As the outsider, I ask for a local road map and try to ask for some directions.

"That is a nice car you have," the disgusting gentleman behind me says.

"I need to find a particular road?" I tell the clerk, ignoring the comment.

"How much does it mean to you?" the clerk asks, laughing with his buddies.

I pay for the map. "Thank you for the map," I say, walking out and listening carefully. The scrambling around behind me is instant. Before I reach my car, I am jumped from behind. The moron on my back goes flying into the nearby wall while I grab the other one by the throat and force him back. Look down into his eyes, I growl, "Where is Shadow Mark?" Trembling, he tells me exactly what I want to know. "I was never here," I say, kicking the other one in the head as he tries to get up. I leave them and slide back into my car.

"Are you okay?" Franky asks with her phone in hand. I nod, driving away to my goal.

"I told you he didn't need any help," my mother says calmly. "He is so much like his father." I quickly look over at her and watch her nod at me. When I find the road, the overgrowth makes it difficult to maneuver, but eventually, "There! Turn there!" my mother shouts. We pull off onto a small, unnamed road, and drive over a bridge into a clearing where a small farmhouse sits as if it hasn't been touched in more than a decade, which I guess is about right.

"Stay here," I say, getting out of the car and roaming around the house before attempting to go in. The doors are locked, so I try to force my way in until my mother taps me on the shoulder. "What are you doing out here? I told you …" She points to the engraved 'J' on the wall. Reaching up, I feel around the edges, pull out a small piece of the wall, and find the key attached to the back. "Thank you," I say earning an obnoxious smile from my mother. Sighing, I walk into the house to find it untouched since my father was here last. There are pictures on the walls of me, Lena, and of Ryan. Even a single photo of Connor sits on a table. The place feels like any other home, except for the dust and the time that has passed. I can find nothing to help me until I see the painting of the angel with its charred wings and smoked filled, churning eyes. Hanging from its neck is a key, a key that matches mine exactly. "You were always about your riddles weren't you Dad?" Feeling along its edges, I find the locks for the painting and undo them. I easily lift the painting from its inset, and behind it, I find the lock that fits my key perfectly. With a single inhale, I open the door to my father's world. The mystery lights up in front of me. The room is covered in notes and boxes of more notes. There are pictures and equipment with one single chair hooked up to a large machine with gauges of all kinds.

"What is this?" I snap my head around to see Franky wandering in.

"I thought I said to wait outside?" I yell.

"Actually, you said 'stay here,' but your mother came in, and I wasn't going to sit out there alone. So what is this room?" She wanders in even farther and looks at the chair and its gauges. "It looks like some kind of electrocution chair. What would your father be doing with this?"

"Strengthening his heart." She looks at me puzzled. "He was trying to make himself stronger. He must have found a formula that would work or that he thought would work."

"You're not going to do this, are you?" Franky asks.

"I don't know yet. I don't even know if it works."

"Oh it works," my mother says, flipping on the switch, causing the loud roaring machine to come alive. "And the formulas work too," she insists, taking hold of some photographs of my father and quickly stashing them into her bag.

I decide to photograph all of my father's notes and forward them to Eddy to help me decipher them. My mother's days of formulas are not as trustworthy to me right now. After I have what I need, I make notes of the location and lock up. Now, to introduce my mother to my wife, and I guess my ex-girlfriend, too.

The gates open to my home, and my mother sits forward while Franky meets my eyes within the rearview mirror. Nicky runs up to greet me the moment, I open the door while Kayla casually walks towards us with my younger son, Brayden, in her arms. The moment Brayden sees me, he squeals and reaches his tiny hands out to me.

"Mom, you remember Nicky, and this is Brayden," I say, kissing his little hands to make him giggle. Taking Kayla's hand, I bring her closer, "And this is my wife, Kayla."

"Nice to meet you," Kayla says as my Mom shyly shakes her hand.

"This is more than I thought for you, Nicholas. A family and a beautiful wife, I never … well I am happy that you are so happy," my mother says, already beginning to retreat again, which frustrates me, but Kayla takes my hand and squeezes, easing my nerves. With a short sigh, I turn to Franky. "And, Kayla, this is Franky an … old friend," I say as the two women greet each other respectfully, but awkwardly.

"Well, please come in. Dinner is almost ready," Kayla says, leading the way to the back of our home. Elijah steps out of my office, smiling wide and already carrying a drink.

"What the hell are you doing here?" I ask.

"I stopped by to drop off some things to you, but then I heard about dinner. No way was I going to miss this. Hi, Franky, it has been a long time," Elijah says.

Franky runs up to him and hugs him. "Oh, Elijah, it is so good to see you." Kayla stands back and stares at her while Elijah smiles fully at everyone. *Idiot is enjoying this too much.*

"Let's all go sit down for dinner," Kayla says.

Dinner is good, but the rest of the evening is terribly awkward, and I want nothing more than to end the night as soon as possible. Franky eyes Kayla, my mother eye my sons, and Kayla switches between them all while Elijah enjoys the whole mess. I try to find a conversation that doesn't lead to my past with Franky or my future with Kayla. Trying to appease everyone is impossible, especially when your best friend finds it fun to bring up all the wrong things. The opportunity to take my mother back and end our night is too welcoming, and I eagerly do just that, except Franky desires more than to simply say goodbye. She calls me into her office on the pretense to discuss my mother, but I know better. I eye her for some time while she fumbles through some folders. "Franky! You always do this," I say, stopping myself when she looks at me funny. "You know what I mean. Stop wasting time. What do you want to ask me?"

She finally jumps up and looks at me. "Do you still have any feelings for me?"

"I'm married, Franky, happily. I love Kayla. I love my children. We were kids, and …"

"And what? And now you feel nothing for me at all?"

"I didn't say that, but no matter my feelings for you, they don't change the way things are now." I stand up and look at her, and tears fill her eyes. "Franky, please, I cannot do this with you. It just isn't possible for us anymore, so why does it matter what my feelings are?"

"It matters to me. I want to know that I wasn't just another girl to you," she cries.

"You were always important to me. Even after I thought you died, I visited your grave all the time. I talked to you like you were always there for me. There was never anyone I had that connection with like I did you. But Kayla, there is no one that matches my feelings for Kayla. You were my best friend, and I love you because of that, but Kayla is the one for me. I love her like I have never loved anyone. I can only hope that you can find the same."

She presses her hand against my chest and looks up at me. "She is nothing like what I thought you would ever want."

"You don't know her."

"No, but I know you, and no matter what happens, I will always be here for you. I will *always* be your best friend." Closing my eyes, I suddenly feel her lips against mine. She pulls away with a smile. "Just like I remembered, soft and warm, perfect lips. Don't worry, I promise I won't sneak that on you again. I am happy knowing that you think so much of me and the time we had together." Still smiling, she walks away from me. "Actually you will be happy to know that I am seeing someone. He is picking me up in a few minutes, so I guess I had better go." She kisses me on the cheek. "It was nice seeing you again, and I am happy that you are happy. You really do deserve to be happy, Nick." She slides her hand across my chest as she walks out.

All I want to do is go home. The moment I get in my car, I begin cursing this day. As I leave, I notice a car pull up to the front of the building and Franky run out and get in. She leans over to the driver and kisses him. I stop my car and watch them drive away - *out of state license plate.* "Good, I am happy for her." I step on the gas and speed home.

Chapter 33

Kayla

I kiss Nick several times before he leaves and stare out the window, watching her as they get into his car. If it weren't for his mother, I would insist on Lionel driving her back.

"Don't worry. Nick won't cheat on you," Elijah says, walking up behind me.

"I know that. Why are you still here?"

"To make sure you are okay. I understand there is a lot going on lately, and I don't just mean an old girlfriend coming back into his life or his crazy mother." I turn towards him. "Yes, I know about Nicky. I wasn't aware that you knew until the other day when Nicky was talking about Adair."

"I'm okay. We have managed to get through a lot of tough times."

"Yeah, tough times, not crazy-eyed psychos." Elijah steps to me and looks at me with a sincere concern. "Nicky is tough. I have seen him do things that scared the shit out of me, but he is my best friend. This guy, Adair, doesn't sound like someone I want to get to know. How bad is he, Kayla?"

I look up at him, and suddenly, my eyes begin to water. "There is something really wrong with him. Connor was terrible and an asshole, but he didn't scare me. Adair scares me. He craves something, and I am afraid it's Nick's life. Unlike Connor, Adair has no fear of Nick, and that can't be good." Elijah wraps his arms around me and lets me be openly afraid. "I have been trying to be strong in front of Nick, but it's getting harder and harder. Tell me he can beat him if it comes down to them one on one?"

"I don't know, Kayla. I don't know enough to understand what Nicky can do."

"I don't want to face losing him again. I can't," I cry, looking up at him. I fall into his arms, and he comforts me warmly. Elijah looks down at me, wipes my tears away, and begins to near my lips. I feel his touch, and I quickly push him away. "What are you doing?"

"I'm sorry, you and your weepy eyes. I don't know how to comfort someone without having sex with them, Kayla."

"That is really sad!"

"Yeah, it is," he says, grabbing his coat and walking towards the door.

"Eli!"

"What, Kayla?" he asks, glancing back at me with a frustrated sigh. I don't know what to say to him. "What happens if he decides he really does love Franky, still?

"What if you two really aren't meant to be, Kayla?"

"But we are Eli."

"Of course you are, so why are you worrying? Do you really think everything would happen like it has, just to find out that it was all for nothing? Don't worry Kayla, I am pretty sure your happy little family will survive. Nicky has always had a way of making things work out."

"Eli!" I yell again before he leaves. He huffs, turning to look at me again. "Thank you. See, you really do know how to comfort someone without having sex with them." The smile he fights to form slowly appears anyway. "I still think you're an ass though." He nods, laughing before leaving me to wait for Nick alone. The moment Nick comes home, I wrap my arms around him and hold tight.

"Everything is going to be okay, Princess. You don't have to worry about anything. I promise I will take care of everything for you." Nick picks me up and carries me to bed, where he holds me tight throughout the night.

Nick spent most of the night calming my fears, and today, I am spending my time out searching for answers. My father is the only one I know who can get me what I need, and as much as I hate to ask him for help, I love my husband too much not to. I walk up to his smiling face, trying to fight my own, but it is no use.

"You look beautiful, Kayla," he says, kissing my cheek joyfully.

"Thank you, you look good too, Mr. President," I say to his nod. "Thank you for flying in to meet me. I know it is difficult to get away. I would have been fine with you sending the information through someone else."

"Well, I wouldn't have been. Any opportunity to spend time with my daughter is one I am not about to pass up. So, Nick's father, huh? Why are you so curious now?"

I smile at him, not wanting to alarm him in any way. "You know, Brayden has been so sick lately, and Nicky is getting older, and I would like to have a full medical history, or at least as much as I can provide for them. I don't want anything more creeping up on us. I would rather be prepared."

"Ah, medical, so then why is it you requested police records and confidential documents following his life? None of that has anything to do with his medical history," my father says, sitting back and eyeing me carefully.

"You know, there are probably some things you shouldn't know, being President and all. I don't want to jeopardize your reelection, Daddy." I smile and receive a smiling nod in return. I manage to change my father's focus and discuss other family matters. "I brought pictures for you." I hand him the photo album I have been creating for him with my children's pictures, to his instant joyful smile.

"A dog? I thought Nick was opposed?" he asks, as I simply laugh and shrug.

After I leave my father, I take out the large packet of information on Nick's father and spread it out in front of me, searching for anything that instantly stands out. Thumbing through notes and pictures, I start to become overwhelmed until I come to a picture of a woman. I don't know her, and she looks nothing like Nick's or Ryan's mother. She doesn't resemble Lena at all, so I become curious and search for more about her. It takes me some time, but eventually, I find another picture, and this time there's a name - Sophia. Her name is Sophia, but I can find no more information than that on her. I clean up everything so Nick doesn't find it and go seek out a friend who might be able to help me.

He sits in his office like someone of importance, and I have to laugh thinking about my goofball friend being Chief of Police. "Don't laugh at me, or I will have you arrested," Brady says, getting up from his chair and giving me a hug. "So, what brings you here? It must be important for you to suffer coming through those doors."

"It wasn't easy, I must say, but what I need is that important," I reply, sitting down in front of his desk as he casually sits himself. "I need your help locating someone. Unfortunately, I don't have much to go on. I know she lived here at some point, because the picture I have shows the old building on 2nd Avenue. Other than this picture, all I have is a name, a first name. Can you find someone with so little information?"

Brady's expression is that of doubt, "I don't know, Kayla. That isn't much to go on. You don't have any other information?" I shake my head and sink back into my seat. "Well, don't give up yet. Let me see your picture."

I hand him the picture of the woman, "Her name is …"

"Sophia." he says, glancing back at me with a serious tone.

"You know her, Brady?"

"I should, she is my father's sister. Where did you get this Kayla?" I shake my head. "She was murdered by Savage, that is why my father went after him in the first place. He was determined to bring him to justice, but it ended up costing him and my mother their lives. If this has something to do with Savage, then you had better tell me everything you know." I stare at him disbelief. "Kayla, you're shaking. I have never seen you look so terrified. It does have to do with him, and you're going to need my help. I don't care what you say or what that stubborn ass husband of yours says. That man is a menace, and he has to be dealt with."

"I don't disagree with you, but I don't think that we can talk here." He nods and begins to tense. "I promise, I will tell you everything I know as soon as I can," I say, taking back the picture and running out of his office. Now, I have to hold him off until I can figure out her connection to Nick's father. I need to talk to Exie.

My friend struts towards me like she has been named queen of the city. "You look fabulous," I say, kissing her cheek. She spins for me as if I was referring to her outfit. "So you got laid this morning, huh?"

She gasps and acts as if I am insulting her. "I will have you know that I am hurt, very hurt. I cannot believe you did not notice my outfit, my new shoes, my …" I sit back, folding my arms. "Okay fine. Yes… I got laid."

"But the shoes look fabulous, too," I say, and she instantly stretches her legs out to show them off.

"Thank you. I bought them to celebrate." Curious, I cock my head to the side. "To celebrate having sex on a regular basis."

"And the outfit?" I laugh.

"To simply celebrate the sex itself. It is so damn good," she gushes. "You know, I thought being sent away with Bo was going to be a nightmare. I was worried they would find us, and I would go to jail or you would go to jail, but the whole time we were gone, he was so comforting and so … oh my. And he is so wonderful with Jerran. He helps him with his homework and goes to all his games." Exie grabs my hand, and excitedly continues, "I think …"

"Really?"

"I know! I can't believe it either, but I love this man. Oh, he is so incredible. At first, I hated him. I was so horny, and with him wandering around all the time looking, oh so damn fine. I thought I was going to go crazy, so I did everything I could think of to try and … you know. But he wouldn't. He kept saying, '*I am working and I don't mix business and pleasure.*' Can you believe that? Anyway, when we got back, I wouldn't talk to him, so he showed up at work a few weeks ago with flowers. Actually, he showed up every day for a week with flowers. He never said a word. He simply put the flowers down on my desk and walked out. There was no card or anything. I finally asked him, 'Why do you keep bringing me flowers and not saying a word to me?' He said, 'Well, you said you didn't want me to speak to you ever again. I am only doing what you told me to do. I will do whatever *you* want me to do. All you have to do ask, Exie. Don't you know that?'" Exie and I both gush. "I know, right?!"

"So you talked to him?"

"Oh we talked, and then we didn't. And I must say, he did exactly what I wanted, but I didn't have to tell him a thing." She smiles, dancing in her chair.

"That's wonderful! I am so excited to see you so happy. I almost hate to bring up my issues."

"No, that's what I am here for. Talk. You know I cannot be happy unless you are." As Exie talks, I spot Adair coming towards us, and I gasp. Exie immediately turns to see what I am looking at. "Whoa… who is that?"

"My issue." Exie looks back at me in shock.

"Kayla," Adair sings deeply as he takes my hand and kisses it. "I don't believe I have had the pleasure. My name is Adair, and you are?" he says to Exie, taking her hand.

"It's Exie. Nice to meet you."

"You as well. I always love meeting beautiful women. Are you dining alone?" I sit back, looking away from him. Adair sits down with us. "Oh, tell me Nick did not let you out of his sight. I can't believe that. I assumed he put you back in your box, to keep you fresh for himself when he returns."

"Nick doesn't treat me like a breakable doll."

"No?" Adair says, tracing a heart on my hand with his finger before I can pull it away from him. "He certainly acts like he owns you."

"No one owns me, but he does love me, and I love him."

"Love changes," he says, dismissing my comment.

"Not for me it doesn't." He doesn't speak, he simply smiles at me. His ego is worse than Elijah's, and I didn't think anyone could be worse than him. "What do you want, Adair? Why are you here?"

"I am here to meet my grandfather, but if I had known you would be here, I would have certainly canceled with him." Adair looks up, "Oh, too bad honey, he is already here. I am going to have to leave you now." I mock his sad expression, making him laugh. "Grandfather, have you met Kayla, Nicholas's wife?"

I turn and look up at the man who sends chills up my spine. He looks me over as if he is trying to decide how he wants to kill me. "No, I have not had the pleasure as of yet. Nice to finally meet you, Kayla, my dear. You are as beautiful as always," he says as I thank him with a simple smile. "I meant to tell you that I was so sorry to hear about your sister."

"You knew my sister?"

"No, I only know of the unfortunate event that took, only her life." His eyes penetrate me, and I feel as if my body is fighting off flames. "I do hope you and Nicholas will be at our celebration for Adair. It is very important to us all."

I stand tall, take his hand, and force a smile at him. "We will do our best to be there, then. It was nice to meet you, Mr. Savage, but I should get back to my friend." He says his goodbye, along with Adair, and they move on to their own table. Suddenly, I am not so hungry anymore.

Our meal was ruined, and all I want to do now is rush home to Nick. "Leaving so soon?" Adair says from behind me.

"Leave me alone, Adair. I am not interested in you at all, and I am most certainly not swayed by you," I say as he slides in between me and my car.

"Incredible how you can do that - deny me that is"

"Not that incredible. You are not all that good looking."

He smiles. "I love your feistiness. I can certainly see why Nick would fight for you."

"Nick doesn't need to fight for me."

"Oh honey, he most certainly does," Adair says, grabbing the back of my head and pulling me to him. "Nick will have to fight me for everything, including his life. That is just the way it has to be. Don't worry though, I will treat you well." He rubs his hand down my face. "I can't wait to force you down in front of me and make our own children." He slams his lips against mine, biting me until he draws blood. "Mmm, you do taste good." I shove my fists into his chest, and start screaming until I gain enough attention to make him walk away from me. I rush home, but before I can get there, Ryan cuts me off.

"Kayla, you need to get home," he yells at me. I jump out of my car and rush over to him, "What are you doing? You can't leave your car there."

"Ryan, where is Nick?"

"He is at a meeting. He asked me to come find you and make sure you went straight home."

"You have to go find him, Ryan! Adair wants to kill him."

"Who the fuck is Adair?"

"Just go find him and protect him. I will go straight home, but go help Nick, *please*," I beg.

"Okay, I will call you when I find him. But you go home!" I nod and jump back in my car, waving him on. Ryan does exactly as he promises. He finds Nick and calls me as soon as he does. I put the boys to bed and wait up for my husband to come home, like he always does.

Chapter 34

Nick

I woke up uneasy this morning, so I told Kayla to stay home today, but of course, her stubborn ass doesn't listen to me. I had been trying to call her for hours, when she finally confesses she is meeting Exie for dinner over my voicemail. She is supposed to call me as soon as she finishes, and as soon as she gets home. I would chase after her, but I have business to take care of, so I send Ryan to find her. He loves yelling at her anyway.

I take Dwayne and Terrence with me to lead five other guards. The entourage of men is typical for days like this, but even with all the guns that I have with me, I still feel vulnerable.

My day is almost over when I have to deal with Nolan Pickard, my informant weasel from customs. He refuses to talk to anyone but me, and I need to calm him down. He needs to be reassured that he will still be taken care of and there is no reason to worry about any prosecution. He rambles on forever before I finally squeeze his flapping lips together. "Nole, shut up. I have listened and listened to your rambling, and none of it is worth me coming down here. So unless you get to the point, I am going to get back into my car and leave you here alone."

"Wait, who is that?" he jumps behind me and points.

Glancing behind me, I see Ryan walk in. "It's only Ryan. You've met him. You talked to him yesterday, remember?" I have to fist my hands to keep from strangling him.

"Oh, yeah. Okay, okay, I'm calm," Nole says as I begin to vibrate with frustration. "Nick, I only wanted to make sure that you have my back. I'm worried…really worried. I think I am putting myself too much on the line for you. I don't think you are understanding what all I am doing for you."

"You want more money?" Taking a step away from me, he nods.

"Just give him the money, Nicholas." I spin around to watch Adair smoothly walk in. He looks over at Dwayne. "Leave, all of you." Dwayne leaves, followed by Terrance and my other guards. They all leave, with no fight.

Ryan, however, steps to him with his chest out. "Who the fuck are you?" Ryan snaps at him.

Adair's jaw drops, and he stares at Ryan wide-eyed. Sensing the tension, Nole runs and hides behind some of the crates in the warehouse. "What are you doing here, Adair?" I ask him.

"It's simple. I wanted to see how truly great you are." Adair turns his head quickly towards Ryan and sends him crashing into the wall. I run after him, and Adair fights me face on. Fire pierces into my skin, like volts of electricity, bringing me to my knees. I try to get up, but he sends me flying across the room, sparking a nearby gathering of papers. The sprinkler system reacts soon after the flames begin to spread. Adair comes at me again, fists ablaze and slamming me with even more force. I stumble to my feet and face off with him again, but the result ends up the same. More fire, more rain, and more of Adair tossing me into one wall after the other. It's a struggle to breathe, but again, I get back to my feet and face him. Adair laughs as if he is playing a game. He taunts me as I eye him down, but my body has little left, and he easily slams me on my back again. All I feel is pain, and all hear is him coming at me.

With his laughter echoing in my head, I stagger back to my feet, exhausted and my vision blurred. Adair causes shooting pains to strike my spine so sharply that I cannot even fall to the ground. He holds me out in front of him like a trophy. I try to search for Ryan, but his lifeless body is too hazy to see. Adair walks slowly towards me, smiling wide and easing his coat off. "You did say to the death, Nicholas. I can't have you running around with the woman meant for me. You are nothing compared to me. You're an embarrassment. I don't know how your father killed mine, for there should have been no possible way for that to happen. We assumed your father was more powerful than we thought; therefore, my grandfather believes that you might be more powerful than me. Now, I can't gain his full respect until you are gone." Adair turns towards Ryan as he slowly approaches us and throws him back into a wall.

Ryan screams out in pain, "Kill him Nick!" He yells before screaming again.

"And whoever he is, he must go too." Adair comes closer, eyeing me down. "Don't worry, I will take care of your family, your sons will have to die of course, but Kayla seems to be a good fuck. I will enjoy making our own children with her. Then, I will kill her, too, once I have what I need." He takes out a knife. "I will slit all their throats," he seethes. "You know, I saw her tonight, your wife. I tasted her lips, and then, I drew blood, to remind myself what it will be like." He motions his knife across his neck, enjoying every second of his taunting.

With every word he speaks, my body heats up more and more. He doesn't realize what he is doing to me. He doesn't realize that my energy has not only increased to full form, but to an even higher level. He comes at me, waving his knife, but for some reason, he decides to toss it and grab my neck with both hands and squeeze. I close my eyes for an instant before reopening them and focusing. With his hands wrapped around my throat, I stand stiff and stare into his swirling eyes, and damn him. The ravaging screams between us overpower everything around us. His skin reflects mine, his body begins to vibrate, and his eyes weaken while mine find new levels of control. I am afraid to move, afraid to break my focus on him. I begin to feel the low rumbling growl emerge from my chest, and then, I toss him backwards, launching him across the floor and into the wall. Ryan acts quickly and wraps a chain around Adair's neck and pulls. Adair wrestles for control, battles Ryan and me both, but in the end, he doesn't have enough to overcome Ryan's hold and my focus.

His last words are a low whisper. "You don't know what he will do to you. What he will turn you into when he gets his chance. You can't say no to him." I flinch, sending Adair screaming in pain to his last breath.

Ryan collapses while my body quakes to an exhausting exhale. When I regain my full breath, I make my way to my brother and check him over. "Are you all right?" His breath is still a struggle, but he nods. A small noise awakens me to the other live person in the room, Nole, who is quietly trying to crawl away through the smoke, broken glass, and falling walls. "Nole!" I yell.

He immediately rolls to his back like a defenseless dog and begs, "Please, I am good. I don't need any extra money. In fact, I am not doing enough for what you are paying me to do now. Oh, please, can I go? There is a shipment of jewels coming in next week I am sure your wife would love …"

"Leave, and do not speak of this night to anyone," I say to him.

"Who would believe me?" he mumbles and runs away.

I slide down the wall next to Ryan and finally breathe normally again. "What the hell was that, Nick?" Ryan asks.

"I have a terrible feeling that was our cousin trying to kill us."

"Oh. Well, I don't care for him too much," Ryan says spitting the blood out of his mouth. "In fact, I liked Connor better than him, and I *hated* him."

"Yeah, me too."

"So, what do we do now?" Ryan asks, looking at me for some kind of answer. I don't think he realizes how many questions that there actually are.

"I think I need to take you and Eddy to Dad's refuge and figure out exactly who we are before it is too late."

Chapter 35

Nick

The debate on what to do with Adair's body has troubled me since Ryan posed the question. Do I make him disappear and hope his disappearance never leads back to me or do I respectfully deliver his body back to where it belongs and let it be known he failed? I choose the latter, and with my men in tow this time, I deliver his body to Savage with only these words, "Whether you knew it or not, he was out to kill me. Now, I am returning his body out of respect for you and you alone. I owe *him* nothing."

Savage walks out to meet me on his ruby-eyed dragon, his breath echoing in my ears. When our eyes meet, I am unsure if he is angry or elated. "I suppose I will have to plan a new party, a masquerade perhaps?" Taking in a deep breath, he exhales with a wide sinister smile. "The job is yours now, Nicholas. Congratulations, you are finally ready."

"No thank you," I say plainly.

He moves slowly until he faces me and sees directly into my eyes. "I didn't give you a choice. It is your responsibility now, and you will finally live up to your birthright," he demands before sitting back on his heels, "For now, I am sure I should probably grieve and bury him, or something.

Damn it! Tomorrow is going to be a busy day," he says walking back into his home and waving his hand to have Adair carried away.

"I have no desire to work for you. You are going to have to find someone else," I call after him.

Savage looks down with a low growl before turning to face me. "You are the most frustrating of them all, even more so than your father. Alright Nicholas, if you want to talk, then let's talk. Come in," he says, walking in ahead of me. The last thing I want to do is go back inside his house, but something tells me I don't have much of a choice. Before I step one foot inside, I look back at my men with their terrified expressions and realize I am going in alone. I walk back through his chilling house and apprehensively sit down in front of him within his office. "What are your concerns about joining me, Nicholas?"

"I don't think you understand. I am happy with the way my life is. I am not looking to change it at all."

"Life changes drastically sometimes. I don't think you would feel the same if your life was much different. No wife. No children to worry about. How would you feel then?" he asks with a glare. I don't speak, and my hands begin to burn. "Your family is nothing to me. What I want is for you to finally take the place your father left and do the work that I need to be done. I have no desire to handle things alone simply because you don't feel like it. This is your heritage, Nicholas. This is where you belong." He sits at the edge of his seat, folding his hands in front of his face as he leans in on his desk closer to me.

"Tell me, Nicholas, do you ever feel as if there is something missing in your life, that there is that piece of the puzzle that just can't be found? Of course you do, that is because you are trying to force yourself to be something that you are not. You belong here. You belong in this family. I can give you everything, all the power you could ever want, and you will never have a lack of respect again. It will not be just this city, Nicholas. You can control so much more, as much as you desire."

His voice continuously flows into my mind. I cannot focus or tune him out. I feel confused and dizzy, so I close my eyes and think of them, my family. "No, that's not what I want. I have what I want. I'm not missing anything."

Savage slams his fists onto his desk, jarring his assistant, Rabbie, into a trembling mess. "Damn you! You do not understand who you are, what you are."

I stand to meet his rage one on one, "Who am I then? Tell me what gives me this power over people. What is the name of this demon that I surely am?"

"You are looking for a name that humans use when they fear the dark. You are looking for a name people scream when hell comes for them, but how could there be such a name if they don't know that you exist? They don't know anything about you until it is too late," he says with a prideful calm.

I stand back, looking him over, "If there is no name then how, why?"

"Well, that is something you will learn over time, too much history to explain in a few sentences. You would know it all now if not for your father shielding you from it." Savage turns to his artwork on the wall. "Asmodeus, one of the princes of the seven hells." He turns back to me as an understanding begins to form within me. "The most powerful prince of them all, the lust demon is your roots."

In an instant, I find my back against the wall, staring at him in anguish, "Are you telling me that I am …?"

"A demon, the devil's helper, the son of the devil for that matter. Name it whatever you like, Nicholas. The fact remains that you have inherited a power that you must learn to use and use it well," he says, and I immediately shake my head. "Do not shake your head at me, you fool. Do not say no to me! I allowed you to have the life you have had as an experiment, a chance for you to grow stronger beyond the others, and you did. You achieved beyond my greatest expectations for you, but now, I need you here by my side," he demands with hardened fists.

"No!" I yell back at him. "Kill me if you must, but I will not be any sort of demon monster for you. I will not subject my family to such horror. I am not what you want. No matter what you say, I am not what you want me to be. I will never be what you want me to be," I say, racing out of the house, ushering my men to quickly remove us from the compound.

Thoughts race through my head, memories become clear, and the voice of my father is louder than ever. I have felt uneasy since I left Savage. I have yet to hear from him or see any sign of him, but I know it is only a matter of time. As we sit down to dinner, Kayla laughs with Nicky and kisses Brayden as she helps him eat. He is still so small, Brayden, and he is always getting sick. He needs protection just from everyday life. Nicky is stronger, but still only a child. Kayla … "Kayla." She smiles at me, still laughing with our sons until she notices my expression.

"What's wrong?" she asks.

I have avoided talking to her, but I can't any longer. She has to know. She should be allowed to run, take our sons, and run even from me. "I need to talk to you." I begin with what I know, and then move on to what I think I know, but I end with, "I don't know what is going to happen if I don't work for Savage." Kayla looks over our sons with fear in her eyes. "I am learning as much as I can. I found my father's work, but there are a lot of notes, and I haven't had time to go through it all." I clench my eyes shut, wishing for a different life for them, and when I reopen them, all I can do is see the love in her eyes. "I love you, Kayla," I whisper, hoping to try and comfort her somehow.

"I love you too, Nick. Don't worry. We will figure it out. We will do it together, just like we always have." She reaches out and takes my hand, instantly setting me at ease. "So who is he, Savage? What is he capable of?"

"I think I can answer that question better than him." Savage walks into our dining room as if invited. I stand up immediately. "Sit down, Nicholas. I am only here to meet the family. I thought joining you for dinner would be a good start." He takes Kayla's hand and kisses it respectfully. "You are a wondrous beauty." Kayla picks up Brayden, puts him in her lap and calls Nicky to her side. Savage sets his cane aside and sits down at the table, waiting to be served. "No servants?" he asks looking around. "No problem, I will use my own." He waves his hand in the air. "Rabbie, please assist me." Rabbie rushes to gather him his food and wine. "So, tell me, Kayla, how did you meet my grandson?" Kayla looks my way with a reality neither of us wanted to believe.

Kayla speaks to him carefully while he watches her every move, and I watch his. "Princess, I think maybe it's time to put the boys to bed. I will see to our guest in the meantime," I say, kissing my sons and gripping my wife's hand briefly before I face my grandfather one on one.

Kayla takes Nicky's hand while Brayden lays his head on his mother's shoulder. "It was nice to see you again, Mr. Savage," Kayla says, looking at me with fear in her eyes.

"It was lovely to see you too, dear. Take care of those boys, although one doesn't seem to need nearly as much care as the other. Tragic news, I must say," he says heartlessly. Kayla rushes them upstairs and hopefully to a place they won't be able to hear a thing. "You have done well, Nicholas. I am impressed, although your home lacks the right ambience for my taste." I grow impatient with his game.

"What do you want?"

"I was thinking you didn't seem excited about your new position. I wanted to make sure you understood fully what your responsibility is going to be now. It is, after all, fairly simple. You do as I say and represent the family properly."

"I am not working for you."

"Again, Nicholas, I don't think you understand. You killed your cousin which puts you next in line. I wish I could say I am disappointed, but I was hoping for that outcome," he says, fisting his hand near me.

"I am sorry, but I am sure there is someone else much more suited for your needs. I have a family I need to be concerned about, a flourishing business, and …"

Savage growls, getting up to meet me face to face, "And, and, AND! Nicholas, enough of this! I gave you time, like your father requested, but now, I need you!" I stand my ground until pain spears into my veins and forces me to my knees.

"Nick!" Kayla rushes in after me, and Savage grabs her by the throat.

"Let her go! AHH!" I scream, falling back against the wall with his cane holding me securely by the throat. The more I struggle against it, the more I am paralyzed by the pain racing through my veins. Kayla's screams escalate while I fight and try to rip my way through the pain to find her.

"Stop please!" I beg.

"I will give you two choices, Nicholas. She dies here, now, and then your son, Brayden, and then you. I will take Nicky with me to take your place. Or you accept your responsibility, and I will spare them for now, giving you a chance to prove their worth to me."

Savage's voice cuts through my pain and releases me, allowing me to finally see again. My eyes immediately jump to Nicky, hiding under the table and crying for his mother while Eey stands guard in front of him with a ferociousness that even I wouldn't dare go near. But then, my focus goes to Kayla. She visibly begins to weaken by his hands, slowly closing her eyes and nearing death while I can do nothing but watch. *I have no choice now …* "Okay. Okay, I will accept the responsibility!"

Savage inhales, releasing Kayla to the floor and smiling supremely as he takes hold of his cane once again. "I will give you thirty days to get your affairs in order, and then, you can learn your duties before your acceptance party, your masquerade ball." Savage smiles joyfully. "Oh what a wonderful idea, Nicholas. I can hardly wait. It is going to be amazing." He turns towards Nicky and holds out his hand to him, but he pulls back when Eey intensifies his stance. "I always hated dogs," he sneers. Savage begins to walk away before turning back again. "Invite your Police Chief friend. We could have some fun with him. Welcome back to the family, Nicholas. It's about time."

The moment he leaves, I crawl to Kayla and Nicky, holding him in one arm while I try to wake Kayla. "Mommy!" Nicky cries reaching for her.

"She's okay, Nicky. She's okay. She's just sleeping," I say, caressing her face and fighting my own tears.

Chapter 36

Nick

I brought them all: Ryan, Elijah, Terrance, Dwayne, Reginald, Eddy, and even Bo Sirra. Lena was also able to help me talk Brady into coming, of course he wasn't about to say no when she agreed to come too. They all look nervous, but Ryan stares at me constantly, vibrating with questions. "Is Kayla doing any better?" he asks.

"She is stronger, but she hasn't woken up yet. I am not sure when she will," I say, staring away from them all.

"I am still not sure I understand exactly what happened," Brady says, breaking the uncomfortable silence.

"I don't either, and in addition to that, I don't understand why I am here?" Elijah asks looking as awkward as they all do. I am not sure how to explain it, so I tell them it was hundred times worse than Adair with no chance of survival if he had not momentarily pardoned us. "Oh, well that sounds lovely. I am so happy to be here then. Thanks for inviting me, Nicky." Elijah nods sarcastically.

"You are all here to help me get stronger so I can kill Savage. Eddy has been helping me go through my father's notes, and if we follow his instructions then … maybe."

"Maybe?" Ryan snaps. "You don't know for sure? I can't believe you are doing this. Let's just fight him together like we did Adair …"

"No! If he finds out about you and Lena, you both will be dead for sure, and I am afraid he will force me to do it," I say, avoiding their eyes on me. "The more you all help me prepare, the better chance I have to get rid of him."

"Prepare how?" Bo asks as we pull up to the farmhouse. I ignore his question and lead them into the house to show them instead. They all follow me in and look around, taking careful notice of my father's things, even the pictures of all his children, from their birth to his own death.

Ryan picks up his own baby picture with a huff. "He wasn't ignoring you on purpose, Ryan. He was protecting you from being known," I say, causing Lena to press her face into Brady's chest. Ryan sets the picture down and looks over at me with a frustrated anger, a feeling I have felt many times over the last few days.

"So, what do you need our help with again?" Ryan asks. I lead them into our father's lab and flip the switch to turn everything on. "What the hell is this?"

"His lab. He was trying to become stronger." Sitting in his chair, I lean back and feel the edges of the seat my father once sat in day after day. "He was preparing to kill Savage himself."

"How?" Ryan looks at me with his arms raised in confusion.

"Learning to take the pain he projects, to overcome it, and use it to kill him," I explain.

Lena gazes over the chair I am in, "Nick … no?" Lena looks closer at the equipment and the chair. "Oh fuck no! Are you insane? You're going to kill *yourself*!"

"It didn't kill him, it won't kill me," I say with only mild confidence.

"Nick! You don't know how far he got and how far he needed to get," Ryan yells at me.

"It doesn't matter." Ryan stomps his feet, fisting his hair and screaming at me. "Protest all you want, but I am doing this, and after each time, I need you all to attack me."

"Excuse me?" Brady asks. "Did I hear you right, or is my constant daydreaming of kicking your ass interfering with my reality?"

"You heard me right. After each level I get to, I want you all to attack me and force me to learn how to regain my energy faster. I need you to motivate me."

"Alright, so when do we get started?" Brady asks with enthusiasm until Lena glares at him. "I'm just kidding baby. I promise, I won't enjoy kicking your brother's ass …too much."

Reluctantly, they all agree to try, and so Eddy sets up the machines and Lena helps monitor me. The rest all back up against the wall across from me, fidgeting, shaking their heads, and staring at me like I have lost my damn mind. *They may be right, but I don't have much of a choice.* Eddy signals to me that he is ready, and after a deep inhale, I nod. *Son of a bitch!* I fight to keep from screaming from the pain, so as not to scare them all off, but it becomes increasingly difficult. Once it's over, Lena releases me and steps back. I motion towards the wall of awkwardness, and even Brady hesitates. "Come on you fucking Pussies! Do you want to kick my ass or do you want Savage to kill you?" It only takes a few more comments to push them to do what I asked. Lena calls them off, and we go again, but neither she nor Ryan are happy about it.

Lena decides to call for a break, and I take the opportunity to pull Elijah to the side and ask him for a favor. "If this doesn't work out, I need you to take care of my family. I need you to talk Ryan into leaving with Sam, force him if you have to. I also need you to take Kayla and the boys away from here."

"What?"

"I see the way you look at her. You said yourself you should have had the family, not me. You are wanting to leave and start a new life, so if this fails, leave with my family and start a new life with them." He backs up and looks at me as if I have lost my mind. "If I start working for Savage, I can't have them in my life. I can't have her see me become something else. As much as I hate to admit it, I know she would be happy with you."

"You mean once I tie her up and drag her off kicking and screaming away from you? Oh yeah, I am sure we will live happily ever after." I don't change my determination and he knows me well enough to know I am not changing my mind. Elijah sighs, closing his eyes. "I promise I will do everything that I can possibly do to make sure they stay safe and happy, if and only if, you can't."

I hold out my hand to him, "Brothers for life?"

Elijah takes my hand, "Brothers for life – Nicky. Always."

I return to the chair and wait to begin again, to Ryan's instant frustration. "Don't start Ryan. Just do what I ask, please." Ryan shakes his head, refusing over and over until I grab him and force him to listen to me. "I have to do this Ryan. We have no other choice. I could do nothing against him. I couldn't even get off my knees to protect my own family. I have to protect them, no matter what. I have to do this so I can save them. So I can save you all. No matter what it does to me."

"And what if time runs out and you have to work with him? What if you become him before we can finish preparing you to take him on? The man has no feelings, no soul. You said yourself that you have felt the world from his point of view. How much will it take for him to change you, for him to force you to forget who you are?" Bo asks, forcing me to think about the worst possibility.

"Who I am? I don't know who I am."

"I know who you are, and you're not him. You don't belong there, Nick. As bad as I thought our father was, he had something about him that forced him to break from that world, and you have it too. I know it."

"I don't know if I do, Ryan. I am not sure how he broke free. Whatever it was, I hope I can find that same inner strength."

"Well, maybe it isn't so much about the inner strength, but some kind of magical cure. Maybe he stumbled onto something by accident," Eddy suggests, trying to find hope where I don't believe there is any.

"If there is, I hope we find it. Otherwise, we are completely dependent on this idea working on its own, and I am not sure I can build up enough rage to kill him and still come back as Nicholas Jayzon and not … The Devil's Son."

Epilogue

Nick

Savage walks into the room as all the masked guests applaud his noble entrance. My own body steadies itself, waiting as the focus changes to me. I should be afraid. I should be fearing him, but as I walk up next to his side, I fear nothing, and I feel nothing. I slowly raise my head and feel the heat, the fire, take over my body. The shadows within my eyes begin to swirl, and, in an instant, I control them all. I control all of them but a select few. Venom begins to flow through my veins and a sudden wrath overwhelms me, and I can see nothing but the few.

"Kill them," Savage says simply.

I concentrate and focus in on my targets. The first is my sister, her fearful eyes are no match for the rage that breaks her neck. My brother scrambles and tries to battle me, but in the end, he is no match and I squeeze his heart to its end.

Brayden, my sickly son, cries and reaches out, a slight twinge within me stops me briefly. "Nick!" A distant voice calls out to me as my son takes his last breath. Nicky backs away from me and runs from me, or so I thought. My headstrong child steps in front of his mother and threatens to destroy me with everything he has. It's a short battle that earns me some scars, but as I hold my oldest son's life in my hands, my wife screams for him. "Nicky! Nick, no! Stop! Stop Nick, stop! What has happened to you?" She cries and cries, and with each tear, I hesitate. I realize I can do nothing more until she is gone. I drop my son and wrap my hands around her neck, perfectly meeting her eyes. "Nick, please … stop. I love you," she cries, and I … tremble.

Gasping, I sit straight up in bed as the sweat from my body clings to me. My nightmare is my worst fear, but the solution it gives me is my best hope.

Kayla. She is my cure.

Printed in Great Britain
by Amazon